My Amish
Boyfriend

Books by Melody Carlson

A Simple Song
Devotions for Real Life
Double Take
Just Another Girl
Anything but Normal
Never Been Kissed
Allison O'Brian on Her Own—Volume 1
Allison O'Brian on Her Own—Volume 2

LIFE AT KINGSTON HIGH

The Jerk Magnet
The Best Friend
The Prom Queen

THE DATING GAMES

The Dating Games #1: First Date

My Amish Boyfriend

a novel

melody carlson

Revell

a division of Baker Publishing Group
Grand Rapids, Michigan

© 2014 by Melody Carlson

Published by Revell
a division of Baker Publishing Group
P.O. Box 6287, Grand Rapids, MI 49516-6287
www.revellbooks.com

Printed in the United States of America

                    Library of Congress Cataloging-in-Publication Data
Carlson, Melody.
    My Amish boyfriend / Melody Carlson.
        pages cm
    ISBN 978-0-8007-2226-5 (pbk.)
    1. Teenage girls—Fiction. 2. Amish—Fiction. I. Title.
PS3553.A73257M9 2014
813′.54—dc23   2013030032

This is a work of fiction. Names, characters, incidents, and dialogues are products of the author's imagination and are not to be construed as real. Any resemblance to actual events or persons, living or dead, is entirely coincidental.

Scripture used in this book, whether quoted or paraphrased by the characters, is taken from the King James Version of the Bible.

14 15 16 17 18 19 20   7 6 5 4 3 2 1

1

As my best friend Merenda and I evacuate the belching yellow school bus on the last day of school, a three-part plan congeals for me. Standing on the curb, watching that gross, smelly contraption growling away in a cloud of diesel smoke, I make my proclamation to Merenda. "I need to get three things this summer."

Merenda ignores my proclamation as we race across the sunbaked parking lot. The asphalt is so hot it might be melting our flip-flops, but my mind is on my plan. To be honest, this plan was probably inspired by my history teacher. "People who fail to plan, plan to fail," he told me as I was leaving his classroom today. Of course, I knew his clichéd challenge was meant to pressure me into signing up for his AP history class next fall, so I answered his cliché with another.

"What about the best laid plans of mice and men?" I asked.

He just laughed. "Quoting Robert Burns, are we?" He rubbed his chin in a thoughtful way. "Methinks you should sign up for AP English as well." So before I left, I promised to consider some AP classes next year. But that's a long way off.

"What were you saying?" Merenda asks as we catch our breath in the shade of the covered walkway next to our apartment complex. "What three things do you need to get?"

I hold up one finger. "First of all, I need to get my driver's license. Sixteen is too old to be riding a smelly old school bus."

"You got that right." She nods eagerly.

I hold up a second finger. "Then I need to get a job."

She looks less enthused about this. "That's two. What's the third thing you need to get?"

"A tattoo." I give her a mischievous smirk.

"Right . . ." Her tone is doubtful. "Okay, I get the license and the job, Shannon, but why do you need a tattoo?"

"Why not?" As we enter the darkened stairwell, I explain my plan to get a monarch butterfly tattooed on my left ankle. "Not too big, but not too small. The butterfly symbolizes rebirth and freedom. This is going to be my summer of independence. Getting a tattoo will be like my badge of courage."

"Like your mom will ever agree to a tattoo." Merenda rolls her eyes. "Get real, Shannon. Your mom's even more conservative than mine, and my mom would have a cow if I got a tattoo."

"My mom will agree," I insist.

"Yeah, right." She shakes her head.

"I'll just have her sign a release form when she's groggy from her meds."

"Really?" Merenda's mouth twists to one side in a skeptical way.

6

"Well, she might agree even without her meds. This sickness has changed her some."

"How's she doing, anyway?"

"Once in a while she has a good day, which only means she can get out of her chair without getting sick. Most of the time she's so dizzy, she can't even stand." I pause to fish my door key from my bag. "That's why I need to get my license, so I can use her car. And then I need to get a summer job to earn some money. I honestly don't know if Mom will ever be able to go back to work . . . and living on Social Security isn't cutting it."

"Well, good luck with your three-part summer plan." Merenda pats me on the back as we pause on the third floor. "Can't say that I envy you on the job part, though. I'm totally looking forward to a *real* vacation this summer. I plan to do absolutely nothing at my dad's house. Well, if I can get away with it." She gives me a slightly pitiful look. "But, hey, it would be so cool if you got your license, Shannon. Especially if you can use your mom's car to go to school next fall. I'd be totally down with that."

"Yeah. Me too."

"And having a job might be kinda cool," she adds hopefully.

"Yeah, especially if I find a good one. I already made my résumé, and I plan to start looking tomorrow. I'll take my driver's test on Monday. I've been studying, and I'm pretty sure I'm ready." I make a cheesy grin. "So while you're at your dad's doing nothing, or vegging out in front of his big screen, I'll be an independent working woman earning my own money. I'll be driving my mom's car and doing pretty much as I please." I feel unexpectedly encouraged to think of it like this. My summer could turn out to be pretty cool after all.

Merenda's mouth twists to one side. "Well, when you put it like that, it does sound kinda appealing."

"Hopefully I'll find a job I actually like. I'm going to apply at Marlee's Thrift Shop to start with. I heard she might be hiring for the summer."

"Keep me posted, okay?"

"Absolutely. And I'll text you a photo of the tattoo as soon as I get it too."

Merenda laughs, then opens her arms for a hug. "I'll miss ya, Shannon."

I hug her back. "Me too."

"Tell your mom I'm still praying for her to get well."

I nod. "Yeah, I will."

"See ya—wouldn't wanna be ya!" Merenda laughs at the old rhyme, waving as she disappears into the shadows of the hallway that leads to her apartment.

As I trudge on up the stairs to the top floor, I try not to feel too envious of my best friend. Despite my teasing Merenda about becoming a vegetable, I know she's lucky to spend summers at her dad's house. Not only does she escape the city, but her dad's house is even by a lake, and her stepmom actually sounds pretty nice. Really, it would be a dream summer to me.

In most ways, Merenda and I have a lot in common. Both of us are only children. Both of us live with a single mom—although my mom is widowed and Merenda's is divorced. And until last spring both of our moms worked full time at the same factory. Then my mom got sick. That's when things began to change.

"Shannon?" Mrs. Wimple pokes her head out of her door. Spying me in the hall, she quickly steps out in front of me and tightens the belt of her raggedy pink bathrobe. Her damp gray hair sticks out like she's just emerged from the shower. "I hoped that was you, dear. I wanted to catch you before you went in."

I smile politely at my elderly neighbor. Mrs. Wimple is a retired army nurse, and she's been a real saint when it's come to helping with my mom these last few months. "What's up?"

Mrs. Wimple's expression grows serious. "I'm worried about your poor mother."

"Oh?" I bite into my lip, bracing myself for the worst. "Did Mom fall down again?"

Mrs. Wimple somberly shakes her head. "No, no, but she was so dizzy she would've taken a tumble if she'd tried to get out of her chair without help. The problem is that she couldn't keep a thing down all day. And it's like an oven in your apartment, but she refuses to run the air conditioner because of the electric bill. I'm concerned that she's gotten herself dehydrated again."

"I'll make her a smoothie," I assure her. "She always likes those."

"There's something else." Mrs. Wimple puts a hand on my arm, stopping me from going. "I don't like to interfere, dear, but I really think you and your mother should go stay with your grandparents—"

"Grandparents?" *Is she serious?* "I don't think so, Mrs. Wimple." I say the words slowly, mechanically. "I mean, from what I've heard, my dad's parents . . . well, they weren't the nicest people, if you know what I mean. They didn't come to Dad's funeral or even send a card."

"I don't mean your father's family."

"But my mom doesn't have any family."

"As a matter of fact, your mother *does* have family." Mrs. Wimple pushes a wet strand of gray hair away from her face.

"Huh?"

"She told me all about it today. Your mother has relatives in Ohio."

"What?" I blink in surprise.

Mrs. Wimple tugs me by the arm toward her door. "Come in here so we can talk. Hurry, before all my cool air escapes into the hallway."

Feeling confused, I walk into the cluttered living room while Mrs. Wimple closes the door, then turns on a floor lamp. "What are you saying?"

"Just a minute." Mrs. Wimple holds up a hand. "I need to get something." She shuffles off to her bedroom.

I stand there waiting, trying to absorb what Mrs. Wimple has told me. *My mother has relatives?* Feeling baffled yet curious, I listen to the cheerful twitters of Mrs. Wimple's parakeets and wonder what's keeping her. Finally I wander into the kitchen to say hi to the birds. Mrs. Wimple has kept birds for as long as I've known her. She calls this pair Pearlie and Pokey and thinks of them as her children, but their rank-smelling birdcage is overdue for a cleaning. Probably neglected because of my mom.

"Here I am," Mrs. Wimple calls out as she returns to the living room.

I leave the birds, returning to the living room to see Mrs.

Wimple with her damp hair combed down so flat that her pale scalp shines through. Still wearing her pink bathrobe, she now has a zebra-print handbag looped over one arm. "I don't know if your mother told you this or not, but my sister and I are taking a month-long cruise this summer. We leave on Saturday."

"That sounds like fun. I hope you have a good time." Thinking that's all she has to tell me, and remembering how older people can sometimes be a little weird, I edge toward the door.

"I've arranged for Pearlie and Pokey to stay with Mr. Warren in apartment 537," she continues as if she feels I need to know all about her vacation plans. "The problem is that I'm worried about your mother, Shannon. What will she do when I'm not here to help her?"

"Well, I'm on summer break now, so I'll be around more," I say, trying to disguise my uncertainty. "Although I might get a job too. At least I'd like to."

"Yes, well, I'm afraid you'll have to put that job on hold for now."

"Why?"

"As I was saying, Shannon, your mother has family. And that is very good news, don't you think?"

"I, uh, I don't know. I mean, I always assumed my grandparents were dead or something. I thought Mom was an orphan. I mean, she doesn't like to talk about it much, but I do remember her saying she lived in some kind of a group home when she was a teen."

"It seems that your mother left home when she was very young, Shannon. Even younger than you are now. And you're right, she was in foster care for a few years during high school. But as it turns out, she does have family, and I've taken the liberty of contacting them for you."

"What?"

"I spoke to them today."

"Seriously?"

"I'm not sure why your mother was estranged from her folks, but she gave me her parents' phone number. I actually spoke to your mother's brother this morning, and I was relieved to discover that he sounds like a decent, God-fearing man. He seemed very eager to have you and your mother come visit the family. They only live about five hours away from Indianapolis. It's been all arranged for you to—"

"Are you kidding?"

"Not in the least." Mrs. Wimple smiles. "Your uncle explained that you'll need to take the bus to Hochstetler."

"Hochstetler?" I feel like the floor has been pulled out from under me. "I—uh—I've never even heard of it."

"Maybe not, but it sounds like a perfectly charming town with lots of delightful little shops. The woman at the bus station told me she's been there before. She said that tourists flock to Hochstetler in the summer." Mrs. Wimple reaches into her zebra handbag. "So I went ahead and purchased your bus tickets today."

"Bus tickets?" I ask weakly.

"Yes, dear. Don't worry, it's my treat." She presses a thin envelope into my hand. "I'll drive you both to the bus station tomorrow. The bus leaves at 10:40 a.m."

"But I don't know what—"

"I know it seems a little sudden, but I do think it's for the best. Strike while the iron's hot, I always say."

"But I—"

"Now, I don't want you to worry about a thing, Shannon. Just make sure you and your mother are ready to leave by 10:00. That'll give us plenty of time."

"What if Mom doesn't want to—"

"Your mother has already agreed that it's the best plan," she says firmly. "For everyone."

"Really?" I feel completely blindsided by this. "Mom *wants* to go?"

Mrs. Wimple's expression grows serious. "She's very ill, Shannon. And you know that she has no health insurance now that she's not working. She's been struggling to get well, and I see her making a little progress, but what will happen when I'm gone for a month? Your mother needs more help and support than you can give her, and it seems her family is ready and able to step up. Truly, it's a godsend, don't you think?"

"Maybe . . . but how long will we be gone?"

"As long as it takes for her to get better. You do want her to get well, don't you?"

"Yes, of course. But is she even strong enough to make this trip? And on a bus?"

"The bus station woman was very helpful. Your seats are reserved in the rear of the bus, near the bathroom, and she made certain no one else would be back there with you. Your mother will be able to lie down and rest. I suggest that you give her an extra dose of her medicine as soon as you board. That will relax her, and I expect she'll sleep most of the way."

"Even so, this is a lot to—"

"It's all worked out, dear. I plan to fix you both some food and drinks to take along." Mrs. Wimple sighs with satisfaction. "All you'll need to do is keep your poor mother comfortable for the duration of the trip and make sure you get off at the right bus stop in Hochstetler. Your uncle has promised to be there to meet you."

I am speechless. Totally blindsided. Is this really happening?

"I don't expect you to thank me, dear. But I want you to do all you can to help your poor mother." She pats me on the back. "Now, you'd better get moving. You'll need to pack for the two of you. Don't forget to bring a couple pillows for your mother. Maybe a small throw blanket too. The woman said the air-conditioning can get a little cool."

"But what about our apartment and—"

"I have a key, and I'll see to emptying your fridge and cleaning up some. And I'll arrange to forward your mail and whatever else needs doing."

"That's very generous of you." I stare at the blue envelope in my hand. "But it's all so sudden. Are you sure my mom is really—"

"She's very relieved, Shannon. Trust me. This is exactly what both of you need." Mrs. Wimple gently nudges me out of her apartment. "I know you must have lots to do. Don't let me keep you."

I feel dazed as I go next door and unlock the door to the apartment Mom and I have shared for the last six years—ever since Dad died and we lost our house, like a lot of other families in our neighborhood did too. As I go inside, I remember how unhappy I was when we moved to this complex back then, but I realize that now this is home. It's all we have. Suddenly the idea of leaving this pathetic little place, or perhaps even losing it if we can't keep up with the rent—well, it feels pretty disturbing. As well as rather scary.

2

I quietly let myself into our apartment. Like in Mrs. Wimple's apartment, the drapes are drawn, but with no air-conditioning, it feels hot and stuffy. Mom, as usual, is sleeping in her La-Z-Boy recliner in the tiny living room. The doctor recommended the chair for her last month because for some reason the reclined position helps with her dizziness. At first he diagnosed Mom with some kind of vertigo with a long name, called BPPV for short. BPPV sounded like a debilitating illness with no real cure or treatment, so I was relieved to find out that was wrong. However, it does make me question how much medical professionals really know.

When the doctor changed Mom's diagnosis to Ménière's disease, it was supposed to be good news. He said Ménière's might be a temporary condition, and he prescribed diazepam to help alleviate her symptoms. While it's nice having medicine to give her, I know these meds are a form of Valium, and according to Mrs. Wimple, they are highly addictive, which is why she strongly encouraged me to control them for my mom. But I have to admit, they do seem to help some. Mom never really gets better, but she doesn't seem to be getting worse either. However, as the weeks and months have passed, the likelihood of her returning to work has seemed to steadily diminish.

"Mom?" I lean down to check on her. "You awake?"

Lying very still, she doesn't even flinch, but I can see she's breathing evenly and seems somewhat comfortable. Satisfied she's okay, I drop my bag on a chair, then head to the kitchen to make her a smoothie. Even if the blender noise disturbs her sleep, it will be worth it to get some fluid into her. Mrs. Wimple is right to be concerned about dehydration. That could result in a visit to the ER, and I know from experience that's expensive.

As the blender loudly whirls the frozen strawberries, milk, honey, and protein powder, I break Mom's frugal rule by turning on the AC. Really, how expensive could a few hours be? Besides, according to Mrs. Wimple's plans, we'll be long gone by the time the bill arrives in July. Of course, our helpful neighbor will probably forward that bill along with the other mail. Our much-needed monthly Social Security check is a direct deposit, though, so we don't have to worry about that. Still, this is so sudden, so unexpected. I try to imagine what tomorrow will be like as I pour the frothy pink liquid into a glass. Will we really go through with this crazy plan?

"Shannon?" Mom's voice sounds raspy. "Is that you in there?"

"Sorry, Mom." I emerge from the kitchen with the smoothie. "Did the blender wake you?"

"Uh-huh." Mom rests the back of her wrist on her forehead.

"Well, that's probably good because you need to drink this." I hand her the glass. "Made with love."

Mom takes a tentative sip. "It's good," she murmurs. "Thanks, sweetie."

"Mrs. Wimple told me about, uh, her plans for us." I sit down on the couch across from Mom. I know I need to say this carefully in order not to upset her. "She said we're going to . . . uh, to see your family?"

Mom sets the half full glass on the TV tray next to her chair. "Yes. I meant to tell you first, Shannon. I know it's a bit sudden."

"That's okay." I try to make my voice sound light and unconcerned. "Mrs. Wimple gave me the bus tickets and explained the whole thing. It sounds like an interesting idea."

Mom's brow creases. I'm not sure if it's from pain or anxiety. "She told you about my parents? My family?"

"She said they live in Ohio, and that your brother will meet us at the bus stop in Hochstetler."

"Oh my." Mom presses both hands to the sides of her forehead and groans quietly.

"Do you need a pill, Mom?"

Mom looks up at the wall clock. "Yes. I think that would help. If it's not too soon."

"Can you finish your smoothie first?" I urge. "Please?"

Mom reaches for the glass and takes another slow sip and then another. Satisfied that she is cooperating with the rehydration program, I return to the kitchen to get her a pill. Having the diazepam this early will probably knock her out for the duration of the evening, but perhaps that will be for the best. Especially if the idea of making this trip is as stressful to her as it is to me. I am well aware that stress only makes Mom worse.

"Here you go." I hand her the pill and wait for her to wash it down with the last of the smoothie.

"Thank you, my angel." Mom picks up the TV remote. "Want to watch the housewives show with me?"

"I'll take a pass this time." I give her a tolerant smile. Those silly reality shows are my mom's one remaining "guilty plea-sure," and sometimes I pretend to enjoy them with her, but mostly I can barely tolerate the shallowness of the spoiled housewives. I wonder what it is about them that Mom finds so entertaining. "You can fill me in on it later," I say as I pick up my school bag.

"Yes, I will. If I don't doze off again."

With so much to get done before the big trip tomorrow, it might be just as well if Mom snoozes in front of the TV this evening. With her asleep, I won't have to keep pretending that I'm down with this plan. I might even be able to throw a quiet little temper tantrum if I want. Not that I would, but it's nice to know that I can. As I pick up the basket of dirty laundry from the bathroom, gathering a few things from the floor to toss in as well, I recall the three-point summer plan I told Merenda about. Well, maybe next year.

After running down to the basement to put a load of laun-dry in a washer, I start getting Mom's suitcase packed. Since getting sick, Mom's go-to wardrobe has consisted primarily of warm-ups. She has four different sets of sweats that she wears 24-7. My biggest challenge has been to make sure there's always a fresh set available, especially since Mom's dizziness and nausea sometimes create laundry issues. It's around 8:00 when I finally bring the clean laundry upstairs and finish packing Mom's underclothes, socks, and personal items. Satisfied that I've thought of everything, I place the filled suitcase by the front door.

I know it's time to pack my own bags, but I don't want to. I even question whether it's necessary for me to go on this unexpected trip at all. If there was any way out of this, I would gladly take it. I start to wonder if I could just put Mom on the bus tomorrow. Make sure she's comfortable and wish her well, and then I could stay here and continue with my original summer plan. I even consider approaching Mom with this idea, explaining how I could get my license as well as a job to bring in some money. I wouldn't tell her this, but if she would agree to my plan, I would even postpone the tattoo. Really, the more I think about it, the more it makes perfect sense.

But when I go back out to check on Mom, I begin to doubt that my plan will work. Mom's asleep in her chair with the TV still droning on. Tiptoeing over, I pick up the remote and quietly push the Power button. With the AC working, the apartment is much cooler, so I grab a throw blanket, tucking it around her. She doesn't even move. I go to the kitchen and gather some rations she might need during the night—a carton of apple juice, a packet of peanut butter crackers, and a water bottle. I quietly carry them back and arrange them on the TV tray next to her.

Satisfied that she has what she needs, I stand there looking at her for a long moment. I've heard the expression "she's just a shadow of her former self," but it never made sense before. Now I realize that it pretty much describes my mom. She used to be so young looking and energetic and vibrant that sometimes people actually thought we were sisters. Now she looks so old and haggard and pale. She's so weak that she could never make the trip alone. It was selfish for me to even entertain that idea.

That means it is time for me to pack. In my bedroom, I close the door and look around my room with uncertainty. How long until we'll return to this apartment? Will we ever be able to come back? I wonder what would happen to all our stuff if we were unable to pay our rent while we were gone. What if I never see this room again? I reassure myself that Mom and I will not let that happen. I feel certain that Mrs. Wimple would not let that happen either.

In the meantime, I need to make some decisions. What to pack? Will we be gone for a few weeks or the entire summer? I don't want to pack too much, especially since I know I'll need to carry both Mom's bags and mine. But I don't want to forget anything important either. I decide on two bags, one midsize and one that's smaller.

I start by gathering up my art supplies. If I have any time on my hands, it might be fun to create something. I pile a couple of sketch pads and some colored pencils, watercolors, and charcoal sticks into the smaller bag. On top of that I place my iPad and cell phone—luxuries we were able to afford back when Mom was gainfully employed. Items I don't take for granted anymore. I neatly coil up the charge cords and earbuds for the gadgets and pack them as well.

Next I go to my dressing table, running my hand over the

top of it. It's an old piece of furniture I found at Goodwill a couple years back, and I totally love it. I painstakingly reinvented this dresser by painting it robin's egg blue, then layering on a white crackly overcoat that made it look even older. To give it some bling, I added some pink glass knobs I found at a thrift shop. I did the same treatment to several other unique pieces in an effort to create my own shabby chic bedroom decor. The end result was so charming that I actually took several photos of my room and posted them on Pinterest.

To my delight, others on Pinterest commented on my decorating skills, marveling that a teenager possessed such talent. Naturally my head grew bigger. And when Merenda saw it, she begged me to redecorate her bedroom in shabby chic as well. Maybe someday, if a career in fine art doesn't pan out like I hope it might, I'll take up interior design instead.

Daydreaming about my future in art and design, I look into the slightly blurry old mirror that sits atop my dresser and notice that the natural curl has returned to my red hair. Thanks to the day's excessive heat and humidity, I could now play the starring role in *Annie*. Knowing I'll be too busy to straighten it out in the morning, and truthfully just wanting to sidetrack myself from packing, I plug in my ceramic flatiron and take my time restraightening my hair. As I work on it, I think about the unknown relatives I'll be meeting tomorrow and wonder what they will think of me.

When I finally set the hair appliance down to cool, I'm pleased with the results, and even though it's nearly 11:00, I don't regret taking the time. When my shoulder-length hair is straight and silky, it's really not so bad. In fact, Merenda always insists my copper-colored tresses are one of my best physical features. I'm aware that redheads are common in my dad's Irish family, but as I stare at my slightly pointy face, I wonder what traits have come from Mom's side. She's always told me that I have her eyes, and I must admit they're similar in the way they slant up at the sides. They're the same shade of greenish blue too. I also have a similar build as my mom; both of us are petites and can share clothes and shoes, although she's been so sick that I'm sure I outweigh her now.

As I wash my face and brush my teeth in the bathroom, I can't help but notice the freckles splattered across my nose and cheeks. These came from my dad. Although he admitted to having been teased for his freckles as a boy, he assured me they looked charming on me and even called them "fairy kisses." But the older I got, the less I liked these spots, and this year I started using a light foundation to cover them up. I remind myself to pack that too.

As I return to packing, I continue to wonder about these relatives I've never met. What will they be like? What will they think of me? Aside from that, I wonder why my mom left her family so long ago. Why is she suddenly willing to go back to them now? Well, besides needing help with her illness, and Mrs. Wimple's helpful "encouragement."

Back in my room, I pack my flatiron, and then, remembering the importance of proper hair drying temperatures for my sort of hair, I decide to pack my dryer as well. I tuck in my usual hair care products, then zip the first bag closed. Progress.

As I start on the larger bag, I keep wondering what Mom and I are getting ourselves into. Just because Mrs. Wimple declared my uncle to be a good man doesn't mean the rest of the family will be delightful. What if we get there only to discover that Mom's relatives are truly horrible people? Will Mrs. Wimple pay our fare to come back home? I doubt that as I set a couple pairs of my favorite jeans in the bottom of the bag. Our neighbor will probably be off cruising the continents by the time we understand we've made a mistake.

I don't even blame Mrs. Wimple. I get why she wants to send us packing. She's been carrying the load of Mom's sickness for nearly five months now. It's no wonder she's sending us to Hochstetler and sending herself off on a cruise. Who wouldn't want to escape all this?

Trying not to feel discouraged and hopeless, I continue layering clothing into the bag: a pair of capri pants, numerous T-shirts, some tank tops, a couple pairs of shorts, and a blue and white sundress. To make myself feel better, I decide to pretend I'm going on vacation, like Merenda and Mrs. Wimple. I pack my swimsuit and a number of other items that promise to make my summer enjoyable. I even put in some paperbacks that I've been wanting to read and imagine myself enjoying them next to a big swimming pool. Who knows? Perhaps visiting my grandparents will turn out to be fun. As I fetch my cosmetics bag from the bathroom, I realize there's a personality struggle going on inside of me. Part of me is a foolish optimist and the other part is an unrelenting realist. I suspect the realist will win out in the end.

As I zip up my second packed bag, the optimist raises her hopeful head, and I begin to wonder if there might be a way to get a job in my grandparents' town. Of course, that just rouses the realist, and she sharply reminds me that despite trying to make my résumé sound interesting, my only real paying job experience so far has been babysitting. Still, it is possible that my grandparents might know a family in need of child care.

My inner optimist reminds me that my dream job, for the summer anyway, has been to work in an antique shop or an art supply store, or even a gallery, if I want to dream really big, although I would gladly settle for a secondhand store too. I remember how Mrs. Wimple described Hochstetler as a small, quaint town. Suddenly my optimist is feeling very hopeful. Hochstetler could be filled with all kinds of interesting shops that are looking for part-time employees. As I get ready for bed, I begin to think that this abrupt change in plans might not be such a disappointment after all.

3

After a fragmented night of sleep interrupted by freaky nightmares about evil alien-like relatives, I manage to wake up in time to help Mom get ready for our big day. With the help of Mrs. Wimple, we get the bags loaded into the trunk of her car, but we can't get my mom out of the apartment until after 10:20. By the time we're on the road, it's nearly a half hour later than what Mrs. Wimple originally planned.

"Will we make it?" I quietly ask Mrs. Wimple as she drives a little too fast through a yellow light.

"Unless we get stuck in downtown traffic," she says with a concerned tone. "Pray that we don't, Shannon."

I nod as if I will do this, but the truth is, I don't pray. In fact, I rarely pray about anything anymore. I used to pray a lot, and I know Merenda still does. But besides being out of the habit, I'm actually hoping that we'll be too late to get on the bus. We'll be forced to return home, and I will tell Mrs. Wimple bon voyage and insist on sticking around to pursue my three-point summer plan.

As it turns out, we reach the bus station right as the bus is getting ready to leave, but thanks to the bus station woman who recognizes Mrs. Wimple and rushes to our aid with a wheelchair, we are able to get my mom loaded onto the bus. Feeling conspicuous and uneasy as curious travelers stare at us, I try to act nonchalant as I help Mom get settled into the vacant seat in the very back. The driver announces our departure as I tuck pillows into the corner by the window and help Mom lean back into them.

Her hands are shaking and her eyes are filled with fear and anxiety as the bus slowly pulls out of the station. Speaking calmly to her, I lay the polar fleece throw over her legs and then hurry to extract a small white bundle from my shirt pocket. I remove a water bottle from the bag of "provisions" Mrs. Wimple gave to me this morning.

"What is that?" Mom's eyes are fixed on my tissue bundle as I fumble to unwrap it, finally producing a diazepam pill. Her eyes flicker with relief as she eagerly reaches for her pill.

"Mrs. Wimple said you should have an extra dose for the trip," I explain as I hand her the water bottle.

She eagerly pops the pill into her mouth, then swigs it down with water. "Thank you," she murmurs.

"That should help you to relax and sleep." I put the cap on the water bottle and slip it back into the bag.

"How long is the trip?" she asks as she leans back into the pillows again.

"Probably about six hours," I remind her. She's already heard this same answer several times this morning. "The trip would be more like five hours in a car, but every stop adds to the time."

"Oh . . . yes . . . I remember now." She takes in a deep breath and, letting out a weary sigh, closes her eyes.

"Just rest," I say quietly. "Hopefully we'll be there sooner than you expect."

For the first few hours, Mom sleeps fairly soundly while I read a paperback. But when she wakes she seems dizzy and woozy and disoriented.

Worried that she might throw up, I grab one of the barf bags that the train station woman handed to me before we boarded the bus. I also reach for Mrs. Wimple's provisions bag, extracting a pack of saltines along with a can of Sierra Mist. "Here, Mom." I pop open the can, handing it to her. "Take some slow sips."

"Where are we?" she asks with a fearful expression.

"On the bus," I whisper as I hand her a saltine. "Eat this."

"What bus?" Mom's eyes dart nervously around. "Where are we?"

"We're on the bus that's taking us to Hochstetler," I explain in a hushed tone. I try not to feel like a freak as some of the passengers crook their heads to curiously stare. Really, are we that interesting? Or are they simply that bored?

"Hochstetler?" Mom's brow creases as she nibbles on a saltine.

"To visit your family," I explain as I hand her a second saltine.

I notice an elderly woman watching us with what seems a sympathetic expression. I give her a stiff smile, then turn my attention back to Mom, encouraging her to have some more soda and crackers. "You'll feel better if you do," I urge. "You need to stay hydrated and keep something in your stomach. I'm hoping you can eat some yogurt."

She makes a face.

I pull out the small carton of yogurt and hold it out to her. "It will feel good on your stomach," I say enticingly.

"Can I have another pill with it?" Her blue eyes grow hopeful.

Mrs. Wimple warned me to try to hold Mom off on another pill until after we arrive in Hochstetler. That way she'll be coherent enough to meet her family. "Can you wait until we get there?" I ask.

"How long?"

I glance at my watch. "Two hours, maybe a little less."

Mom's lower lip slips out into a pouting expression as she stubbornly pushes the yogurt carton away from her.

I know this is all backward and bizarre. It's like I'm the mom and she's my child—and I'm sure it appears totally weird to onlookers. But that's the way life is right now, and I have to accept it. I love my mom more than anyone on this planet. Even though helping her is awkward and inconvenient and sometimes, like yesterday, I just want to be selfish, I am determined to stick by her. I want to get her through this illness. I think I would do almost anything to help Mom get back to her old self.

"I'll make a deal with you," I tell her. "If you eat the yogurt and some crackers and drink the soda as well as some juice, I'll let you have another pill."

She brightens a little, reaching for another cracker.

I feel slightly like a traitor as I watch her struggling to eat and drink. I honestly don't expect her to put away the short list of things I've given her, but after a few minutes, she's polished it all off and is holding out her hand for another pill.

I feel torn now. Is it crazy or irresponsible of me to have made that agreement with my mom? "Are you sure?" I ask with uncertainty.

"Yes, Shannon." Mom keeps her hand out. "The other pill has worn off completely. I'm sure it's because of the stress. I need another pill."

I nod, thinking that makes sense. Also, I remind myself, Mom is the adult here. These really are her pills. Who am I to play the drug police? So I dig through my purse, unzip the pocket where I've tucked her prescription bottle, remove a pill, then re-cap the bottle and carefully zip it back into the pocket. Mom washes down the pill with the last of her water and is soon peacefully sleeping again.

It's only an hour later when I hear the bus driver announce that we're arriving in Hochstetler. "Really?" I say to no one in particular since Mom's still soundly sleeping. "We're already there?"

"That's right," the elderly woman up ahead tells me. "This is Hochstetler. Are you getting off here?"

"Yes!" I say urgently, scrambling to gather up our stuff. I peel off the blanket, trying to wake my mom.

"All out for Hochstetler," the bus driver calls out after the bus stops moving.

"Come on, Mom." I tug on her arm, removing the pillows from behind her and shoving them into the bag I brought to carry them in. "We gotta go, Mom."

"You need a hand back there?" the driver asks as he comes down the aisle.

"Yes, please," I tell him. "My mom is really sick, and she's on medication. I'm not sure she can even walk."

He nods with a kind expression. "You go on out. Take your things. I'll help her get out."

I thank him, then hurry on ahead, eager to get out of the bus. The sun is still high in the sky as I stand on the sidewalk next to a restaurant, waiting. Glancing around, I wonder if my mom's family is somewhere nearby. Will they come to our aid?

"Here you go," the bus driver says as he and another man help maneuver my mom down the steps. Her eyes are open now, but she looks totally spacey and out of it. "Let's get her onto that bench there," the driver says.

I follow them over to a cement bench, watching helplessly as they set her down like a limp rag doll. I hurry over to sit next to her, holding on to her shoulders so she doesn't slide off and crumple onto the ground.

"Which are your bags?" the driver asks me.

I quickly describe our luggage, and before long he's plunked them down next to the bench. "You gonna be okay?" he asks me with a concerned frown.

"Yes, thank you," I assure him. "We have family meeting us here."

He tips his hat. "I hope your mom gets better soon."

I nod. "So do I."

He and the other man climb back into the bus, the door closes, I hear the hiss of the brakes, and just like that, the bus pulls out, leaving us behind. Suddenly I miss it and wish we were still on it. I.glance up and down the street, looking for someone—anyone—who could be here to help us. But no one even makes eye contact.

I've never felt so alone, and I'm starting to freak. What if none of Mom's family shows up? Mrs. Wimple gave me my grandparents' phone number along with a twenty-dollar bill, but she seemed convinced I wouldn't need either of them. Now I'm not so sure. But to get into my purse might mean spilling Mom onto the ground, so I simply squint into the bright sunshine and look around, hoping to spy someone who is looking for a pair of weary travelers.

"Mom?" I say quietly. "Can you wake up? Please?"

She moans softly, her head wobbling back and forth like one of those bobblehead dolls in slow motion. Although I refused to pray earlier today, back when Mrs. Wimple asked me to pray to get through traffic, I decide it's time. I'm usually the first one to admit that I don't take my faith as seriously as some people—like Merenda or Mrs. Wimple or even my mom—but put me in a helpless situation or back me into a dark corner, and I will most definitely call out to God for assistance.

As I'm praying, with my eyes wide open, I notice something's different in this town. I feel like I've gone back in time or I'm watching a historical movie being filmed here, because every so often, I see a horse-drawn carriage going down the street. I also observe some people dressed in old-fashioned clothes moving about this town. Finally, when a couple of young women in long dresses and crisp white bonnets walk past me, I get it. They are Amish. I know this from having watched a couple of reality shows about Amish teenagers, although I've never actually seen a real Amish person before.

Everything starts to feel entirely surreal as I sit here on the bench in this strange little town. The hot sun beats down on my head as I try to support my mom and keep her from sliding off the bench. I look down at her, realizing that she probably looks like a drunk. Besides being strung out on diazepam, her hair is messy and her clothes are rumpled and dirty looking—and I notice she's missing a shoe! Fortunately, it was only a worn ballet flat, and I packed a couple other pairs in her bag. I glance down at the mishmash of bags and suitcases surrounding us, knowing that we must look both desperate and pathetic.

I look up and down the street again, hoping beyond hope that a nice air-conditioned car will pull up and take us home where our family will take care of us. Perhaps my grandparents have a swimming pool, although I'd happily settle for a nice long shower. As I study the cars and passersby, I notice that Hochstetler is rather busy for a small town, and it definitely has a slightly touristy feel to it. In fact, it actually seems like a clean and attractive community.

Of course, that just seems to spotlight how Mom and I do not belong here. We're like a messy little blotch on an otherwise pretty picture. I suspect this is not what Mom's family expects to find when they come to pick us up. That is, if they are coming to pick us up.

Is it possible that the mysterious relatives have already passed by and, spotting our embarrassing spectacle, decided to simply continue on their way, pretending they didn't know us? I think of the cars that have driven slowly past, looking at us like we're sideshow freaks. Maybe Mom's family checked us out from a safe distance and then went on their merry way.

I'm about to lay Mom out on the bench like a dead body in order to dig out my phone and call the number that Mrs. Wimple gave me this morning when one of those horse-drawn carriages stops right in front of the bench.

"Anna Hershberger?" a man wearing a straw hat calls out to me.

I shake my head. "No, I'm not Anna Hersh—" I stop myself, staring up at him and wondering if that's the name Mrs. Wimple wrote down with the phone number. "My mom's name is Anna," I quickly say, before he can drive away. "Anna McNamara. She's come to—"

"Anna!" he exclaims as he hops down from the front of the boxlike carriage, hurrying to Mom's side. "It *is* Anna. What is wrong with her?" he asks me.

"She had some medicine," I explain. "It made her go to sleep."

He frowns at me. "Sleeping out here? On the street?"

I simply hold out my hands. What can I say?

"You must come with me," he says with authority. "We will go now."

"Who are you?" I demand. I suddenly feel wary about taking my drugged-up mom anywhere with a perfect stranger. Even if this dude does look relatively harmless with his concerned blue eyes and goofy beard.

"I am Benjamin Hershberger," he solemnly tells me. "I have come here to pick up my sister Anna and her daughter Shannon." He peers curiously at me. "That must be you. Shannon?"

"Yes!" I nod eagerly. No way could he know both our names if he wasn't a relative.

34

He kneels down by the bench, peering curiously at my mom. "Anna?" he says with concern. "Come now, Anna, it's time to go home."

"She can't hear you," I say. "Her meds have knocked her out. I wouldn't have given them to her, but I didn't realize we'd get here—"

"I will help her." He scoops up my mom, cradling her like a child in his arms as he climbs into the back of the strange little carriage. "Come," he calls to me. "Help me with her now."

Grabbing the bag with the pillows, I hurry to climb into the boxy carriage, quickly shoving the pillows onto the firm bench as I try to help Mom recline somewhat comfortably without falling off. Meanwhile he gathers up our other bags and sets them inside too. Then, without saying a word, he climbs into the seat in front, and just like that, we start moving down the street.

As I sit next to Mom, holding on to her to keep her from sliding off the bench seat, everything begins to feel very surreal again. The sound of the horse's hooves clip-clopping on the pavement, the bumpy swaying of the carriage as it rumbles along—it's so unlike anything I've ever experienced before that for a moment I honestly think I'm hallucinating. Or perhaps I'm still asleep in my bed, having another strange dream.

I watch in wonder as we slowly move through the town, then take a turn that leads us down what eventually turns into a country road with small farms spotted here and there along the way. I begin to accept that this is not my imagination. It is for real. I peer up at the strange man driving the horse. It seemed like he was really my mom's brother, which would make him my uncle. But studying him as he drives the horse, with his old-fashioned looking black jacket, his yellow straw hat, and his black leather boots, he seems like someone from another world, maybe even another planet. I begin to wonder—*where on earth is he taking us?*

4

We're still rumbling down the country road when Mom starts to wake up. Not surprisingly, she looks startled and afraid. "Where are we?" she demands, clasping my hand so firmly that it actually hurts.

I quickly explain about her being asleep when we arrived in Hochstetler. "Your brother Benjamin picked us up." I point to the driver of the carriage. "I'm not sure where he's taking us, though."

"Benjamin?" She says his name slowly.

"He is your brother, right?" Suddenly I'm worried. What if I've let some crazy person kidnap us? But with a horse and carriage?

"Yes, yes." Mom sits up now, holding on to her head as if she's getting dizzy. "Oh, dear! Please, can we stop? I feel sick."

I call out to Benjamin and he stops the horse, turning around to peer inside the carriage.

"My mom's feeling sick," I explain to him. "The motion of the carriage makes her dizzy."

"Oh?" He rubs his chin. "Does she want to walk?"

"No, no, I don't think so." I dig through the bag, looking for a water bottle and some saltines. "She's too weak to walk."

He gets down and comes around to the side door to peer inside. "Anna?" he says in a gentle voice. "How are you?"

"Oh, Benjamin." Mom's voice chokes with emotion. "I'm not very well."

He nods. "*Ja*. I can see that. Does the buggy make you sick?"

"Everything makes me sick," she says as I hand her a saltine. Pointing to her head, she sighs. "I have a sickness that makes me dizzy."

"Oh." He frowns. "How will we get you home?"

"Just give us a couple minutes," I assure him. "Sometimes crackers help. And a little water. Then we can go." To be safe, I remove one of the emergency barf bags and keep it handy.

"Okay," Mom declares after a couple of crackers. "Go ahead and drive the buggy, Ben. Don't worry about me. Just get us there."

"*Ja*." He nods. "You can rest better at home."

Once again we are moving down the road. I consider offering Mom more diazepam but don't want her to fall asleep again. "Your brother seems nice," I say.

"He's a good guy."

"Is he Amish?" I ask tentatively.

"Yes."

"What about the rest of your family?" I ask.

"They are all Amish, Shannon."

I try not to act as stunned as I feel. "They're all Amish? Does that make you Amish too?"

"No. I am *not* Amish. That's why I left." She leans back, closing her eyes again.

"Oh." How am I supposed to wrap my head around this? I want to ask her to explain herself, but I know this isn't the time or place—I don't want to stress her out. So we sit there without speaking, hearing only the rumbling of the buggy's wheels, the rhythmic beat of the horse's hooves, and an occasional car passing by.

"I'm sorry I didn't tell you, Shannon."

I can't even think of a response to that. I mean, I appreciate that she's sorry, but keeping something like this from me? Especially when I always thought that we were so close? Well, it's more than a little disturbing, and I wonder, when did she intend to tell me?

I think about an hour or more passes before the buggy turns off the main road onto a narrower one. We are deep in farm country now, going past one farm after another, and all of them look strikingly similar. Most have a white two-story farmhouse and a big red barn with numerous outbuildings and tall silos all neatly laid out around it. Because it's late June, everything growing around these farms looks green and lush, and the landscape has a peaceful, pastoral feeling. Like something you might see in a children's picture book. Very unreal.

Mom is sitting up straight now. I can tell by her expression that she still feels woozy, but there's a light of interest in her eyes too. "Up there." She points to a house and barn coming up on the right. "That is my parents' home."

"That *was* our parents' home," Benjamin calls over his shoulder as he turns the horse and buggy onto a gravel road. "Now it is where I and Katrina and the children live."

"Oh?" Mom looks slightly concerned. "What about Mamm and Daed? Where do they live?"

"In the dawdi house."

"Dawdi house?" I ask.

"Grandparents' house," she explains.

"See that little house on the other side of the barn?" Benjamin points toward a small white structure. "We built that for them not long after Isaac was born."

"Isaac?" Mom asks him. "I remember your boys Samuel and Joshua. Did you have another son?"

"*Ja*. Isaac is our third son. He is twenty-three."

"Born after I left," Mom says quietly.

"You left twenty-three years ago?" I ask.

"I was fifteen." She looks up at Benjamin. "So you have three sons?"

"Four sons. Jeremiah is the last son. He's twenty-one. Then we have two daughters. Grace is nineteen. She got married last month. Our youngest is Rachel. She is seventeen. And that is all."

"Six children." Mom sighs loudly. "How nice for you."

"Six children and three grandchildren. Samuel married Abigail Miller, and they have three girls."

"Oh my." Mom looks surprised. "My big brother is a grandpa."

He slows down the buggy in front of the small white house now. "You will stay with Mamm and Daed," he declares as we come to a complete stop. "They are expecting you."

"Oh, Shannon." Mom reaches for my hand and grips it tightly. "I don't think I'm ready for this."

"You and me both," I nervously tell her.

Benjamin reaches into the buggy to assist her. "Let me help you, Anna."

After some struggling, together we manage to get Mom out of the buggy and on her feet in the driveway. "Hold on to me," I tell her as I begin walking us toward the little white house. It looks so tiny, I can't imagine they will have room for us. Benjamin joins us, carrying all our bags.

"Anna!" The front door pops open and a woman wearing a long, dark blue dress waves toward us. "Welcome!" She has a spring in her step as she hurries to meet us, but when she gets closer, I can see that she is old. Her gray hair is pulled back tightly and hidden under a small white bonnet.

"Mamm!" Mom's voice cracks with emotion as the older woman wraps her arms around her.

"Oh, Anna!" she exclaims. "You came home. At last you came home."

Both of them are crying and holding on to each other, and I feel unnecessary and uncomfortable. Ignoring the reunion, Benjamin takes our bags up to the house, and I just stand here, watching.

"Mamm, this is Shannon," Mom is saying now. "My daughter."

Suddenly I'm being hugged by the gray-haired woman in the long dress. "Shannon," she places both her hands on my cheeks, staring directly into my eyes. "Welcome, child."

"Thank you," I say as she releases her grasp on my face.

"Shannon is sixteen," Mom tells her.

"Sixteen?" My grandmother shakes her head with a dismayed look. "All grown up and I am only meeting you now?"

"What should I call you?" I ask her.

"Mammi," she declares.

"That means grandma," Mom explains as Benjamin emerges from the little white house.

"I put their things in the other room," he tells Mammi.

She thanks him and then he excuses himself, saying he has work to finish before the sun goes down.

"Now come inside." Mammi puts her arm around Mom's waist. "I know you have been sick, Anna. And you must be weary from travel. You do not look good to me. Too thin. Too pale."

The inside of the house seems very stark with its wooden floors and plain wooden furnishings, but everything looks clean and neat. However, the space seems very small, and it feels even smaller when all three of us are standing in the living room together. I wonder how there can possibly be room for Mom and me in this miniature home.

"Your room is here." Mammi opens a door right off of the living room to reveal a very tiny room with a full-sized bed pushed up against one wall.

"Oh?" Mom tosses a concerned look at me as she sits down on the edge of the bed.

"We'll both sleep here?" I ask Mammi.

"*Ja*. Is it a problem?"

"Maybe I can sleep on the floor," I offer halfheartedly.

"You don't want to sleep with your mamm?"

"She's been *really* sick," I explain. "And I'm a very restless sleeper. I'm afraid I'd disturb her if we shared the same bed."

Mammi frowns. "Oh . . . *ja, ja,* I see what you are saying."

"I don't mind sleeping on the floor," I declare weakly. However, the hard wood floor doesn't look inviting.

Mammi looks uncertain, but then she nods. "*Ja,* that is fine. You can sleep on the floor. Come with me, Shannon. I will show you where there is more bedding."

"Maybe you should stay here and rest," I tell Mom.

"Yes. That might be wise."

I pull the two spare pillows from the bag. "Maybe we can prop you up with these so your head will be up."

"Thank you." She waits for me to arrange the pillows against the wall behind her.

"I'm afraid you're going to miss your La-Z-Boy," I tell her.

"What?" Mammi gives Mom an odd look. "You have a *lazy boy?*"

"It's a chair, Mamm." My mom leans back against the pillows and wearily closes her eyes. "A very comfy chair."

"A chair that she can sleep in," I explain to Mammi. "It leans back like this." I use my hand to show her. "It's called a La-Z-Boy."

She makes a confused frown. "That does not sound good to me. Laziness is sinful."

Feeling almost as dazed as Mammi looks, I tell Mom to get some rest and then follow my new grandmother out into the main room where she opens a closet that has a sparse selection of sheets and towels and blankets.

"Tonight you can get what you need for your bed from here," she says as she closes the door. She opens another door. "This is the bathroom."

I peek into the tiny and rather odd-looking bathroom.

The toilet looks normal enough, but the shower space is very small and the sink has a strange faucet. Still, I don't feel comfortable questioning every little thing.

"It was your uncle Benjamin who said we must have indoor plumbing," Mammi tells me. "Jacob—that is your dawdi—he did not want pipes in the house. But Benjamin insisted." Her gray eyes twinkle when she smiles. "I am glad that he did. Especially in the wintertime."

Next she shows me another small room with a bed the same size as the one Mom is resting in now. "Your dawdi and me, we sleep here."

"Dawdi?" I ask. "Does that mean grandparents or grandfather?"

"*Ja, ja*. It's both." She nods as she opens the window to let some air into the stuffy room. I am curious as to why there are no curtains over the windows, but then I am curious about a lot of things. "I forget you have been raised as an Englisher."

"A what?"

"Englisher," she says a bit sharply as she turns around to face me. "The ones that live outside and are not Amish. They are Englishers. Your mamm did not tell you about that?"

"No. But she didn't tell me that she was Amish either."

"She is *not* Amish." Mammi scowls. "She left us."

"I know," I say quietly.

Mammi's dark countenance brightens. "But now our Anna has come home to us. And she has brought you." She reaches over to touch my hair, twirling it in her fingers. "Such a color."

"My dad had hair like mine."

"Amish girls must pin up their hair and cover their heads—when they are out of the house." She removes some pins from her white bonnet, then slowly lifts it from her head and places it on a shelf by the door. "Our prayer covering is called a *kapp*," she tells me. "It is to be treated with respect."

"Did my mom used to wear these clothes too?" I ask.

"*Ja, ja.* All the girls here dress like this." She looks down at my khaki cargo pants, then shakes her head. "English girls who dress like boys. I do not understand."

Feeling self-conscious, I turn to leave the bedroom. "You have a nice house," I tell her when we are in the living room again. It isn't a heartfelt compliment, but I can't think of anything else to say.

"Our home is small and humble, but it is enough." Her stern countenance softens again. "But you have not seen the best room yet."

"What's that?"

"The kitchen." She tilts her head to the other end of the house.

To my surprise, the kitchen is by far the largest part of the house. But it is unlike any kitchen I've ever seen. The big sink has what looks like a pump for a faucet, and there are no modern appliances whatsoever. In the center of the room is a long, wooden table with a chair at the end and a bench on either side. "Looks like you can have lots of people for dinner here."

"*Ja.* We always have plenty of room at our table." She goes over to open the door on an old-fashioned black stove. I notice some pieces of wood and wood shavings stacked neatly but am surprised to see Mammi striking a match and lighting the stove.

"You're making a fire on a hot day like this?" I ask her.

"I can't cook supper without a fire in the stove."

"You cook in that thing?"

"*Ja.*"

I look around the kitchen now, remembering something I've read or heard before. "You don't have electricity, do you?"

"No. No electrical wires can come into our homes."

"What do you use for lights?" I ask.

She points to a kerosene lamp hanging on a hook by the sink. "This is good light. Also candles. And we have some battery lights too."

"So batteries are okay?"

"*Ja.* Just no wires to the house."

I wonder how I will manage to charge things like my iPad and phone. "What about phones?" I ask. "My neighbor said you have a phone. She gave me a number. Is it a cell phone?"

"Benjamin put a phone into the barn. It is to be used for business. Since the wires don't come to the house, it is allowed."

"Allowed?" I consider this. "So the Amish have a lot of rules?"

"We have our Ordnung."

"Ordnung?"

"*Ja.* Our Ordnung lights the path to a godly life."

So many questions are running through my mind now, but I don't even know where to begin. I feel like I'm visiting a foreign country.

"Would you like to help me make supper?"

"Sure," I tell her. "Although I'm not much of a cook."

Her brow creases. "Your mamm did not teach you to cook?"

"Not really."

She says a word in another language, but it doesn't sound

like a happy word. "Get the milk," she tells me as she sets a big kettle on top of the stove.

"Milk?" I glance around the kitchen. "Do you have a refrigerator?"

"It's out there." She tips her head toward a screen door that appears to lead to a back porch.

Curious if it's an electric appliance, I go out to the porch, and sure enough, there's an old-fashioned looking refrigerator. Inside of it I find what looks and smells like a pitcher of milk, so I carry it back to the kitchen.

"I thought you didn't have electricity in the house," I say as I hand the pitcher to her. "What about that refrigerator?"

"It runs on propane."

"Ah." I nod as if that makes sense. The truth is, I've never heard of such a thing.

But I think I'm starting to get it. These people are green. They like keeping life simple, and they obviously know how to live off the grid. I must admit that as I work with Mammi in the kitchen—asking questions and hearing some rather interesting answers—it is all becoming pretty intriguing. There's no denying that this kind of life has an appealing sort of charm. I'm wondering more than ever why my mother ever left this place.

5

"Anna is not coming to the table to eat with us?" Mammi asks me for the second time.

"She can't," I explain. "Sitting up in a chair and eating will probably make her sick to her stomach."

"She needs to eat," Mammi insists. "To get strong again."

"She'll have to eat in bed," I tell her.

"Eating in bed?" Mammi frowns as she removes something she calls shepherd's pie from the oven.

"She's not really used to eating too much solid food either."

"You think she cannot eat this?" Mammi asks.

"I'm not sure." I sniff it. "It smells delicious. The potatoes on top are soft, so it might be okay. But most of the time, I just fix her things like soup and smoothies."

"Smoothies?"

"That's when you put fruit and yogurt and things in a blender."

"Blender?"

"It's an electrical appliance that blends food."

She nods. "*Ja, ja*, I think I've seen that before."

Having convinced Mammi that Mom needs to have her meal in the bedroom, I proceed to fix a plate of food that I hope might tempt her to eat. But when I take it in to her, she holds up her hands. "I can't eat that."

"The shepherd's pie smells yummy, Mom."

"I'm sure it is." She leans back with her hands pressed to the sides of her head and closes her eyes. "But I can't."

"Yes, you can," I tell her. "At least you can taste it. I know you can eat the applesauce and the bread and butter. You can get those down if you'll try. I know you can."

"No, I *cannot*." With her eyes still closed, she juts out her jaw.

I don't like to do this, but I know it's time to resort to bribery again. "Well, Mom," I say in a firm tone. "If you can't eat your dinner, I can't give you your pill. You know you shouldn't have diazepam on an empty stomach."

Her eyes pop open. "But I need my pill, Shannon."

"I know." I hold out the plate to her. "You need to eat too. Besides, it will hurt your mom's feelings if you don't at least try to eat what she's worked so hard to fix for you."

She frowns, and I can tell I have her now. Although I feel sorry for her, I will not relent. After a long moment, she reaches out for the plate. Not trusting her, I remain by her bedside, watching as she takes a tentative bite of the applesauce. I stay there until I see her sample everything and I hear Mammi calling me to come to the supper table.

"You're doing great," I tell Mom as I go to the door. "Keep it up, and I'll give you your pill when I come back."

When I return to the kitchen, Mammi is already sitting at

49

one end of the table and a weathered old man with a gray fringe of beard circling his chin is sitting at the other end. He is wearing a disgruntled expression, and I suspect it's because I've kept them waiting.

"Sit down," Mammi commands in a stern tone. "It is time to pray now."

I sit down on the closest bench and bow my head, waiting for the man I assume is my grandfather, although no introduction has been made, to say a prayer. When no one utters a single word, I glance up. They both still have their heads bowed down and eyes closed. I feel confused. Do they expect me to say a blessing for them? If so, why didn't they just ask me? But suddenly my presumed grandfather lifts his head and, seeing me looking at him, scowls as he says, "Amen," and picks up his fork.

"Amen," Mammi echoes, giving me what feels like a warning expression.

"Amen," I say quietly.

"Jacob," Mammi says sweetly, "this is Shannon. Anna's girl. Your granddaughter."

"I know who she is," he grumbles as he sticks a large bite of food into his mouth.

Pleased to meet you too, I think as I slowly butter a piece of bread.

What little conversation that transpires at this table seems related to farm chores and church services. None of it includes me. I could be invisible and it would make no difference. From what I can see, my grumpy grandfather either is an old curmudgeon or else resents having guests in his tiny home, or maybe both. To make matters worse, he starts talking to

Mammi in a different language. At first I think he's pulling my leg, but I can tell by her face that she understands what he's saying. I'm pretty sure they're talking about Mom and me. Gramps does not seem happy about us being here. At least that's what I'm thinking.

When Gramps is finished, he shoves back his chair loudly. But as he stands, he lets out a growling sound, rubbing his elbow as if in pain. Without saying a word—not even a thank-you to Mammi for the nice meal—he leaves the kitchen through the back door, slamming it noisily behind him.

"Is he in a bad mood?" I quietly ask Mammi.

"A bad what?" Her brow creases as if she doesn't understand.

"I mean, he seems to be angry about something," I explain.

"Oh no, Jacob is not angry. It is sinful to be angry. Jacob hurt his arm doing farm chores yesterday. It is paining him some. That is all."

"Oh."

After supper, I check on Mom and am relieved to see that she's eaten most of her food. I give her a pill and then help her to the bathroom.

"Indoor plumbing?" she says in surprise. "That's something new."

"You still have to pump the water into the sink," I explain. Mammi already showed me how this room works.

"Yes, but even so, it's a big improvement from what I grew up with."

"The shower comes out of that bucket." I point to the bucket hanging from the ceiling. At the bottom of the bucket is a funny-looking showerhead. "Mammi says you fill it with hot water from the kitchen, with some cold water too, of course. She says if you do it just right, you can make one bucket work for a shower." I frown. "But I seriously doubt one bucket can really get you clean. I plan to bring an extra gallon of backup water with me."

"At least you are figuring things out here, Shannon. Good for you."

"I guess." I shake my head as I close the door, giving her some privacy. I have a feeling I have barely scratched the surface on figuring things out here.

As I wait for Mom to finish, I can't help but think about how strange everything here feels. In a way this Amish lifestyle reminds me of the time I went camping with Merenda and her dad. Except that was outside. And only for a few days.

After I get Mom settled back into her bed, I return to the kitchen to help Mammi clean up. Neither of us talks much as we work to wash the dishes. It's bad enough to have no dishwasher, but besides that, I have to hand pump cold water into the sink and then warm it up by adding hot water from a kettle on the stove. Then I have to refill the kettle to make more hot water. My initial impression of the charming Amish lifestyle is swiftly fading. This is hard work, and I can imagine how it could get old in time.

After the kitchen is cleaned, Mammi invites me to come outside to see her garden. "I enjoy being out here this time of day," she says as she pauses to pull a small weed.

"It's a nice garden," I tell her as I examine the tidy, even rows of green, tender plants.

"It will be nicer next month." She stoops down to pull another weed. Slowly standing, she holds the weed out to me. "It is easier to pluck the weeds when they are small."

I nod.

She points to a weed by my foot. "Go ahead, Shannon."

I bend down to pull out a weed, and before I know it, I am pulling out more weeds with my industrious grandmother. We work together like this for about an hour. When we finish our chore, my back is starting to ache. As we walk back to the house, I rub my lower back to get the stiffness out.

"You are not used to hard work?" Mammi asks as we go into the kitchen.

"I guess not."

"Bend the tree while it is young," she says mysteriously. "When it is old, it is too late."

"Huh?"

She shakes her head as she opens the pantry. She begins pulling out canisters and jars and things.

"What are you doing?" I ask curiously.

"Getting things out for baking," she says simply. "In the summer, I like to do my baking in the cool of the evening."

"Oh?"

"*Ja* . . . and then we have what we need for tomorrow."

I know I should offer to help her, but the truth is, I am exhausted. Completely and utterly exhausted. It feels like this has been the longest day of my life. So I tell Mammi that I think I should get my bed ready.

"*Ja, ja*," she says without looking up from where she is measuring flour into a bowl.

"I might just stay there with Mom and read awhile," I tell her, "before I go to bed."

She gives me a tired-looking smile. "*Gute nacht*, Shannon. *Schlaf gut*."

"Huh?" I peer curiously at her.

"Good night. Sleep good."

"Oh, yeah. You too. Good night, Mammi."

As I walk through the living room, I nearly collide with my grandpa, who has just come in the front door. As before, his expression is grim, and he simply grumbles as he passes by me on his way to the kitchen.

"Good night," I call out to him.

"*Gute nacht*," he mumbles back at me.

I go to the closet and select some things that I hope will make a comfortable bed, although as I carry the meager pile to my room, I have my doubts. I see that the pills have taken effect and my mom is soundly sleeping with her head still propped up on the pillows against the wall. I try to be quiet as I attempt to make a bed across the room from her. There is only a narrow pathway between her bed and mine. I hope she doesn't decide to get up in the middle of the night and accidentally step on me.

It's hot and stuffy in here, so I open the window to let some fresh air in. I wonder again why there are no curtains. Worried that Mom might get chilled in the night, I pull her blankets up over her. As usual, she's fallen asleep in her clothes, but at least she looks comfortable.

I wedge my bags against the wall beneath the window, fumbling around to find my favorite sleeping T-shirt as well as a paperback. But once I'm settled into my hard-as-a-rock bed, I notice that it's dusky out and getting darker, and there is no light to read by in here. If only I'd known we were time-traveling to a previous century, I might've packed a flashlight. Lying in the semidarkness, I am wide awake and well aware that I never go to bed this early. I consider powering up my iPad but doubt there's any internet to connect to in these parts, and knowing I can't recharge my battery, I don't want to waste it. However, I do recall seeing a pair of kerosene lanterns on a little side table in the living room. I don't see why anyone would miss one.

Wearing my oversized T-shirt, I crack open the bedroom door and peek out to see that the living room is empty. I see a warm, golden light coming from the kitchen and smell something delicious baking in there—and for a moment I feel like I'm living in a fairy tale. As I tiptoe out, I can hear my grandparents' quiet voices. I pick up the smaller of the two lanterns but then realize I'll need matches to light it. I look around and notice a little metal box hanging on the wall, and upon closer inspection, I see that it contains matches. I'm getting a small handful of wooden matches when I hear heavy footsteps coming.

I turn just in time to see my grandfather emerging from the kitchen. He stops in his steps as if he's shocked to see me. His eyes grow so wide it feels like he's caught a burglar red-handed in his house. I imagine how strange I must look wearing only my sleep T-shirt. We lock eyes for an uncomfortable instant, and then without saying a word, feeling completely embarrassed by his scornful expression, I scurry back to my room with the filched lantern and matches in my trembling hand.

I wish Mom was awake so I could tell her all about my weird encounter. Is it possible that mean, old, creepy guy is truly her dad . . . my grandpa? He certainly hasn't gone out of his way to make me feel welcome here. As I make a couple of feeble attempts to light the kerosene lantern, getting down to my last match, I think I'm starting to get why she left. Finally the wick ignites, with flames leaping so high I'm surprised my hair doesn't go up in smoke. I fumble to figure out how to turn the wick down to reduce the flame, and when I feel it's relatively safe, I replace the glass chimney and set the lantern where it won't get knocked over. Even so, I seriously wonder how Amish people manage to keep their homes from burning down.

As I set the lantern on the wooden floor next to my make-shift bed, I must admit that it puts out a nice cozy light. Once again I have the feeling that I'm camping. Indoor camping. If only I'd thought to bring a few necessities like an air mattress and flashlight, I might have a better attitude. As it is, I don't even have a pillow. I roll up my bag and put it behind me as a pillow, lean back, and read until my eyes refuse to focus.

I have no idea what time it is when I blow out the lantern and slide it safely into a corner of the room. The house is so silent that I begin to wonder if anyone else is even here. I suppose my grandparents are probably sleeping. The evening air drifts into the room, and I can hear the sounds of crickets and frogs outside, as well as an occasional hoot of an owl, all reinforcing the feeling that I'm on a campout. If I knew I only had to rough it for two or three nights, I think I could live with it. But the idea of being here all summer . . . perhaps even indefinitely . . . well, that's just plain freaky!

6

The next morning my body aches from sleeping on the rock-hard floor. I'd be better off sleeping outside in the grass. In fact, as I'm sitting outside on the front porch, getting some fresh air while Mom is using the bathroom, I decide that tonight I will do precisely that. After everyone has gone to sleep, I'll sneak my blankets out here and camp outside. I scratch a mosquito bite on my elbow, one of about a dozen I got last night, and decide that sleeping outside can't be any worse than being in that bedroom with no screen on the window.

Curious to investigate the prospects, I walk barefoot through the long grass, rounding the corner to the side where our bedroom window faces. I figure that if I make my bed right here, I'll be able to hear Mom if she calls out for help during the night.

"What're you lookin' for?" a gruff voice demands.

I turn around to see my grandfather watching me. Although his face is shaded by his broad-brimmed straw hat,

I can tell he's scowling. Or maybe his expression is permanently sour.

"Nothing," I tell him. "Just looking around."

"If you got nothing to do, your mammi has plenty a' work in the kitchen."

"Okay." I shrug and walk past him into the house. Before I go to offer my assistance in the kitchen, though, I make sure that Mom is safely back in the bedroom and relatively comfortable.

"Do you want to try to come out for breakfast?" I ask.

"No, I don't think I can manage that." She sighs. "Besides, I'm not hungry, and I'm sure I won't be able to keep anything down anyway."

"You need to eat something," I insist. "That is, if you want a pill."

She narrows her eyes. "I know what you're doing, Shannon."

"What?"

"Blackmailing me with food in order to get my diazepam." She frowns as she eases herself back into the pillows.

I give her an innocent look. "I'm following Mrs. Wimple's directions. She said you need to have food in your stomach before you take a pill."

"Mrs. Wimple is not here." Mom folds her arms across her front, clearly annoyed. Not that I particularly care.

"Yes, and that's why I'm in charge," I remind her.

"Just because I'm sick doesn't mean I have no rights."

I want to point out that I'm the one who seems to have no rights, but I know starting an argument with her would be worse than pointless. "At least you're lucky to be stuck in this room." I slide my feet into my flip-flops.

"Lucky?"

"Yeah. You don't have to be around your parents."

"Oh." She looks slightly concerned as she rubs her temples with her fingertips. "Are they really bad?"

"Well . . . your mom's okay, I guess. I mean, except for being a total workaholic. But your dad . . ." I lower my voice. "Well, I think I understand why you left."

"Really?" Her hands slide down to her lap. "Daed used to be easier to get along with than Mamm."

"Maybe things have changed."

"I'm sorry, Shannon."

I go over and put my hand on her shoulder now. "I'm sorry too, Mom. I shouldn't complain. It's just that everything feels so weird and backwards and upside down." I rub my backside. "And I'm sore from sleeping on the floor."

"Oh, Shannon." She looks as if she's about to cry, and I realize I've said too much.

"Other than that, it's kind of fun being here," I say quickly. "Mammi is a really good cook. In fact, I should go help her with breakfast. And I think she made sugar cookies last night."

"Sugar cookies?"

"Yeah. Want one with your breakfast?"

She seems to consider this.

"I'll bring you one," I say as I leave. "If you don't want it, I'll eat it myself."

I find Mammi at the stove. She's stirring a pan of oatmeal in the back, tending to bacon in front, and scrambling eggs—all at the same time. She greets me, then immediately puts me to work setting the table and fetching items for her.

I explain that Mom still doesn't feel able to sit at the table, and she helps me fix her a bowl of oatmeal with applesauce and cream. "I think she might like a cookie too," I say as I pour a glass of apple juice.

"*Ja, ja.* That's a good idea, Shannon. We need to fatten her up."

To my relief, Mom doesn't seem terribly opposed to the breakfast I present her with. "You know what to do," I say as I start to leave. "I mean, if you want a pill."

"Yeah, yeah." For some reason when she says this, I'm reminded of Mammi, and it's like I can almost see how they have some similarities.

When I get back to the kitchen, my grandpa is hanging his hat on the peg by the back door, and before long we are sitting at the table once again. Just like last night, my grandparents bow their heads, and once again not a word is spoken until he says, "Amen," and she echoes it. They must be praying silently. I have no problem with that since it's the only way I know how to pray anyway. Not that I'm in the habit of doing it as often as I should.

After the nearly silent breakfast ends, my grandfather opens a cabinet and removes what appears to be a big black Bible. Instead of abruptly leaving the table, he opens the Bible and begins to read. However, he is reading in a different language. I do not understand a single word. As badly as I want to excuse myself and escape this madness, I get the feeling that would be perceived as very bad manners. So I sit there like the proverbial bump on a log. Or maybe I'm a bump on a bench.

Finally, he bows his head and Mammi does the same.

Assuming they are praying, I imitate them, and eventually they do the amen thing again. It does occur to me that I might actually attempt to pray while they are praying, but something about this whole thing feels so strange, I'm not even sure I could pray a sincere prayer under these conditions.

Gramps slowly stands, then puts the Bible back into the cabinet, reverently patting it before he closes the door. Then, just like last night, he rubs his arm, grimacing as if he's in severe pain. But without saying a word, he gets his hat and leaves.

"I need to go check on Mom," I tell Mammi. "It's time for her medicine."

"*Ja, ja.*" She nods. "Tell Anna I will come in and visit with her soon."

"Okay." I hurry back to the bedroom, hoping that Mom's not too irritated at having to wait for her pill.

"What took so long?" she demands as soon as I'm in there.

"Sorry." As I go to dig out the bottle of pills from my purse, I explain about her father's Bible reading. "It was all in a foreign language," I say as I shake out a pill.

"Pennsylvania Dutch."

"They speak Dutch?"

"It's not Dutch. It's actually a form of German. High German."

"But they call it Dutch?" I frown as I hand her the pill. "Is everything that backwards here?"

She gives me a half smile as she puts the pill in her mouth and uses the last of her apple juice to wash it down.

I gather up her breakfast dishes, relieved to see that she's made a good dent in the oatmeal. "Did you like the cookie?" I ask as I open the door.

"Yeah. It was pretty good. Thanks, Shannon. Tell Mamm thanks too, okay?"

"Sure." I study her for a moment. "Are you feeling any better?"

She shrugs. "Hard to say. I think I'm worn out from the trip."

"Yeah, that makes sense."

"And I miss my TV."

I frown. "Yeah, I wondered about that."

"Coming here is kind of like electronic cold turkey, huh?" she says.

I force a smile. "Maybe it's good for us."

"Yeah, they say what doesn't kill you makes you stronger, right?"

"Right." I consider offering her one of my paperbacks, but I know reading makes her dizzy. Seeing she's already closing her eyes, I quietly let myself out.

Mammi has already cleared the table, but as I join her in the kitchen, I get an idea. "How about if I clean up by myself this time?" I suggest.

"On your own? Do you know how?"

"Yeah. You showed me how to do everything last night. I think I can handle it." I make what I hope is a confident smile. "Maybe that will give you time to visit with my mom. I mean, before she falls asleep again. She just took a pill, and she'll probably doze off before long."

Her face brightens. "*Ja, ja.* That is a good idea. *Danke,* Shannon."

After she leaves, I scrub down the top of the wooden table. Then I make sure that the kettle on the stove is full of hot water. I rinse the dishes in cold water, then I stack them next to the sink. Next I clean out the sink, then pump cold water into it. I add some soap and finally the hot water. I am finishing washing the juice glasses and oatmeal bowls when Mammi returns.

"Your mamm is asleep now," she says a bit sadly.

"Did you have a chance to talk to her much?" I ask as I set a mixing bowl into the warm soapy water.

"*Ja, ja.* Enough for now. I will talk to her again later."

I notice she has something white in her hands. "This is for you," she tells me as she sets the bundle on the kitchen table. At first I think it's a pillow and I'm so grateful I could hug her, but on closer inspection, I see it's some kind of clothing. Hopefully she doesn't plan to dress me up like an Amish girl.

"What is it?" I ask as I dry my soapy hands on the back of my shorts.

"A nightgown," she tells me. "Your dawdi said you have need of one."

"But I don't—" I stop myself as I remember my run-in with my grumpy grandfather last night. I'm sure he thought I looked indecent. He probably thought that same thing this morning when he saw me in these shorts. Not that I care particularly. I mean, it's one thing to be stuck in a place like this for a couple of weeks—if we even make it that long—but for them to attempt to enforce their weird dress code upon me too? Well, that is just too much.

"I made this myself." Mammi holds up the plain white nightgown, shaking it open to show me and smiling as if it's the most beautiful garment in the world.

To be polite, I finger the fabric. "It's soft," I admit.

"*Ja, ja.* It is good for sleeping."

"Thank you." I make a stiff smile. "I—uh—I'll wear it tonight."

She holds it up to my shoulders. "Not too long. I think— just right." She pats my cheek. "I am so happy to give it to you, Shannon."

I thank her again, and then she informs me she's going out to work in the garden while the air is still cool. After she leaves, I return to the dishes. It seemed like a good idea to volunteer like this, but I'm quickly discovering that it's more work than expected. It turns into even more work when I slop water onto the floor, which now needs mopping.

Without Mammi here to help, everything takes longer than I think it should, but eventually I've got everything cleaned and put away. I even remember to refill the kettle and replace it back on the stove to soak up the remainder of the stove's heat, since I get how that's the only source of warm water in this house. I give the counter one last swipe, glancing around this space in satisfaction, hoping that I didn't miss anything. For some reason it feels important to me to win Mammi's approval.

I check on Mom, but she's sleeping soundly. I drop my new nightgown onto my messy pile of belongings in the corner near my makeshift bed. This tiny room has no closet, but there are pegs on the wall. I assume these are for hanging clothes, so I pick up some of our stuff, and before long I've utilized all the pegs. Problem is, Mom and I both have more clothes than there are pegs.

Still feeling stinky and sweaty from KP duty, I consider taking a shower but then remember the hot water situation. I know the kettle water is probably lukewarm at best—and besides that, I'm not sure I'm ready to tackle that bucket shower device yet.

Instead I decide to go outside for some fresh air. I slip out the front door and sit in the shade on the small wooden porch. Staring blankly at the green landscape that surrounds this house, I try to wrap my head around the weird situation I find myself in. *Mom and I are living with the Amish.* I wish I'd thought to grab my phone, because I'd like to text Merenda about this strange turn of events. However, I know that my phone battery was low from being on all day yesterday. Plus there's no place to recharge it today. I also have no idea what kind of cell phone coverage there is out here. For the time being I think I'll let it go. I used to brag to Merenda how I'm not addicted to electronics the way that some people are, but to be honest, I feel like I'm experiencing a little withdrawal right now. Or maybe I'm just having withdrawal from normal.

But what is normal? I ponder this question as I sit here on the porch. To my Amish grandparents, living out in the sticks with no electricity is perfectly normal. To me it's like visiting another planet. I honestly wonder how long I can last here. In fact, as I watch a horse-drawn buggy slowly moving down the road in the distance, I make a decision. Before I give Mom another pill today, I'm going to insist we talk this whole thing through. I can think of numerous reasons why we would be much better off in our apartment back home.

Having reached this conclusion, it's easier for me to relax here on this little porch. It's really not such a bad place to be. My grandparents seem to prefer the back porch door for coming and going. Besides, it's cool and shady here right now. Even better than that, it has a lovely view. While the back door looks directly toward the barn and silos, this porch looks out over a peaceful meadow fringed with trees. About a dozen cows are grazing out there, and I can hear birds happily chirping and singing. Very bucolic. I can imagine painting a watercolor of this scene. If we stay another day or two, maybe I will. But I plan to convince Mom that we should pack up and get home as soon as possible.

Just as I'm deciding that a three-day visit should be more than enough to satisfy everyone, a quiet growling sound starts to disturb the quiet peacefulness of this spot. I look over and see my grandfather huffing and puffing as he pushes some kind of motorless grass-cutting device through the tall lawn that surrounds their house. He obviously doesn't see me perched here in the shadows, and I watch with interest as he struggles to maneuver the mower through the tall grass. I can tell by the way he's favoring one arm that his bad arm is hurting. The twisted grimace on his face shows that he's in pain—and I feel unexpectedly sorry for him. In that same instant, I leap to my feet and run over to offer my help.

"Want me to do that for you?" I ask, thinking he'll probably turn me down.

He frowns at me, looking me up and down as if sizing me up. "You think you are strong enough to cut this grass?"

"Sure," I say, trying to appear confident and at the same time wondering why on earth I'm doing this. "Why not?"

He looks on the verge of amusement as he takes his hands off of the handle, pausing to rub his sore arm again. "*Ja*," he says slowly. "You go ahead. Work is good for you."

Slightly surprised but not willing to back down now that he's agreed, I nod. "I don't mind a little work," I tell him.

"Remember, child, half done is far from done."

I want to ask him what that's supposed to mean, but he turns and walks away. Now it's just me and the mower. I give it a tentative push and discover it does not roll easily. I lean into it, pushing with all my upper body strength. As a result, I make it all the way to the edge of the grass. I look back to see a long strip, about a foot wide, of neatly cut grass. However, I still have about a thousand more strips to go. At this rate I'll still be out here pushing this thing well into the night. Maybe that's what my grandfather meant about a half done job. He's certain that I'll never finish it.

I'll admit it looks impossible. Still, I refuse to give up. I want to prove to Gramps that I can do this, that I don't give up that easily. I tell myself that I'm climbing a mountain and that I'll be a bigger, stronger, better person when I make it to the peak. I can do this!

After more than an hour, I am dismayed to see that I've barely made a dent on the lawn. Not only that, but this pathetic mower seems like it's getting more stubborn. It's almost like it's gone on strike, refusing to move at all. I'm really, really tempted to give up, but then I imagine Gramps's face scowling down at me with smug disapproval.

I take in a deep breath and really lean into it now. With my arms extended, I'm leaning so far forward that I'm nearly at a forty-five degree angle. My toes dig into the rubber soles of my flip-flops as I put all my weight into it.

"Easy there," someone calls out from behind me.

In the same instant the mower jerks, and I fall flat on my face into the freshly cut grass. I want to cry. Instead, I sit back on my knees and glare at the straw hat–wearing figure rushing toward me. At first I assume it's Gramps, but as the person gets closer, I realize it's actually a young man.

A concerned pair of brown eyes gazes down at me. "Are you all right?" he asks as he extends a hand, firmly helping me to my feet.

I nod, brushing grass clippings from my sweaty tank top as I try to slip my foot back into one of my flip-flops. "Thanks," I mumble as I shove my other foot into the other one.

"That looked unsafe," he tells me sternly.

"Falling on my face?" Placing my hands on my hips, I study his squared chin and nice straight nose. Despite his funny shirt and strange pants complete with suspenders, plus a hat that looks identical to Gramps's, it is obvious that this guy is extremely good looking.

He grins, exposing a nice set of white teeth. "No, I mean the way you were handling that push mower. It looked dangerous." Now he seems to be checking me out from head to toe as he reaches over to pluck some grass from my hair. "You must be one of the Englishers visiting at Jacob's."

"Huh?" I continue to brush grass clippings from my shirt and shorts, suddenly concerned with my appearance.

"I heard the Hershbergers' daughter and granddaughter are visiting." He points to my clothes. "I figure you're the granddaughter."

I stand up straighter, push my hair away from my face, and smile. "Yeah. I'm Shannon McNamara." I stick out my hand in a silly formal way.

"I'm Ezra Troyer," he tells me as he takes my hand, shaking it as if this is totally normal. "My friends call me Ezra."

"Ezra?" I try to decide if he's being funny.

He nods. "*Ja*. You can call me Ezra too."

In this very instant, what previously felt like a strange and alien world—Amishland—is transformed into an enchanted and lovely and wonderful place. It's as if the sunshine is cleaner and brighter and the birds are singing in perfect harmony. My life has gone from drab to fab.

7

Here's your problem right here," Ezra explains as he kneels down, using a stick to dislodge some impacted grass cuttings from the mower.

"Oh." I nod. "No wonder it wasn't working."

"The reason the grass jammed like that is because these blades are too dull to cut properly." He stands up. "Come with me, English girl."

Gladly, I think as I follow him. *Anywhere.*

"I came over here to return a tool my daed borrowed from Jacob," he explains as he leads us toward the barn. "I wondered if I'd get to see you."

I snicker. "Not only did you get to see me, you got to see me do a belly flop."

He laughs. "That was something to see. Good thing you didn't get hurt. I was afraid you were going to land on the mower. Even with dull blades, that could've hurt a lot."

"Yeah, I guess so."

He turns to gaze down at me. "And it would be a shame to mess up that face."

I feel my heart fluttering and don't quite know how to respond. "So do you live around here?" I ask, feeling like I'm walking in a dream.

He nods his head to the right. "See that barn over there?"

I peer in that direction. "Yeah."

"That's my family's farm."

"It looks nice."

He laughs. "It looks just like every other farm around here."

"Yeah, well, I'm from the city," I explain. "The countryside looks nice to me."

He looks into my eyes again. "Really? Do you think this is better than living in a city?"

I shrug. "I'm not sure. I mean, it's so different, and I just got here yesterday. The truth is, I think I'm having culture shock."

"Culture shock?"

"It's something people get when they visit a different country. Kind of like everything is backwards and upside down."

"*Ja*. I know. We are like a different country to the Englishers." He turns and enters the barn now.

As I follow him into the shadowy interior, I wonder about the tone of his voice. "Don't you like it here?" I ask him.

He glances around the barn as if to see if anyone is in here, then, seemingly satisfied that we're alone, he shakes his head.

"Really?" I stare at him. "You don't like being Amish?"

Now he looks uncertain. "Sometimes I like it good enough, and I like farming all right. But sometimes I think I'd like to see the rest of the world. I wonder what's out there."

"Oh." My eyes have adjusted to the dimness in here, and I look up at him, trying to figure him out. "Have you ever been away from here?" I ask quietly.

He shakes his head. "Not beyond Hochstetler."

I try not to act shocked. "Well, I haven't seen too much beyond Indianapolis."

"Indianapolis?" His eyes brighten. "Where they have that big car race?"

I can't help but chuckle. "Yeah, they have the Indy 500 there."

"Have you seen it?"

I slowly nod. "My dad took me once when I was a little kid . . . before he died."

His eyes grow dark. "Your daed's passed on?"

"Yeah. I was about eight when he died."

He sighs, but without saying anything else, he turns his attention back to the lawn mower, lifting it up onto a big wooden workbench. He takes down a couple of big metal tools that are hanging on a board behind the bench and goes to work on the mower blades. First he cleans them off, then he starts to rub a long piece of metal over the blades. "See how the metal on the blade is starting to shine there?" He moves his head so that I can see the edge of the blade. Our heads are so close that I can feel his breath on the back of my neck. And it feels good!

"Yeah," I whisper.

"That means it's getting sharper," he says. "But I have to do all of them, on all sides. I'll make this mower so sharp that it can whack off a finger or toe." He pauses to look down at my feet. "You need to wear shoes to use this now."

"Okay."

I watch as he finishes sharpening the blades and oils them all, wiping the drips with an old rag. Now he sets the mower on the ground and gives it a push, and I see the blades whirling around freely.

"Wow," I say, impressed. "That looks like it could chop off a toe."

"Let's go see how it works," he tells me as he starts wheeling it out.

Back on the lawn, Ezra takes a trial run. "Cuts the grass like a hot knife through butter," he tells me. Then he frowns at my feet. "You need to put on your shoes before you try it out."

"Oh, right. I forgot."

"You go get your shoes while I do another row."

I hurry into the house in time to discover Mammi and Mom on their way to the bathroom. "I called for you," my mom says weakly, "but you didn't come, Shannon."

"I'm so sorry," I say quickly. "I was mowing the lawn for your dad and—"

"Oh? You're helping Daed?" Mom shuffles her feet along, leaning on Mammi. "Well, I needed you to help me."

"Do you want me to take—"

"I've got her," Mammi assures me.

"Okay." I turn from them and hurry to my room, fumbling through my bags and stuff until I finally locate my sneakers, which I hurry to put on and tie. I go back outside and discover that Ezra has done several rows.

"Looks like it's working great," I tell him as I go over.

"Wanna give it a try?"

"Sure." He hands it over to me. I give a tentative push and

am shocked to see that it works fine. Sure, it takes a little energy to push it, but nothing like before. I pause to look at Ezra. "Thank you so much," I tell him. "It really works!"

He grins. "Take good care of your tools, and your tools will take good care of you."

I'm sure I must look starry-eyed and smitten as I continue gazing up at him. "That's very wise," I say.

"I can't take the credit. It's what my daed says."

"Well, thank you for helping me. I really appreciate it."

He removes his straw hat now, running his fingers through his curly golden hair so that it sticks out all over—but not in an unattractive way. "I like you, Shannon," he says. "I'd like to get to know you better."

I try not to look shocked. "I'd like to get to know you better too," I say.

"How about if I come by later on, after my work is done. After supper?"

"Sure," I say eagerly. "I'd like that."

"We can take a walk," he says.

"Great," I agree. "That sounds good."

"See ya then," he tells me as he starts to leave.

"See ya!" I call out happily, watching him as he strides away. If anyone would've told me yesterday that I would fall in love with an Amish boy today, I would've told them they were certifiably nuts. But as I watch him hopping over a fence and cutting through a pasture, I know that my heart is going with him.

Don't be a total idiot, the realist side of me warns as Ezra slowly fades out of sight. But my dreamy optimist side is not listening. I return to cutting the grass, easily pushing

the mower down one row after the next. I am still amazed at
how nicely it works since Ezra stepped in. Almost like magic.

I've just finished up when Mammi comes out and announces that it's time to eat. "Come in for the midday meal,"
she tells me.

I look at my hands. "I better wash first," I say.

"*Ja*, but hurry. Jacob is hungry. I already took Anna her
dinner."

I jog up to the house, rush into the bathroom, pump out
the water, and hurriedly wash my hands. I'm tempted to check
out my image in the little shaving mirror, which I suspect
belongs to my grandfather, but don't want to waste the time.

They are already bowing their heads when I slide onto the
bench. I bow my head too, waiting until they say, "Amen,"
and echoing them. I'm surprised to see that Mammi has made
macaroni and cheese, biscuits, and green beans with bacon.
For lunch, this seems like a feast. When I mention this, my
grandfather only grunts, but Mammi smiles. "We eat hearty
because we work hearty." She glances out the window. "And
you have been working too, Shannon."

"Yeah, I didn't know that mowing grass was such hard
work," I admit, glancing at my grandfather, who seems intent
on his food. "But it's fun too."

He looks up at me with a surprised expression.

"Good girl," Mammi tells me. "It is good you enjoy hard
work."

It feels good to have her appreciation, but it would be even
better if Gramps would give me a kind word. However, it
does not seem to be in the works for today.

"Ezra Troyer came by," I say to both of them. Mammi

simply nods, but Gramps looks curious. "He returned one of your tools," I say to my grandfather.

"*Ja*, I saw that."

"And he helped me fix the mower," I continue.

"The mower?" His scowl returns. "What is wrong with the mower?"

"The grass was stuck all over it and the blades needed to be sharpened."

"The blades were sharp," he tells me.

I consider debating this but know it will only cause more problems. "He seems like a nice guy," I say absently. "So helpful."

"*Ja*, Ezra is a good boy." Mammi nods as she reaches for a biscuit. "His father Silas is a good man. The apple will not roll far away from the tree."

"But it will roll," my grandfather says in a somber voice.

While this is the most conversation I've been part of at my grandparents' table, it comes quickly to an end, and before long it's time to clean up. Remembering that Mom is due for a pill, I excuse myself to check on her.

"It's about time," she tells me when I open the door. "Where have you been all day?"

"Cutting the grass," I say. "Remember?"

"Did you cut the whole hayfield?"

"No." I remove her dishes, which still have a fair amount of food left on them. "You didn't eat all your lunch," I tell her. "You know what that means?"

"Shannon," she says with irritation, "you didn't see how much food Mamm brought me. It looked like enough for three people."

"So you ate enough?" I ask.

"More than enough." She gives me a weary smile. "And now I would very much like a pill, if it's not too much trouble."

"You really need it?" Looking at her, I'm thinking she looks better than usual. Is it possible that this fresh country air and good food are improving her health?

"Of course I need it," she snaps.

"You know what the doctor said, Mom. You're only supposed to take them as needed. The more you take them, the less effective they'll be."

"I'm telling you, I need a pill, Shannon. Are you going to get it for me, or do I have to stumble over there and dig it out for myself?"

"I'm getting it," I assure her. As I dig through my things, trying to locate my purse, I comment on the size of the room. "I've seen bigger closets," I say as I shake out a pill. "And this room doesn't even have a closet."

"Mamm said you might be welcome to stay at my brother's house. They have more room."

"Would we both go there?"

Mom frowns. "I don't know. I've never really gotten along that well with Ben's wife, Katrina. If I'm going to be beholden to anyone in this settlement, I'd rather it be my own parents."

"Oh." I hand her the pill and the last dregs of her tea.

"But you could go over there if you want." She takes the pill, swallowing it with the tea. "Ben's daughter is about your age."

"And leave you here on your own?"

"I wouldn't be on my own, Shannon. Mamm is here. She'll take care of me."

I frown. "You wouldn't even miss me?"

She makes a sad smile. "Of course I would. But I feel guilty making you sleep on the floor."

"It is a little hard."

"Why don't you ask Mamm to walk you over to Ben's house so you can talk to Katrina and Ben about it?"

"Right now?"

"Why not?"

I'm thinking about my "date" with Ezra tonight. He's coming here to meet me. No way do I want to risk not being here. "Maybe I should wait until tomorrow," I say. "Mammi and I could go over there in the morning."

"You don't mind sleeping on the floor again?"

I consider this, then shrug. Maybe I'll be sleeping out on that freshly mowed grass tonight. Not that I plan to tell her this.

"Well, I suppose it makes sense to wait until tomorrow," she admits. "Gives you more time to spend with your grandparents. How is it going with them, anyway? You helped Daed mow the lawn?"

"I mowed it all myself," I tell her. "Well, mostly." I explain about how Ezra came over to help. "He was returning a tool, but he knew just what to do to make the mower work."

"What's his last name?" Mom asks sleepily.

"Troyer," I tell her. "Ezra Troyer."

Her eyes pop open. "Silas Troyer's son?"

"Yeah, I think Mammi said his dad's name is Silas. Why?"

She waves her hand. "Nothing."

"What?" I demand. I can tell by her eyes there's more story here, and I want to hear it. "Who is Silas?"

"Just an old friend."

"Just a friend? Or something more?"

"Oh, I probably thought of him as a beau."

"Really?" I lean forward with interest.

"Yeah." She shrugs, leaning back into her pillows. "But I obviously didn't like him well enough to stick around."

"You think if you'd stayed here, you might've married Ezra's dad?" I am incredulous.

"Well, he wasn't Ezra's dad back then, Shannon."

"I know . . . but it's weird." Is it possible that Mom was in love with Ezra's dad and now I'm in love with Ezra? Okay, I know saying I'm in love is pushing it, but I certainly do feel something.

Mom is still reclined on the pillows, but her eyes are fixed on me. "Why is it so weird, Shannon? Is there something about this Ezra fellow that I should know?"

"No, of course not."

"Shannon?"

"He just seems like a nice boy, Mom. He helped me with the mower and was polite. That's all."

"How old is he?"

"I don't know, Mom."

"Your age?"

"I guess. I didn't ask him."

Mom studies me now.

"Don't make this into a big deal," I tell her. "An Amish boy was helpful and I appreciated it. End of story."

She sighs and closes her eyes.

"I'll let you rest now," I say quietly.

"Don't forget to talk to Mamm about moving over to Uncle Ben's house."

"Uncle Ben?" I laugh. "Like the rice?"

"Yeah." She smiles sleepily. "Like the rice."

I pick up her dishes and quietly go to the door, silently opening it and slipping out. I can't help but see the irony of this—me falling for a boy that is the son of Mom's old beau. But I don't see any reason for Mom to get all up in arms about it. Would she try to put the brakes on a summer fling? Because as much as my optimist side is imagining Ezra and me, true love forever, my realist side knows that this is just something to brighten up my summer in Amishland. And really, don't I deserve a break like this?

8

With both Mammi and Gramps out of the house in the afternoon, I decide to take my first bucket shower. My goal is to be clean and lovely for my date this evening. Okay, I know it's not really a date. But meeting a guy like Ezra and taking a walk, well, I'm guessing by Amish standards, it might be a date. Not that I know much about such things yet.

To my relief, the cookstove is still quite hot, so I take in the water kettle from the kitchen and use it to fill the shower bucket along with some cold water. Then I refill the kettle and return it to what looks like the hottest spot on the stove. I hurry back to the bathroom and arrange my bath products and hair things on the narrow space next to the sink. Because I snuck a peek in Gramps's shaving mirror, I know that my hair is a mess of grass and dirt, and the only way to remedy this is a shampoo. I also know that without electricity, I run the risk of looking like Little Orphan Annie, unless I use a good dose of conditioner and then comb my hair until it's nearly dry, so it might not be so curly.

I'm right in the middle of conditioning my hair when my bucket runs dry. I wouldn't mind rinsing in cold water, but I haven't even gotten half of the grit off of me, and I wanted to shave my legs. Plus I'm sure that the kettle is probably warm now and might be just enough to finish up if I'm careful. I look at the sad excuse for a towel and wonder if it will even wrap around me, but knowing no one is in the house, I decide to give it a try. Wearing the tiny towel, I make a dash through the house and into the kitchen, and I'm reaching for the kettle when my grandfather opens the back door and steps into the kitchen.

He looks at me with a horrified expression, then turns around, marches out, and slams the door behind him. Feeling like a complete idiot, I grab the kettle and dash back to the bathroom. Okay, I'm sure I must've offended Gramps, but I can't help but feel a little indignant. I mean, *hello*? If these people had proper plumbing or bigger towels or even electricity—well, give me a few basic amenities and we could've totally avoided that embarrassing incident altogether.

I finish my shower and am somewhat satisfied by the results. I got the general grime, grass, and sweat off, but my hair is going to pay the price. I suppose I should be thankful for the lack of mirrors in this house. As I sit on my floor bed with Mom soundly sleeping, I attempt to smooth out my hair and try not to obsess over Gramps and how I feel like he despises me. But it's impossible to forget the disgusted looks he's given me in the past twenty-four hours. For sure, I'm not eager to see him at the supper table tonight. I plan to keep my eyes on my plate while I'm eating. After that I'll help Mammi do the dishes and then make myself scarce until Ezra shows up. It seems a doable plan.

To pass some time, I pull out my cell phone and turn it on. I want to text Merenda about my upcoming date with an Amish guy. I can imagine her shock to read it. She'll think I'm making this up. To my relief there is still a little charge left in the battery. But to my dismay, there is no connection. I don't know if that's because of my cell server or because we're out here in the sticks. I turn off my phone and toss it back into my purse. Talk about feeling totally cut off. I glance over at Mom, propped against the pillows that are propped against the wall. She reminds me of my cell phone—barely running and not connecting.

The evening meal is the quietest one so far. I can tell by my grandparents' expressions they do not approve of my attire. I thought putting on my sundress might please them. I mean, it is a dress, after all. But Gramps gives me his disgusted look again. To say that I've worn out my welcome with this man is definitely an understatement. But with Ezra preoccupying my mind, I'm not sure I even care. After supper, I help Mammi wash up and then go to check on Mom. To my surprise, she is attempting to stand up.

"Do you need help?" I ask.

"I'm not sure." She holds on to the wall to steady herself. "I was feeling a little better and I thought I should give this a try."

I nod, watching as she works her way toward the door. She's weaving a little but seems determined. I stay nearby, following her out of the bedroom, ready to catch her if she falls.

She makes it all the way to a chair in the living room, slowly sits down, and finally lets out a big sigh.

"Good job, Mom!" I grin at her.

"Oh, Anna," Mammi says as she comes into the room. "You are up! Are you feeling better?"

"A little better," Mom tells her.

Mammi sits down in a chair across from Mom, smiling with satisfaction. "It is like I told Jacob. Good food, fresh air, family . . . all are good for making you well again."

Mom gives her an uncertain smile. "I hope you're right."

"Me too," I agree.

"I told Shannon your idea for her to go stay with Benjamin and Katrina," Mom tells Mammi.

"*Ja.*" Mammi nods eagerly. "It is a good idea. Rachel has a big room all to herself. You will share it with her."

"Rachel?" I ask with hesitation. I didn't realize I'd have to share a room with a stranger. Maybe I'd be better off here with Mom.

"Rachel is your cousin," Mammi says.

"Oh." I'm still trying to wrap my head around all these new relatives.

"Rachel is seventeen," Mammi explains. "Only a year older than you. She is a good girl. I think you will be happy to know her."

I give Mom an uneasy look. "What about you? Will you be okay without me?"

Mom looks a little uncertain but makes what seems a forced smile. "I am feeling better, Shannon. And Mamm will help me when I need it." She looks at her mother now.

"You do not need to worry," Mammi assures me. "Your

mamm will be fine. I will take very good care of her. I will feed her good food, and she will soon be well again. You'll see."

"You'll be much more comfortable at Ben's house," Mom tells me. "It's the house I grew up in. It has four bedrooms."

"Does it have indoor plumbing?" I ask. I remember Mom's surprise to see indoor plumbing here.

"*Ja*," Mammi says. "Katrina asked Benjamin to make some changes to the house."

"Well, if you both think it's a good idea, and if Uncle Ben agrees, I'm willing to stay over there. But I think we should wait until tomorrow." I glance outside now, curious as to when Ezra will show up. Should I be waiting outside?

"*Ja*." Mammi nods. "You and I will go over after breakfast in the morning, Shannon. I will introduce you to your relatives and speak to Katrina about this idea."

"Then it's settled," Mom declares.

"Good," I tell them. "Now, unless you need me, Mom, I'd like to take a little walk outside. The countryside is so pretty here. I thought I'd take my sketch pad and do some drawing."

Mom looks pleased to hear this. "Yes, that's a lovely idea, Shannon."

"I will help Anna if she needs it," Mammi assures me.

I go into my room and dig out my sketch pad and a pencil. This was a last-minute idea, but I think it's perfect. By the time I'm going out the front door, Mammi is helping Mom into the bathroom. Suddenly I feel free—and it feels good.

I stroll outside with my sketch pad tucked under my arm. I pretend to be looking for something to draw, but I am glancing toward the barn where I suspect Gramps is probably working on something. I want to find a spot where his ever-present scowl and disapproving eyes cannot find me, yet I want to be visible to Ezra when he comes. Finally I decide to sit under a tree next to the pasture that's between Ezra's farm and my grandparents' house. From this vantage point I can see my uncle Ben's house too. It's a tall white house just on the other side of the barn. I almost get the impression that the dawdi house (where my grandparents live) was positioned where it is in order to put the barn directly between the two houses. This way they're near each other, but neither house is visible to the other.

I flatten down a section of tall pasture grass right next to the tree, then sit down, using the tree's trunk as my backrest. I open up my sketch pad, pull out my pencil, and pretend to be sketching. I'm really keeping my eyes peeled for a certain young man in a broad-brimmed straw hat. I hope I'm not making too much of this. It's possible that he's simply being neighborly and trying to make me feel at home. However, I feel that it's something more. I hope that it is. I can't even explain the feeling I get just thinking about him. Oh, I know we live in totally different worlds, but in some ways I find that extremely romantic. Kind of like forbidden love. Like Romeo and Juliet. At least that's how I'm imagining it.

The sun is getting lower now, and I'm getting worried that Ezra has forgotten all about me. Even so, I plan to remain out here until the sun sets. Maybe longer. It really is pretty and peaceful. Totally unlike home. I wonder if I could be happy living in a place like this. I almost think that I could, except for one thing: my grandfather. I feel certain that he hates me. In fact, I'm sure that's the primary reason Mammi wants me to stay at Uncle Ben's house. Gramps probably told her about me running around the house wearing only a towel. Yes, I'm sure they will both be glad to be rid of me.

I see something moving in the grass now. At first I think it's a cow, but as it gets closer, I can tell it's human. Then I can see that it's Ezra. I suspect he can't see me sitting in the shadows of this tree, so I stand and, stepping out, wave to him. He waves back and hurries toward me. I feel like I'm in a scene from a beautiful movie—the girl in the sundress stands under the oak tree as the handsome man rushes to sweep her into his arms. Of course, once he gets to the tree, there is no sweeping going on. Well, except in my heart. He has definitely swept that away.

"Hello," he says shyly, removing his hat and holding it in his hands. "I wasn't sure you'd really meet me."

I hold up my sketch pad, trying to act nonchalant—and not like my heart is pounding happily inside of my chest. "I was just doing some drawing," I tell him.

His eyes light up. "You're an artist?"

I shrug. "Well, I love doing art."

"Can I see your drawing?" he asks eagerly.

"Well, I—"

"Please," he urges. "I would love to see it."

I slowly flip open the pad, revealing the first page, which is a study of a park bench. I was working on shadows and light.

"That's good." He nods.

I flip to another and another, and each time Ezra praises my work with what seems genuine admiration. I feel like my heart is swelling inside of me. "Thanks," I murmur as I finally close the pad.

"Want to walk over to the pond?" he asks.

"There's a pond?"

"*Ja*. It's shared by several farms." He points to the east. "Over there."

"Sure." I nod. "I'd love to see it." I hold up my sketch pad. "Maybe I'll leave this by the tree and pick it up later."

"*Ja*." He waits as I set it there, then tosses his straw hat down next to it. "Right this way." He holds out his hand like I'm supposed to take it, so I do—and a wonderful tingling rushes through me as our hands clasp. It runs like electricity from my head to my toes and back again.

"You are a very pretty girl," he tells me as we walk together through the tall grass.

"Thank you," I murmur.

"When I saw you this morning, fighting with that push mower, you caught my eye."

"You mean when I fell on my face?"

He laughs. "No. Although that was funny. But it was you that caught my eye. Your beautiful hair . . . and, you know, *everything*." He squeezes my hand.

"Well . . ." I wonder how much I want to say. "You caught my eye too, Ezra. I mean, at first I thought you were my grandfather." I giggle. "But that's only because of your clothes. I'm still getting used to the way the Amish dress."

"It's a lot different than what you're used to."

"That's for sure." I look down at my sundress. "I think my grandfather is pretty unhappy with how I dress."

Ezra chuckles. "I'm sure that is true."

"I don't understand why clothes are so important. It seems like what's beneath the clothes should be more important."

"*Ja*, I'd have to agree with that." Ezra laughs.

Okay, I get it. He thinks I'm talking about our bodies. My mistake. "I mean what's inside of us," I clarify. "What kind of character we have, what sort of talents, what we believe . . . you know?"

"*Ja*. And the Amish do think those things are important too. In fact, the reason we dress like this is because it is supposed to reflect our insides."

"How so?"

"It's all about humility. We are supposed to be humble both on the inside and on the outside."

"But why do people have to dress alike?"

"So no one stands out."

"I suppose I stand out."

He nods. "*Ja*. In a good way, though. Anyway, that's how I see it."

"You seem somewhat disenchanted with your lifestyle."

He frowns but says nothing.

"Are you happy being Amish, Ezra?"

"I'm not sure. I guess it's something I need to figure out."

"How do you go about that? I mean, figuring it out."

"It's not easy." He opens a gate. It's part of a wire fence that's surrounding some shrubbery. "The pond is in here. We keep it fenced so when the cows are in this field they can't get into it." He leads me through an opening in the bushes, and there before us is a big pond that's reflecting the pinkish rays of the sunset.

"Oh, Ezra, this is beautiful," I exclaim. "I would love to paint this."

"You should paint it," he tells me as he leads me over to a log, inviting me to sit with him.

"The way the light hits the pond," I say. "The grasses growing all around it. Those willow trees over there. It's really pretty."

"I like it." He turns to face me now. "It's almost as beautiful as you are, Shannon."

I feel that warm rush running through me again. I cannot believe I am here with him like this, or the way he is looking into my eyes. It is magical, wonderful, intoxicating. He reaches over to touch my hair, running his fingers through my curls and smiling.

"Your hair in this light . . ." He sighs. "Beautiful." He leans toward me, and suddenly he is kissing me, and I feel like I'm floating . . . like I'm in some kind of heaven . . . like I never want this moment to end.

But it does. "I'm sorry," he says. "I probably shouldn't have done that."

"Oh?" I keep looking at him, lost in those big brown eyes.

"I couldn't help myself, Shannon. You're so beautiful."

"It's okay," I murmur.

He kisses me again and again, and it keeps getting better and better, and I feel myself being swept away. I mean really swept away. I realize that I need to slow this down. I pull away from him, struggling to catch my breath. "Oh . . ." I let out a long sigh.

"*Ja.*" He sighs too.

"Ezra," I say, "that was really cool, but I feel like this is moving too fast."

He nods, looking down at his hands in his lap. "*Ja* . . . I think you're right."

"I mean, I liked it," I confess. "But, well, we only just met. And I really, really like you."

"I like you too, Shannon." He looks up into my eyes again. "I more than like you."

I smile. "I more than like you too."

He reaches over and touches my cheek. "I can hardly keep my hands off of you."

"I know." I giggle nervously. "But because I feel this way toward you"—I control myself from using the word *love*, although it's all I can think of—"I want to get to know you better. In fact, I want to know everything there is to know about you, Ezra."

"*Ja*. That's how I feel too, Shannon. When you showed me your drawings, I felt like I was seeing inside of you."

"I want to see inside of you too, Ezra. I want to know more about you."

"Ask me anything," he says eagerly. "I will tell you anything you want to know."

I don't know where to begin but decide to start with my most pressing question. "You said you have to figure out whether or not you're happy about being Amish. I guess I'm curious what that means."

"It means I have to decide whether or not I am Amish."

"I thought you were Amish. I mean, you live here, you dress in Amish clothes, your parents are Amish. Doesn't that make you Amish?"

He shakes his head. "That's not how it works."

"How does it work?"

"We are brought up in the Amish traditions," he explains. "We are taught the Amish ways. We go to an Amish school until eighth grade. And—"

"That's all? You stop going to school after eighth grade? What happens then?"

He nods somberly. "Mostly, we work on our parents' farms. But some men learn a trade."

I'm trying to wrap my brain around this. Education ends at eighth grade? How is that even legal? And boys go to work when they are only fifteen? What about child labor laws? Maybe those laws don't apply here. But how can part of the United States be exempt from the law? Okay, I feel confused. And I can understand why Ezra feels so frustrated.

9

The sunset sky is turning the pond all sorts of amazing colors, but my eyes remain fixed on Ezra as I continue to press him with questions.

"How old are you?" I ask in a flirtatious voice.

"At least that's an easy question. I just turned nineteen."

"Oh." I nod, wondering what my mom will think to find out I've been off with a nineteen-year-old.

"How old are you?"

"Sixteen . . . last January."

He nods. "That's perfect."

"Perfect?"

He grins. "A man should be older than a woman."

I love that he thinks of me as a woman. But I still have a lot of questions. "So, tell me," I say, "what happens *after* you finish eighth grade? That would've been about four years ago for you, right?"

"*Ja*. After our schooling ends, we're expected to make some very important life decisions."

"What kind of life decisions?"

He pushes his hand through his hair in a frustrated way. "Do you really want to know all this?"

"Yes. I actually do. If you don't mind telling me." I imagine myself reaching for his cheek, running my hand over the slightly bristled surface. But I don't move a muscle. "It will help me to know you better. To understand you."

He sighs. "And after I answer your questions, will you answer mine?"

"Absolutely. I promise."

"All right then. After we finish school, we're in a time known as *rumspringa*."

"I think I've heard of that before." I don't admit to having seen some reality TV because I'm afraid it doesn't portray the Amish as they really are. "But what does it mean?"

"*Rumspringa* means running around."

"Running around?" I laugh. "So is that what you do? Run around?"

"Not really. During the week we work hard. Just like the older men. But on the weekends . . . well, there is some running around going on then, for sure."

"What kind of running around?"

"Oh, parties and such." He gives me a sly look. "There is one tomorrow night, since it's Saturday. Would you want to go to it with me?"

"Sure," I easily agree. "But right now I want to hear more about these life decisions you have to make."

"Between the ages of fifteen and nineteen, we are given a lot of freedom. More so than anyone else in the settlement. In some ways, it's odd, but it's because our parents want us to fully experience life—both the good and the bad. They hope we will grow weary of the bad and long for the good." He grins. "That is why I can be out here with you tonight, Shannon. Because I'm still in *rumspringa*, I'm free to do as I like."

"So your parents would be okay with this—us being together?"

He tilts his head to one side. "Well, they wouldn't like knowing I'm with an English girl, that's for sure. But they wouldn't stop it either."

"Really?"

"They believe that we need this freedom to make our decision."

"What decision is that exactly? Whether to be Amish or not?"

"We have to decide if we are ready to declare our faith and be baptized. Anyway, that is what our parents hope we'll do. If we make that decision, we spend a year meeting with the bishop and taking classes, and when he says we are ready, we get baptized." He holds up his hands. "Then we are Amish."

"Oh." I'm trying to grasp this. On one hand, it sounds convoluted. On the other hand, it sounds as if the parents just want their kids to make a confession of faith. Nothing terribly strange about that. "What happens after you are baptized? Any more decisions?"

"Then we're expected to choose a wife and get married, and have children, and participate in the community, and go to church, and work and work and work . . . until we die."

I frown. "You make it sound rather bleak. Like life's not much fun for the Amish."

"Sometimes that's what it looks like to me. I read about things the English get to do. Like car racing. Or flying in airplanes. Or traveling around the world. Or I see the kinds of clothes the English wear." He fingers the thin shoulder strap of my sundress and smiles. "Sometimes I feel like I am missing out."

"I get that . . . but I suspect there are English people out there who would gladly trade places with you. Our world isn't always as fun as it looks."

"I suppose you're right." His somber expression warms up a little. "And maybe if I married a woman like you"—he runs his fingers through my hair again—"maybe I would not mind being Amish at all."

"I think if you're with the one you love, you can be happy anywhere." Okay, I'm starting to feel light-headed again.

"I think you might be right, Shannon. I think I could be happy anywhere with you by my side." His frown returns. "Except that you aren't Amish."

"My grandparents are." It's getting dark now, but I have no desire to leave. I feel like I could stay here—with Ezra—forever. "What if I wanted to become Amish?" I ask tentatively.

He chuckles. "Then I would say you're crazy."

"Why?" I reach for his hand again, feeling the warmth of it as he clasps it around mine. "You live in a beautiful place. There are a lot of things to love about this lifestyle."

"Like what?"

"You have family all around you."

"That can be miserable sometimes."

"Maybe . . . but having grown up with only my mom and me for family, it sounds rather sweet to me."

"What else is good about being Amish?" His face is closer to mine now. I can tell he wants to kiss me again.

"The food." I giggle.

"*Ja*, I hear the English food is not very good." He's running a finger down my cheek and then on down my neck, giving me shivers that actually make my entire scalp tingle. Who says the Amish don't have electricity!

"What is going on here?"

We both turn to see my grandfather with a lantern in his hand, and I swear, if he had a scythe in the other hand, he would look exactly like the Grim Reaper. Even without the scythe, he is seriously frightening. I cower next to Ezra as if I expect him to protect me.

"Good evening!" Ezra says nervously.

"What are you doing here?" The Reaper holds his lantern out toward us, illuminating Ezra's shocked face.

"Just talking," I say, standing and stepping into the light. "Ezra was telling me what it's like to be Amish."

"Ezra can tell you about being Amish in the daylight hours," my grandfather says sternly. "Right now your mamm and mammi are worried for you, Shannon."

Gramps holds out what looks like Ezra's straw hat. "Go home," he commands. Ezra takes his hat, tosses me an uneasy glance, and takes off running. Now Gramps hands me my sketch pad and shakes his head as he turns around. "Come on," he calls. "Time for bed."

I hurry to catch up with him, thinking maybe it's time Gramps and I had a little showdown. "I know you don't like me," I say when I'm next to him. "But I don't think it's—"

"I never said I do not like you." He stops walking, holding

the lantern up so that he can see my face. Once again, he is scowling.

"You don't have to say it," I tell him. "It's written all over your face."

He looks slightly perplexed now.

"I'm sure you hate the way I dress and act and talk and everything about me. I'm sure you hate me."

"I do not hate you, Shannon." His expression softens a little. "I am worried about your soul. I do not want to see my granddaughter go to hell."

"Go to hell?"

"*Ja*. You are not baptized. You will go to hell."

"I was baptized," I tell him. "When I was thirteen I got—"

"That is not what I mean," he says sternly. "You English can pretend to be baptized, but it is not real baptism."

"It was real to me."

He shakes his head as he starts walking again. "You do not know the Ordnung. You were not brought up in the church. You cannot begin to understand what baptism means." He exhales loudly. "You are *not* Amish."

"Ezra was telling me about what it means to be Amish," I say quietly but firmly. "What if I wanted to become Amish?"

He looks at me, and in the lantern light, I can see his features softening a little. For the first time I think I can see some kindness in his eyes. "You want to become Amish?"

"I don't know . . . maybe I do." I shrug. "There are a lot of things I like about the Amish. You live in a beautiful place. You have family nearby. The food is good."

"*Ja*, that is all true. But that is not what being Amish means, Shannon. Being Amish means putting God above all else. It means living a life that is obedient and humble and simple. It is keeping the Ordnung and working hard. You Englishers do not understand how to live like we do."

"But I'm here now," I tell him. "I've been trying to work."

"*Ja*, that is true. I like that you help out." His face actually softens into a smile as we stop in the yard in front of the house. "I like that you did not give up on cutting this grass today."

"Really?" I feel my heart unexpectedly warming to him.

"*Ja*. You did a good job, Shannon."

I cannot describe how happy this makes me.

He points at my dress. "But your clothing." His old scowl reappears, even grimmer than usual. "It is an insult to my home. Your mammi does not want to speak to you of it, Shannon, but I will. You are disrespectful in your dress. Disrespectful to me and your mammi. Disrespectful to yourself."

I frown at him. "Are you saying I should dress like Mammi?"

"*Ja*. While you are under my roof, you should do so out of respect. I should demand you do so. Both you and your mamm. But I know you are English. And your mamm is sick. So I keep my mouth shut." He shakes his head. "It is not easy to do."

Suddenly I get it. I see his frustration. Not only have the English invaded his calm, peaceful, orderly world, but it's like we're flaunting our Englishness in his face. "Dawdi." I say the word slowly, using the name Mom told me to use for him. "I'm sorry that my clothes have offended you."

He looks surprised. "*Ja?* You are?"

I nod. "But these are the only clothes I have."

He rubs his bearded chin in a thoughtful way. "We can give you Amish clothes, Shannon. Would you wear them?"

"Is it okay if I wear them? I mean, because I'm not really Amish?"

"*Ja*. It is all right. It is better than the clothes you brought with you."

I think about Ezra now. I remember how he said he might like to be Amish if I were Amish. Maybe it's time for me to really sample this culture. "Okay," I say lightly. "I will dress like an Amish girl. At least I'll try it out."

He slowly nods as he turns to go inside the house. "I will tell your mammi about this. She will help you tomorrow."

Other than his lantern, the house is dark. "*Gute nacht*," he says quietly as he blows out the lantern and heads for his bedroom.

"*Gute nacht*," I echo, standing there in the darkness. What a strange night this has been. I wish my phone worked so that I could call Merenda and tell her all about it. I don't feel tired, and the idea of sleeping on that hard wooden floor again is not inviting. I remember my resolve to sleep outside tonight. I know the freshly cut lawn will be softer than the floor. However, I'm not sure if my grandfather would approve, and after making such amazing progress with him tonight, I am reluctant to put our relationship at risk. But I can't think of any reason that it would be wrong.

I tiptoe into the bedroom, and hearing Mom's even breathing while she sleeps, I slip into the long white nightgown, which is surprisingly soft and comfortable. I make sure the window is open, gather up my blankets and things, and quietly slip outside. I creep around the side of the house to where our bedroom window is and arrange my funny little bed right next to the window so I can hear Mom if she needs me.

Once I'm settled in, enjoying the softer surface beneath me and the sweet smell of freshly cut grass, I look up at the stars and feel completely and utterly stunned. The stars are so clear and bright and breathtakingly beautiful—it's like nothing I've ever seen before. I stare and stare, wondering why they are so stunning. Maybe it's because with no electricity, there are no lights around here to diminish the darkness of the sky and the brightness of the stars. Or maybe it's because I'm so totally smitten by Ezra, so hopelessly in love, that everything around me looks bigger and brighter and better. Or maybe it's God's way of calling out to me—with a sky like this, it just seems like I should be talking to the One who created it.

I used to pray all the time. I made my first real commitment to God when I was twelve, and for several years I took my faith very seriously. Like I told my grandfather, I got baptized, and I believed in it 100 percent. But over the past year, I've felt myself slipping away. Merenda has pointed it out to me a few times. Of course, I always deny it, and I am always promising myself that I'll get my spiritual life together eventually. Then Mom got sick, and instead of going to God for help, I continued pulling away from him. I feel bad about this now, but I'm not quite sure how to come back.

Besides, it is easier to think about Ezra right now. Instead of praying to God like I suspect I should, I gaze up at the gorgeous sky and replay everything that happened tonight— every word, every touch, every kiss. I want to press it all into my memory so that I can pull it out at will whenever I want. I have never been in love before. Oh, I've had a couple of crushes. I even had a guy I thought was my boyfriend last year—Austin Moore from my youth group. But comparing any of those boys to Ezra is like comparing an anthill to Mount Everest.

I feel myself slipping off to sleep and hope that my dreams will be filled with images of Ezra. Ezra and me. I wonder, what would it be like to become Amish, and to live here in Amishland and marry Ezra, and be together forever?

10

"Your aunt Katrina is a good woman," Mammi tells me as we go outside. Breakfast is over and cleaned up, and it's time for me to meet my other relatives. "She is diligent in her obedience to the Ordnung."

"Oh?" I can tell by Mammi's flat tone of voice that there is something more going on here. "Do you get along well with her?"

Mammi gives me a curious glance. "*Ja, ja*. Certainly I get along. She is my son's wife."

Still, I'm not convinced. I'm getting a strong impression that something is wrong here. "I'm surprised she hasn't come over to visit my mom," I say carefully.

"Oh, well, Katrina is very busy. She is an industrious woman." Mammi opens a gate by the barn, letting us through. "She encourages Benjamin too. Katrina hopes Benjamin will be the bishop someday. Already he is a minister."

"Does that mean he's in charge of your whole church?"

"The bishop is the head of the church. Then we have

two ministers. One is Joseph Miller and one is your uncle Benjamin."

"Did my uncle get trained to be a minister?" I'm curious about this since I know education ends by age fifteen.

"No. It is not like that," she tells me as we walk through the grass.

"So how did he get to be a minister?"

"Any married man can be chosen to serve." Mammi gets a thoughtful look, as if she's wondering whether it's appropriate to tell me more, but then she continues. "After a communion service, the members gather, and names are whispered to the deacon. Each man whose name is whispered three times or more is written down. If everyone is in harmony, we ask God to choose the right man."

I turn to peer at her. "How does God do that?"

"A Bible verse is written down and placed into a songbook. Then the men all kneel down—the ones being considered—and each one is given a songbook. They all open the songbooks, and the man who has the Bible verse in his songbook is God's choice." Mammi smiles happily. "It was such a good day when Benjamin was chosen. I was very happy for him."

We're heading toward the big white house now. "So my uncle Benjamin is an important man?" I say.

"*Ja*. But he is a humble, obedient man. A good man."

"He seemed very nice when I met him. He was kind to my mom."

Mammi stops walking and turns to look in my eyes. "Your aunt Katrina, she is concerned. You and Anna . . . you are not Amish." Mammi glances over her shoulder. "Do you get my meaning?"

I nod. "Yes. I think I do. Is she worried we might do something to embarrass her or Uncle Benjamin?"

"She would not say this, but it is true. And as you know, your mamm is shunned."

"Shunned?"

"*Ja*. When Anna turned her back on God and left the settlement, she was shunned by the community."

"Is that why Aunt Katrina hasn't come to visit her?"

"*Ja*." Mammi looks troubled.

"But what about you and Dawdi? Why aren't you shunning her?"

"Your mamm needs our help. And we always hope that those who have fallen will confess their sins. We want your mamm to repent and return to her faith. Then she will not be shunned."

"What about me?" I ask. "Am I shunned too?"

"No, no. You are English. You cannot be shunned."

I look down at my jeans and T-shirt. "I'm guessing Aunt Katrina will not approve of my clothes."

Mammi shakes her head with a slightly amused expression. "No, Shannon, Aunt Katrina will not approve. Not at all. If you stay with her, she will expect you to dress properly. She and Rachel will have what you need. I'm sure of it."

Despite promising Dawdi that I would dress Amish, I feel myself growing resistant to this idea now. It's one thing to compromise myself for my grandfather. But for this aunt, who doesn't sound so nice? I'm not sure I want to become a pushover. But as we get closer to the house, I remember Ezra, and I realize that changes everything. I wouldn't want to admit this to anyone, but I would gladly wear silly old-fashioned clothes for him.

"Mammi!" A tall, slender girl in a periwinkle blue dress comes running toward us. As she hugs Mammi, I study her. Even in Amish clothes, I can see she's very pretty. Her dark shiny hair, smoothed away from her face, is neatly tucked under her white *kapp*. Her strikingly blue eyes are big and bright, and her smile is clear and sweet. She is altogether lovely. Picture perfect, even.

"Rachel," Mammi says happily. "I want you to meet your cousin Shannon. She is almost your age. Sixteen."

Rachel looks directly at me, reaching out to grasp my hand. "It is a pleasure to meet you, Shannon. I have looked forward to this."

"Yes," I say nervously. "I'm happy to meet you too. I can't believe I have a real cousin."

"*Ja*. You have plenty of real cousins. But you are my first English cousin." Rachel grins. "Mamm is very curious to meet you too."

"I told Shannon that your house might have more room than the dawdi house," Mammi tells Rachel as we turn toward the big house. "She's been sharing our spare room with Anna, but Anna is very sick, and poor Shannon is sleeping on the floor."

Rachel holds my hand in hers as we walk. "Shannon is welcome to share my room, Mammi. Now that Grace is married and gone, I have a spare bed."

"I had hoped you would offer it." Mammi gives me a reassuring smile.

"Today is quilting day," Rachel says as we go inside the enclosed back porch that leads into a big, tidy kitchen. "But the women won't be here until 11:00."

"It is Saturday," Mammi says. "I almost forgot that."

"Mamm!" Rachel calls out as we go through a rather stark dining room area that opens into a living room with a staircase coming into it.

"What is it, Rachel?" a woman's voice says sharply from upstairs.

"We have guests," Rachel calls out sweetly.

"Oh. I am coming." The voice becomes more pleasant. Then a smiling woman wearing a dark blue dress comes down the stairs, but seeing Mammi at the foot of the stairs, her smile fades. "Guests?" She frowns at Rachel. "It is only Mammi."

"Mammi and my cousin Shannon." Rachel points to where I am standing slightly behind the staircase. "Come and meet her, Mamm."

"This is your aunt Katrina," Mammi quietly tells me.

"Welcome to our home, Shannon." Katrina looks me up and down with a perplexed expression.

"Thank you, Aunt Katrina. I'm pleased to meet you."

"*Ja.*" She peers curiously into my face. "You look some like Anna. Except your hair." She turns to Mammi with an uneasy look. "You know I have women coming to sew quilts today. We haven't even set up the tables and frames yet. I have much to do."

"*Ja, ja.* I am sorry," Mammi tells her. "I forgot it is Saturday."

"But they can stay," Rachel tells her mother. "Can't you stay?" she says eagerly to Mammi. "Mamm made chicken casserole for dinner. I made your potato salad recipe. We also baked strawberry rhubarb pies last night. Six of them!"

"That does sound good." Mammi tips her head toward

me. "Maybe Shannon can stay to help sew. I must go back to tend to Anna." She looks at Katrina. "She is very ill."

"I'm sorry." Katrina's pale blue eyes remind me of an icy pond as she presses her lips together, still studying me with what seems a disgusted expression. Then she says something in Pennsylvania Dutch to Mammi. I suspect, by the way she quickly tosses some glances my way, she is talking about me.

"Rachel has offered to share her room with Shannon," Mammi tells Katrina. She seems to be answering her in English for my benefit. "It is very kind and generous of Rachel. Poor Shannon has been sleeping on the floor. With her mamm so sick, they cannot share a bed. It would be good for her to be here with you, to get to know her relatives."

Katrina looks fit to be tied right now.

"*Ja*, Mamm." Rachel eagerly grasps my hand again. "A cousin who is almost my same age. We can get to know her."

"An English cousin," Katrina says coolly.

"Does not the Bible say to love our neighbor as ourselves?" Rachel asks her mother. "Are the English not our neighbors too?"

Katrina adjusts the strings of her *kapp*, smoothing them down next to her cheeks. She seems clearly annoyed, and I feel like crawling under a rock.

"Shannon has brought only her English clothes, but she is willing to wear a dress," Mammi tells Katrina. "Perhaps Rachel has something she can use."

Katrina's face lights up a little. "*Ja*. That is a good idea." She turns to Rachel, saying something in the other language, then back to me. "If you stay here, Rachel will help you to dress with modesty."

"*Ja*," Rachel says before I can respond. "I will do that, Mamm."

Mammi thanks Katrina, excusing herself. "I must go home to check on Anna."

"I'll go with you. To get my things," I say to Mammi. Mostly I want an excuse to get out of this place where I'm clearly not wanted. Well, at least not wanted by my aunt. My cousin seems welcoming enough.

"Hurry back," Rachel cheerfully tells me.

"*Ja*," Katrina says with less enthusiasm. "Do hurry. You will need time to ready yourself before our guests come."

As Mammi and I walk back to the dawdi house, neither of us speaks, and I can tell she feels uncomfortable. "Shannon," she says when we get inside her little house. "If you do not like staying with Aunt Katrina and Uncle Benjamin, you are welcome back here. Jacob and I will fix you a real bed to stay in your mamm's room with her. If you would like that better."

I look into Mammi's eyes and once again am reminded that she truly is a kind woman. "Thank you," I tell her. "That's good to know."

"Your aunt Katrina works hard," Mammi says. "She wants everyone in her household to work hard too. It is her way."

"I will try to be a good houseguest," I promise Mammi.

"*Ja*." She nods. "I know you will."

As I pack my things, which will probably be useless to me in my aunt and uncle's house, it dawns on me that I'm starting to talk like them. Not that they speak so differently, but the way they talk is very simple. Very much to the point. Considering they haven't gone to school past the eighth grade, I guess it makes sense. I realize that I sometimes use words they don't know. As I zip up my bag and kiss my snoozing mom good-bye, I remind myself that I should try to be more like them. *When in Rome . . .*

Before I go, I hand off Mom's bottle of pills to Mammi. "These are prescription pills," I explain. "From the doctor. From what I can tell there's only enough left for about a week or so. After that, I suppose we could have them refilled in town."

"What do they do?" she asks as she peers at the label.

"Mostly they make her sleepy."

"Oh?" Mammi frowns. "Is that good?"

I shrug. "Sometimes I wonder, but I know she can be pretty miserable when she's awake and dizzy." I explain a little more about Mom's mysterious illness, and Mammi seems to be even more confused. "I don't know if the doctor really figured it all out," I confess. "But these pills do seem to help." I bite my lip now, wondering how much to say.

"Is there something else?"

I look into her eyes, thinking, *This is my grandma and I can trust her.* "Yes," I say quickly. "These pills are highly addictive." I study her. "Do you know what that means?"

She frowns. "I'm not sure."

I sigh, thinking what a wonderful world she must live in to be unaware of things like addiction. "It means that she may *think* she needs them more than she actually needs them. It's like they make her feel better, but maybe they don't really make her better. Does that make sense?"

"*Ja, ja.*" She nods, setting the amber bottle up on a high shelf.

I feel guilty, like I've betrayed my own mom. "You will take good care of her, won't you?" I ask.

"*Ja*, Shannon, you know I will. I love your mamm. I want her to be well. I will give her good food, and I will try to get her out of bed too."

I consider this. "Well, that might be good."

"Now you must go." She gives me a gentle push. "Aunt Katrina wants you to look like an Amish girl before the guests arrive."

"*Ja, ja,*" I say in a joking tone.

Mammi laughs. "On with you then."

As I walk back to my uncle's house, my mind is on Ezra. I'm replaying our time from last night. In the harsh light of day, it feels as if it were a dream. Did that really happen? I remember him asking me to go to a party with him tonight. I said I would go. At the time I didn't think about the fact that I might be relocated by then.

As I walk through my aunt and uncle's yard, I get worried. What if they refuse to let me go with Ezra tonight? What if they think they're supposed to be the boss of me? What if they lock me in Rachel's room? Not only that, but I'm worried Ezra won't know where to find me. I glance over my shoulder in the direction of his house, wondering if I should drop my bags and dash over there to attempt to find him. But I imagine his parents' shocked faces to see an English girl, dressed like I am, wanting to see their son. I know it would be a mistake. *Rumspringa* or not, I doubt they would approve.

"There you are!" Rachel comes out of the house to meet me. "Mamm was getting worried that you'd show up after the women arrive." She laughs. "We couldn't have them see-ing our English cousin 'dressed in men's clothes.' They might faint from shock."

I smile at her. I like that she has a sense of humor. And that she is kind.

"Come on up to my room," she tells me. "I already got some things out for you. Mamm stored some dresses that I outgrew a few years ago. She was saving them for my nieces. But the little girls won't be big enough for these garments for several years yet."

Rachel leads me up the stairs, down a hallway, and into a room that's not much bigger than the one I was sharing with Mom, but it has two twin-sized beds on opposite walls. On one bed three dresses have been laid out, resembling the cool side of a rainbow. One is a purplish blue, one is a medium blue, and one is a greenish blue.

"This one would be good on you," Rachel says as she picks up the teal dress, holding it up to me. "It used to be my favorite, back when I was still in school, before I got taller."

"It's a nice color."

"It matches your eyes," she tells me. She proceeds to help me dress. I never knew I needed help getting dressed—well, not since I was too young to remember. I soon realize that Amish clothes are rather uniquely challenging, though. First of all, there are all these layers of undergarments, which go in a particular order. Although they are cotton and lightweight, they feel like overkill in this warm summer weather.

"Don't you get hot with all these clothes?" I ask as I pull on the long, black stockings.

"*Ja*. But when we are at home, with no one visiting, we can go barelegged and barefoot if we want." She looks at my feet. "What size are your feet? You are short, so they are probably smaller than mine."

"Well, my feet are kinda big for my height," I admit. "Eight and a half."

She nods as she points out a black, flat-heeled shoe. "Well, mine are nines, but I have a pair that is on the small side. You can try them or just wear your own shoes if you like. Mamm prefers black shoes for us, but lots of girls wear what they want."

She helps me pull the teal dress down over my head. To my surprise, it has no zipper or buttons. When I ask her why, she tells me it's against the Ordnung.

"Are you serious? Zippers and buttons are against the rules?"

"Modern devices like zippers are English. We are Amish. We don't want to be like the outside world."

"What about buttons?" I ask as she reaches for a little box on her dresser.

"Buttons used to symbolize the military. Certain brass or silver buttons specified ranks. The Amish never wanted to be confused as the military," she explains as she slips some straight pins between her lips.

I try not to laugh at this. Amish and the military? Seems like a real stretch to me. "Are you going to sew something?" I ask.

"No, I'm going to fasten your dress." She steps behind me and proceeds to close up my dress—using straight pins!

"What if the pins slip out and poke me?" I ask after she's done.

"If you do it right—and I did—they will stay put."

"I still don't get it," I say. "So much concern about clothing. Why does it matter so much?"

"Our clothes help to set us apart. Just as God has set us

apart. Amish history explains why this is important." She reaches for what appears to be an apron, similar to what she is wearing. "Our people were massacred back in the sixteenth century—because of our beliefs. That is why we moved to this country. Religious freedom. The way we express our religious freedom is to live according to the Bible and the Ordnung. In a way that pleases God." She pins the apron onto me, then nods with satisfaction. "All we need now is your covering."

"Covering?" I imagine myself draped from head to toe in a burka.

Rachel taps her head. "A prayer *kapp* to cover your head. We don't usually wear them at home, but because we have guests coming, Mamm expects us to dress properly. But first we have to do something with this hair." She chuckles as she reaches for a comb. "I don't think it'll be easy."

I look at her glossy brown hair, pulled back so sleekly. "If it's supposed to look like yours, good luck."

"First we comb it all back." She works to get the comb through my curls. "As smooth and flat as we can get it. Then we secure it with a band." She contains my wild hair into a ponytail. "Then we make it into a bun and pin it into place."

I wait as she secures my bun, curious as to how this is going to look.

"Then we put a hairnet over it."

"A hairnet?" I imagine a cafeteria lady.

"*Ja.*" She pins a hairnet over the bun. "And over the net goes your covering."

"Why do you wear coverings or *kapps* or whatever you call them?" I ask as she reaches for a *kapp* that looks identical to her own.

"We do it out of obedience to Scripture. In First Corinthians 11:5 the apostle Paul instructs women to cover their heads." She reaches for more straight pins.

"You're not going to use those to pin it to my head, are you? That'll hurt."

She laughs. "They just go through the *kapp* and through your hair and back into the *kapp* again. I promise it will not hurt at all."

I stand very still as she does this final pinning. No way do I want a pin pricking my scalp.

"There," she proclaims. "Finished." She nods with approval. "You look like a real Amish girl."

"So I won't embarrass your family now?"

She shrugs as she puts the comb away. "I don't mind being seen with an English girl."

As I follow my pretty cousin downstairs, where I can hear the voices of other women, I try to imagine what it would be like to be a real Amish girl. What if my mom had never left this place? What if I'd been born here like Rachel? What if this simple life was all I knew? Would it be enough?

11

My aunt responds to me completely differently now that I'm dressed in appropriate clothes. Even though I find this somewhat aggravating, I am also pleased. It's kind of like how I feel when I take a math test—I despise taking it but am happy to pass it.

There must be close to thirty women here, inside and outside of the house, all of them working on big quilting frames and happily chattering amongst themselves. The quilts they are stitching are really beautiful—geometric creations in shades of purples, blues, greens, grays. I would love to paint a picture of this scene. Even more than that, I would love to learn how to make a quilt, but Rachel and I are kept busy getting their midday meal ready.

"What are the quilts for?" I ask Rachel as we set things out on the dining room table, which has been moved outside.

"It's Mamm's business," she explains. "Mamm does all the work of cutting the quilt pieces and sewing them together to make a top, but when it comes time to quilt them, she invites her friends to help. At first it was only a few women. Two or three." Rachel lowers her voice. "Mamm always makes them a good dinner and they have a good time—in time more and more women wanted to come."

"What do you mean it's your mamm's business?" I ask as we go back into the kitchen. "Does she sell the quilts?"

"*Ja.*" Rachel nods as she checks the teakettle to see that it's hot. "Mamm sells them to a shop in Hochstetler. For good money too. The quilts sell as fast as she can make them."

"Interesting."

As Rachel and I help with the food and drinks, I get to meet various women. All the women are pleasant to me, and although I'm introduced as Rachel's cousin, only a couple of the women who are somehow related to me seem to piece together that I am the daughter of Anna Hershberger (the shunned). I can tell that when they switch over to Pennsylvania Dutch, they are talking about us, probably saying things they don't want me to hear. It almost makes me wish I understood their weird language.

I try to remember all the women's names, but like their clothing and hair, their names are very similar. Most of them sound like they came from the Bible. And there are two Rebeccas, two Sarahs, and three Katies. I figure if I forget someone I met, I'll just call her Katie—and the odds will be in my favor.

However, I do manage to remember one particular woman's name: Ruth Troyer. The name *Troyer* catches my attention, and when she tells me she lives on the neighboring farm, I ask if she is related to Ezra Troyer.

"*Ja* . . . ?" She gives me a curious look. "I'm his mamm. You know my Ezra?"

"*Ja*," I echo. "He returned a tool to Dawdi and I met him."

"Ezra is a good boy. Works hard."

I nod, feeling her eyes on me as if she's measuring me up. "Would you like more tea?" I ask politely.

"*Ja*, please." She holds up her cup for me to refill it.

The quilting party goes on merrily until close to 4:00, but then the women suddenly start getting up, talking about getting supper and evening chores, and in what seems mere minutes, they are all gone.

As Katrina packs up the quilting things, Rachel and I clean up the kitchen. I've never seen such a mountain of dishes. "Do Amish people ever use paper plates?" I ask as I dry the umpteenth plate.

"Many do." Rachel chuckles. "But Mamm likes to do things . . . *her* way."

I get the feeling that my aunt is fairly strong willed, at least for an Amish woman. Compared to the meek, mild souls who were helping her with her quilts today, her personality seems dynamic and overpowering. I wonder if that ever causes problems in this culture. Watching my grandparents these past couple of days, I am aware that men have authority over women. I wonder if my uncle Ben ever has a power struggle with his wife.

"Mammi told me that your father is a minister," I say to Rachel as I place a small stack of dishes on the open shelf.

"*Ja*. Daed was chosen last winter when Jeremiah Troyer passed on."

"Troyer?" I say with interest. "Is that Ezra Troyer's father?"

"No, Jeremiah was his dawdi." She looks curiously at me. "You know Ezra?"

"*Ja.*" I smile shyly. "And I met his mother today too."

Rachel tilts her head to one side. "How did you meet Ezra?"

I can feel my cheeks warming as I dry a teacup. "I was mowing the grass," I begin slowly. "Dawdi's mower wasn't working right. Ezra happened to be around, and he stepped in and helped me."

"That sounds like Ezra. Always poking his nose in other people's business."

"You don't like him?" I ask her.

She shrugs as she scrubs a casserole dish. "Ezra is a good man." But as she says this, I hear something else in her voice. Almost as if she doesn't fully approve of him.

"He seems nice."

"*Ja.* Time will show us."

I think I have my opportunity, but I get the feeling I should tread carefully. "Ezra told me about a party tonight—"

Rachel drops the dishrag into the water. "What?"

"He said the young people get together on Saturday nights."

"He told you about that?" She looks close to angry now.

"*Ja.* Is there something wrong with it? He explained rum-springer—"

"*Rumspringa,*" she corrects me.

"Yeah, well, he said that it means running around and all that."

"*Ja,* I'll bet he did." She returns to scrubbing the dish.

"Anyway, I told him I'd like to go tonight." I take in a deep breath. "Do you think your parents will mind?"

She continues scrubbing, focusing all her attention on getting the casserole dish sparkling, as if her life depends on it.

"Did I say something to upset you?" I ask.

"No." She shakes her head. "My brother Jeremiah will probably go to the party. Mamm and Daed will not stop you from going with him, if that's what you want to do."

"Don't you ever go to the parties?"

"I *used* to go." She stops scrubbing and turns to look at me. "But I stopped. I do not think those parties are good, Shannon. I do not think you will enjoy yourself. There are other ways for young people to get together. Singing groups or volleyball or—"

"Is there some young people activity tonight?" Katrina asks as she comes into the kitchen with a couple of neatly folded quilts in her arms. "Maybe you should take your cousin with you, Rachel."

"*Ja*, Mamm, we were just talking about that," Rachel says in a wooden sounding voice. "I said Jeremiah could take her."

"You do not want to go?" her mother asks.

Rachel's brow creases. "*Ja*. Maybe I will go, Mamm."

"Good," Katrina declares. "Young ones need to gather together. I remember those times." She looks at me. "It is how I met your uncle. I was not even seventeen when we first met. And Rachel will be eighteen in September."

Rachel looks as if she'd like to throw the dishrag at her mother.

"Those are beautiful quilts," I say to my aunt, mostly to change the subject but also because it's true.

At first Katrina seems pleased by my praise, but then she gets a solemn look. "They are good and well made. But they are *not* beautiful, Shannon. They are not meant to be beautiful."

"Is it wrong for something to be beautiful?" I ask her.

She smiles in a tolerant way. "The best things in life are not things," she tells me. "And the best kind of beauty is the kind the eye cannot see."

"Oh." I try to absorb this.

"Rachel," she says abruptly. "Did you check to make sure there is enough leftover food for supper tonight?"

"*Ja*," Rachel assures her. "There is plenty for sure."

"Good. We will not have to cook again."

"I set aside a pie for tomorrow's dinner too," Rachel says.

"Good. Finish in here and then go see to the milking. Shannon can help you." My aunt peers at me. "Do you know how to milk?"

"A cow?" I ask.

She looks slightly amused. "Rachel will teach you."

After I've finished cow milking 101, earning a grade of D–, I help Rachel get the table set and supper ready to serve. At 6:00 sharp the table quickly fills up. Besides my aunt and uncle and Rachel, two of Rachel's older brothers join us. Isaac, who works on the farm, is twenty-three and recently engaged. Jeremiah is twenty-one and also works on the farm. Both of these guys look big and strong, probably from doing farm work. They are quiet and polite and seem mostly intent upon the food.

Although there's more conversation at this table than at my grandparents' table, it is mostly about the farm and what happened today. Of course, this makes sense. It's not like they would talk about world events or politics or the latest crime spree. In fact, it's rather refreshing. Not to mention stress free.

121

"So what do you think of this place?" Uncle Ben asks me as we're having dessert.

"I like it," I tell him.

"You do?" He looks slightly surprised.

"Yeah, I do. I'll admit I didn't really like it at first. I think I was in shock."

Uncle Ben chuckles. "You should have seen her face when I picked them up in Hochstetler," he tells his family. "She did look shocked."

"I didn't know I had Amish relatives," I explain.

"Your mamm never told you about us?" my aunt asks.

"No. Not at all."

The table gets quiet now.

"Even if she had told me," I say quickly, "I don't think I would've understood. I think it takes being here, living right among you, to understand what being Amish means."

"You think you understand what being Amish means?" My uncle is challenging me.

"Not exactly. But I know that you aren't Amish just because you're born here," I say to him and he nods. "I get that it's a commitment, and that you must be baptized and follow the Ordnung."

My uncle looks impressed. "You've learned a lot in only a few days."

I smile at him. "I guess I've had good teachers."

We talk for a while longer, and I feel encouraged to be part of this family. Sure, my aunt intimidates me a little, but I respect that she's a strong woman. I'm a little surprised to see that she's very respectful of her husband. I'm not sure why I thought she wouldn't be, especially knowing that he is a minister. Even though Uncle Ben is a minister, he seems fairly easy to talk to. All in all, I feel fairly good about being here. To be honest, that surprises me.

After dinner I help Rachel wash the dishes and clean the kitchen. Their kitchen setup is almost identical to Mammi's, except that there is more space, which is probably good since their family is bigger. "There used to be eight of us sitting at that table," Rachel tells me as I'm scrubbing the dining table and she's sweeping the floor. "Before Samuel—that's my oldest brother—married Abigail and moved to her parents' farm to help out. Then Grace got married and moved too," she continues. "And then Joshua . . . um . . . left."

"Left?" I ask. "Where did he go?"

She pauses her sweeping. "We're not supposed to speak of him."

"Oh . . . but he's your brother, right?"

She nods and lowers her voice. "He would be twenty-six now."

"Did he die?"

She shrugs. "Maybe he did. I don't know."

"Really?"

"He left," she whispers. "Went into the—*the army*. We are not supposed to mention his name again, ever."

"Oh . . . I'm sorry." I'm guessing that means he's like my mom—shunned. "That must be hard."

"*Ja*. My brother was taught pacifism. Not war." She returns to a normal tone of voice. "So when all the kids still lived here, it could be noisy sometimes."

"Noisy? That's hard to imagine."

"Well, it was noisier," she explains. "Unless Daed said, 'Quiet,' and then it wouldn't be so noisy."

It's so weird to think about how my aunt and uncle could exercise that kind of control over six children—six! Of course, according to Rachel, Joshua didn't seem to fall into the being controlled category. He joined the army. I wonder if he's ever sorry about leaving. What would they do if he wanted to come back? Do they believe in the prodigal son?

Rachel and I spend a little time, though not much, cleaning up to go out to the party. She seems a little unhappy about going, and I'm curious as to why, but I'm afraid that if I ask, she might change her mind. So I keep my mouth shut. Every once in a while, I sneak a peek out the window. I keep wondering if Ezra might stop by my grandparents' house and ask about me. If they tell him I'm over here, is it possible he'll show up? And if he does show up, what will I do?

When Jeremiah announces that he's hitched the horse and buggy and it's time to go, I don't see any sign of Ezra. Rachel and I get into the back of the buggy, and I look out the window in the direction of Ezra's farm.

"Don't worry," she tells me. "He will be at the party."

"Who?" I try to act like I don't know what she's talking about.

"Ezra," she says plainly. "He will be there. Count on it."

"*Ja*," Jeremiah says from in front. "Ezra will be there for sure."

Feeling satisfied, I lean back and wonder how Ezra will react to seeing me in Amish clothes tonight. I know he liked how I looked in my sundress, but I hope he'll appreciate me making the effort to dress like this too. Besides, I remind myself, if I didn't, I probably wouldn't have been allowed out tonight. So, really, I did it for Ezra. I gaze out at the sun, which is starting to dip low in the sky. With the clouds and what looks like smoke in the distance, it appears the evening will be another colorful show. "Looks like a pretty sunset tonight," I say lightly to Rachel.

She nods, looking out. "*Ja*. Peace is seeing a sunset and knowing who to thank."

I turn to look at her. "Wow. That's a cool thing to say."

She tips her head to one side. "It is just something my daed says sometimes."

"The knowing who to thank part, that means God, right?"

"*Ja*. He is the one who makes the sun to rise and to set."

"And the moon and the stars," I say dreamily.

She gives me a funny look, like she's wondering what's up with me.

"Last night the stars were absolutely amazing," I explain.

But as the buggy rumbles down the graveled road, it's not the stars or the sunset that occupy my thoughts. No, my mind is fixed on Ezra Troyer, and my heart is beating with anxious anticipation. I cannot wait to see him again, to look into his brown eyes, to feel his rough hand touch my cheek . . . to kiss him. Just thinking of these things makes me light-headed and giddy.

12

'm not sure where we are when Jeremiah finally stops the buggy, but I hear someone mention Yoder's barn. I have no idea who Yoder is and don't really care, but as Rachel is climbing down from the buggy, I notice a number of young men, all dressed in dark pants with suspenders and all sporting the same kind of straw hats. They're milling about the door to a barn that looks very much like the one Dawdi and Uncle Ben share. Suspecting that Ezra might be amongst these guys, I try not to trip over my long skirt as I get out. I don't want to fall on my face again.

The light is getting dusky now, but I can make out the faces of these guys well enough to spot Ezra. I'm about to wave to him when he suddenly turns away from us, and just like that, he seems to disappear around the corner of the barn. I'm not sure if this is a snub or perhaps an invitation. As we walk toward the door, I wonder if I'm supposed to follow him. I'd like to.

"Come on!" Rachel grabs my hand. "Let's go inside."

I want to protest, but feeling like an intruder on foreign turf, I decide I'd better follow her lead. I have no idea how these kids act in a group like this. Will they be prim and proper? However, as we go past the guys clustered by the door, they call out cheerful greetings. "Good ev'nin', Rachel," a dark-haired guy says in a slightly slurred voice. I pause to look at him, certain that I can smell beer on his breath, and I spot a shiny can in his hand.

"Are they drinking beer?" I whisper to Rachel as we go inside the barn. Music is playing and the interior of the barn is lit with a few lanterns, but it still looks fairly shadowy in here.

"*Ja*," she says in a slightly disgusted tone. "Those boys don't think it is a party without their beer."

"Oh."

A trampoline is set up on one side of the barn, and a couple of barefoot girls are jumping on it. Holding onto each other's hands, they giggle as they bounce, and their full skirts balloon up around them each time they land, exposing more leg than I'm sure is acceptable. The guys and girls watching the pair laugh and joke—sounding almost like some of the kids I go to school with. Except that they are *different*.

I can feel eyes on me, and before long Rachel begins introducing me to some of her friends—or maybe they're just acquaintances, because she doesn't act particularly friendly to any of them. She seems stiff and unnatural, and I'm certain she would rather not be here—and doesn't care who knows.

"Are you the English girl?" a guy named Levi asks me.

I nod. "Yeah."

He grins. "Want a beer?"

"No, she does *not*," Rachel answers sharply for me.

"Why can't she speak for herself?" Levi demands.

Rachel folds her arms across her front, glaring at him.

"No thanks," I tell Levi. I glance around the barn, hoping to spy Ezra again and wondering if it would sound odd if I asked about him.

"Ezra was here earlier," Levi tells us.

"I know," Rachel says. "I saw him."

Levi glances at me now, as if to see whether I'm interested in hearing more about Ezra. I decide to risk it. "Ezra invited me to come tonight," I explain. "I thought I'd get to talk to him."

Levi nods with interest. "*Ja*, I thought he would want to talk to you too."

"Why?" Rachel's brow creases and she makes a deep frown as she glares at Levi.

Levi looks uncomfortable. "I, uh, I don't know."

I'm getting a little fed up with my uptight cousin. "Maybe I'll go look around," I say lightly, hoping to pry myself away from Rachel. She seems determined to ruin my fun.

I wander around the barn now, smiling and saying hello to people I've never met before. To my surprise, they are all pretty friendly to me. Some of them ask who I am and why I'm here. I simply tell them I'm Rachel's cousin, and that seems to satisfy their curiosity.

"You don't seem much like Rachel," a skinny blonde girl named Phoebe says to me. She's got a beer can in her hand, and I suspect it's not her first.

"I don't know," I say. "To be honest, I don't know Rachel that well."

She frowns. "But you're cousins?"

"*Ja.*" I try to sound Amish now. "I live far away."

"Oh, *ja*." She nods. "You want a beer?" She holds up her blue and silver can. "To loosen you up?"

"*Ja*," I tell her, knowing this is probably a stupid mistake. I have no intention of drinking, but I hope that holding a can in my hand will help me to fit in better with this crowd. Besides that, if Amish kids think it's okay to drink beer, maybe it's not such a big deal.

She walks me over to a cooler by the door and plucks a dripping can from the icy water. "Here you go." She grins. "Bottoms up!"

I laugh nervously as I pop open the can and pretend to take a swig. I sampled beer last summer at a friend's house, but I decided then and there that it was nasty and not for me. Still, I pretend to be sipping this foul-smelling brew as I look around the barn. "Ezra invited me to come here tonight," I tell Phoebe. "But I don't see him around."

"He was here earlier," she tells me.

"Uh-huh." I pretend to take another sip.

She gives me a curious look. "You and Ezra?" she asks with a teasing tone.

"What?" I act innocent.

"Do you *like* him?" she asks with twinkling eyes.

"Sure," I say offhandedly. "He's a nice guy."

"And nice looking too." She grins. "*All* the girls like Ezra."

"Really?"

"*Ja*. All the girls are interested in Ezra Troyer, but he has only been interested in one girl."

I smile, thinking that, like Levi, she's heard about Ezra and the English girl. "Who is that?" I ask innocently.

She laughs. "You must be joking."

I giggle, taking another fake swig of beer.

"Your cousin," she tells me. "Didn't she tell you?"

I'm confused. "Tell me what?"

"About her and Ezra."

I blink, then glance over to where Rachel is talking to a girl. "What about her and Ezra?"

"They used to be together," Phoebe says in a conspiratorial tone.

"Really?" Suddenly I feel off balance, like the earth beneath my feet is tilting slightly. I know it's not the beer since I've only inhaled the fumes.

"*Ja*. But Rachel broke it off."

"Rachel broke it off?" I echo dumbly.

"*Ja*." Phoebe glances around like she's worried someone's listening, then lowers her voice. "Rachel's daed is a *minister*, ya know?"

I nod. "*Ja*. I know."

"Rachel is studying for baptism now. I think she plans to join the church this summer."

"Oh . . ." I recall what I've heard about baptism and how it's a life commitment that makes a person really Amish.

"But Ezra isn't ready for that yet," Phoebe tells me.

"I know."

Phoebe's eyes light up again. "But you and Ezra . . . ?" She grins. "*Ja*, that makes sense."

I frown. "Maybe so . . . but where is he?"

"He might be outside with some of the other boys," she suggests.

"Should I go look for him?" I ask her.

"*Ja*," she says eagerly. "I'll go with you."

Grateful to have her company, I let her lead me out a side door in the back of the barn. I don't look at Rachel as I exit. I suspect she wouldn't approve of me going outside with Phoebe, but the truth is, I don't care. All I care about right now is seeing Ezra. I feel like I would swim across a raging river, climb a steep mountain, walk over hot coals just to see him again.

Outside, the air feels fresh and cool. I look up to see the stars shining brightly and spy the moon coming up through the branches of some evergreen trees. "What a beautiful night," I say to Phoebe as she leads me over to where someone has built a bonfire back behind the barn. A number of guys are standing around it, plus a couple of girls. All are drinking beer and seem close to being intoxicated.

"Anyone seen Ezra?" Phoebe asks loudly.

"*Ja,*" a guy tells her. "He's around about here somewhere."

"I saw him sitting by himself on a wagon over there." Another guy jerks his thumb over his shoulder.

I peer in the direction of his thumb, but it's so dark I can barely see. "I guess I'll go look for him," I mutter. This sets some of them to laughing, and as I hurry away, I can hear them making jokes at my expense. I don't care. All I want is to find Ezra so I can find out what's going on between us. I'm worried that he didn't recognize me, dressed like this. Or maybe he didn't like it. Or maybe it's something else—something to do with my pretty cousin.

As my eyes adjust to the darkness, I see the shape of what looks like a wagon, but I don't see anyone sitting on it. Just the same, I continue over there, thinking I might sit there by myself and hope that he will return.

"Who's that?" a voice says in the darkness. I think it's Ezra and a rush of hope surges through me, but I am not certain.

"It's me," I say pleasantly. "Shannon."

"Shannon?" Almost in the same instant, a figure leaps from the wagon and runs over to grab me, sweeping me into his arms. "I'm so glad to see you."

I can smell beer on his breath, but I don't care. "Why are you out here hiding?" I ask as he leads me over to the wagon with his arm still around me.

"I'm not hiding." He pauses now, peering down at me in the moonlight. "What are you wearing?"

I giggle.

He taps my white *kapp*. "What is this?"

"You know what it is."

"But why?"

"Because it was the only way I could get out of the house." This isn't exactly true, but I don't think it's exactly untrue either.

He points to the can in my hand. "I see you got yourself some brew."

"*Ja.*" I nod, acting like this is nothing out of the norm for me.

Ezra puts his hands around my waist now. "Up you go," he says as he hoists me to a sitting position on the wagon's tailgate. Then he sits beside me. "Look at that moon," he says as he pops open a can of beer and takes a swig.

"Yeah," I say, watching as its nearly round shape crests the tops of the trees. "Beautiful."

He slips his arm around me, snuggling close. "Not as beautiful as you, Shannon. I'm so glad you came tonight."

"You didn't seem glad," I say in a slightly hurt tone.

"What do you mean?"

"I mean when Rachel and I got out of the buggy." I peer at him. "Didn't you see me?"

He looks puzzled. "I saw Rachel," he says quietly.

"But not me?"

He takes another swig of beer.

"Was it because I was wearing Amish clothes?" I ask hopefully.

"*Ja,*" he says quickly. "I never saw you dressed like this before."

Part of me doesn't believe him, but the rest of me doesn't care. It's almost as if I've switched off my ability to care—or maybe I checked my brain at the door. But I shut down the inner voice that always seems to question everything. Before long we are kissing again. Tonight it feels even more passionate and breathtaking than last night. Was that only last night? I find myself getting lost in his kisses . . . and liking it.

I'm not sure how it happens, and I suspect I'm intoxicated—not from drinking beer, but from being with him—but soon we are lying down in the wagon. I can feel and smell hay, and I can feel his body pressed close to mine. "I love you," he mumbles into my ear, sending a fresh new thrill through me.

"I love you too," I tell him.

His hands are starting to wander, and although a part of me isn't comfortable with this, another part of me likes it and doesn't want him to stop. Oh, I know I will have to draw a line eventually. But I don't mind going right up to that line first.

"There she is!" a male voice exclaims as a blindingly bright lantern is held up to the wagon.

I scramble to push Ezra away and sit up, smoothing my rumpled clothes, squinting into the light.

"What are you doing?" a familiar voice demands.

Shielding my eyes from the light with my hand, I see that it's Jeremiah.

"What does it look like she's doing?" the other guy jokes.

"*Ezra?*" Jeremiah holds the lantern over where Ezra is slowly sitting up, rubbing his eyes and looking slightly confused as well as sheepish.

"Hey, Jeremiah," he says in a slurred voice.

"Rachel is worried about you." Jeremiah reaches for my hand, pulling me down from the wagon and onto my feet. "You shouldn't be out here like this, Shannon. Daed would not like it."

"But I—"

"Come on," he says, tugging on my hand. "I'm taking you back to Rachel."

I turn to look at Ezra, but he seems slightly disoriented, and I suspect he's had more beer than I thought. "See ya," I call over my shoulder. He says nothing, not even good-bye.

I can't help but feel embarrassed as Jeremiah and his buddy escort me back into the barn, which seems brighter than before. I brush loose pieces of straw and hay from my bodice and my skirt, trying to appear more together than I probably look.

"You found her," Rachel says to Jeremiah with a scowl.

"*Ja,*" his buddy says in a teasing tone. "We found her, all right."

Rachel reaches over to pluck a piece of straw from my hair, tossing it to the ground. "What were you doing out there, Shannon?"

"She was with Ezra," Jeremiah quietly explains.

Rachel gives me a disgusted look, then turns to her brother. "I want to go home."

"Already?"

"*Ja*. Already," she insists.

He frowns. "But it's still early, Rachel."

She folds her arms in front, glaring at him. "If I told Daed that I wanted to go home and you refused to—"

"Why don't you drive the buggy home," he suggests.

"Jeremiah!"

"I can drive you," the other guy offers. I can tell by the way he's looking at Rachel that he'd be more than happy to take her home.

"Thanks, Jonah," she says lightly. "But I'll drive Shannon and myself home." She points a finger at Jeremiah. "Do not forget we have church in the morning!" she says sternly. Then she grabs me by the hand like I'm a six-year-old and marches me out of the barn.

I feel like protesting and demanding to stay here, but her power over me is overwhelming. Besides that, she's taller than me and probably stronger, and it's as if I can feel her personality dominating mine. Rachel is definitely a force to be reckoned with. And I get the distinct feeling that she is more than just disgusted with me—she is angry!

13

"You know how to operate this thing?" I say lightly to Rachel as she climbs into the front driver's seat. I'm sitting in the back because I have a feeling she doesn't want me up there.

Instead of answering, she does something with her foot, then snaps the reins and says something I don't catch—probably to the horse—and soon we are going back to where we came from. I consider attempting to start a conversation with my disgruntled cousin, but I suspect she does not wish to speak with me. I lean back and daydream about Ezra.

However, my happy daydream seems to have frequent interruptions, almost like an obnoxious commercial popping into my favorite reality show. I can hear the comments Phoebe made about Ezra and Rachel and how they used to be "together." I wonder what that means. At the same time, I do not want to know. Although I've never had a real boyfriend before, I've observed others. I'm well aware that some relationships begin and end in less than a week. Perhaps that was how it was with Ezra and my cousin. Nothing serious. Besides that, it's history now.

What seems most important is that Ezra loves me. He said those words tonight. And I love him. What difference does it make that he has a past with my cousin? They were obviously not meant for each other. Not the way Ezra and I seem to be, anyway. If my cousin is feeling out of sorts because she sees someone else enjoying what she obviously didn't want, why should I be concerned?

In fact, I have as much right to be irritated as she does. Perhaps even more. She's the one who ruined my evening, dragging me away from a party that I was enjoying immensely. I look out of the slow-moving buggy, realizing that I could just hop out. I might take a little tumble, but it wouldn't be enough to get seriously hurt. Then I could jog on back to the party and pick things up right where we left them. Rachel is so zoned out, she probably wouldn't even notice I was gone until she got home. Then she'd have something to think about.

However, I'm not sure that I want to go back and pick things up right where we left them. The truth is, I think I was partially relieved that Jeremiah and his buddy showed up when they did. I wasn't looking forward to telling Ezra that it was time to stop. I didn't even know what I was going to say to him to make him stop. Their untimely intervention (or was it timely?) kept me from having to deal with an uncomfortable situation. I can act miffed and outraged at Rachel, but really I'm not. And on some level I feel kind of sorry for her. I know what it feels like to be the only person who's acting responsible when everyone else is acting like immature juveniles. Yet, at the same time, I think maybe it's my turn—maybe it's time for me to enjoy being a teenager. I suppose it's ironic I would experience this sort of thing in Amishland.

The house looks dark when we pull up. Without saying a word to me, Rachel drives the buggy up to the barn, then gets out and starts doing something with the horse. I suspect she has to get the harness stuff off of him and put everything away. If she had been a little friendlier to me, I would offer to help her. As it is, I think she wants to be alone, so I go back to the house, quietly letting myself in through the back porch door. It's so dark in there that I have to go slowly. I consider finding a lantern and lighting it, but I like the idea of sneaking through the house in the dark. I find my way to the stairs and go up, reminding myself that Rachel's room is to the right and clear down on the end. At least I hope that's right. I don't like the idea of crashing in on my aunt and uncle or my cousin Isaac, all of whom must be soundly asleep by now.

To my relief, I open the correct door, and thanks to the moonlight flooding through the window that faces east, I can see my small pile of bags on the floor by my bed. It takes me a while to unpin and remove my layers of strange clothes, which I toss in a heap on the floor. Then I retrieve the nightgown Mammi gave me, slip it on, and hop into bed. I plan to pretend to be sleeping when Rachel comes in. I've decided I have no more desire to speak to her than she has to speak to me.

However, this makes me sad. I remember how much I liked her when we first met. She was so kind and friendly and helpful. She seems fairly smart too. And there's no denying she's pretty. But knowing that she used to be involved with Ezra—my Ezra!—no matter how briefly . . . well, that changes everything.

As I lie still in the narrow bed, listening for my cousin's footsteps, I think that I would've been better off staying with my mom at the dawdi house. Sleeping on a hard floor—or out beneath the stars—seems preferable to sharing a room with the *other woman*. Okay, I know that's a little over the top. Rachel is only Ezra's ex. Lots of people have exes. And tonight Ezra proclaimed his love for me. Whatever Rachel was to him—if she was anything—is in the past. I need to get over it and act as if nothing whatsoever is wrong. And that is exactly what I intend to do. Tomorrow.

I hear footsteps in the hallway. Quietly the door opens and closes and I can hear her rustling about in the darkness. I suppose I could tell her it's okay to turn on a lantern, but I'd rather just play possum. I hear her go to use the bathroom and realize I probably should've done this myself, but now I feel like I need to keep up the illusion that I'm asleep.

After a while she returns and I hear her getting into bed. It's very quiet in here, and I'm thinking she must be asleep and I can sneak out to use the bathroom, when I start to hear something. I can't figure out what it is. It's kind of a snuffling sound. Then it hits me: she is quietly crying in her bed.

Even though I don't really see what it has to do with me, I get the haunting feeling that it is totally my fault. I feel guilty and sad. I feel like my being here is making her unhappy. Yet I don't see why. It's not like I've stolen Ezra from her. Even if they were a couple—or whatever—it was obviously over with long before I stepped into the picture. Besides, I reassure myself, there is no way that her relationship with Ezra was anything like mine, because if it were, they would still be together, and clearly they are not. Still, I wish she wasn't crying. I wonder if there might be some way to make it better for her. Maybe tomorrow.

The room is bright with sunlight when I wake up, but to my surprise, Rachel's bed is empty and neatly made. I also notice that the dress and things I threw onto the floor last night are now tidily hanging from a peg on the wall by the door. I must've been sleeping hard. But since it was the first night I've slept in a real bed since arriving here, I suspect I was more tired than I realized.

I yawn lazily, stretching in bed, enjoying this unexpected spell of alone time and peace and quiet. Then I get up and, still wearing only my nightgown—which might not be good manners but is a necessity—scurry down the hallway to the bathroom. I hope no one's in it, but if so, I am prepared to dash downstairs and outside to use the outhouse that Rachel said was mostly for the fellows. To my relief, the bathroom is empty.

When I emerge from the bathroom, I look both ways up and down the hall before I dash back to the bedroom. The place seems so quiet that I wonder if everyone is downstairs having breakfast. The faint smell of cooking tells me that someone's been in the kitchen.

I go back down the hallway, leaning over the stair rail to listen. The house really does sound as if it's been deserted. I tiptoe down the stairs, listening carefully as I go, but hearing nothing, I go all the way through the living room and dining room and clear to the kitchen. No one is here, but on the kitchen table is a short, simple note.

Dear Shannon,
  We have gone to church.
  Please have breakfast and make yourself at home.
  We will be back in a few hours.

Aunt Katrina

Feeling unexpectedly happy to have the entire house to myself, I do a happy dance and, still in my nightgown, take my bowl of oatmeal out on the porch. As I sit out there I gaze over toward where I know Ezra's house lies. I wonder if he, like me, is lounging around this morning. I imagine him sitting on his porch wearing only his trousers. It's a nice image.

But then I wonder, what if he went to church with his parents? Since he's not English like me, most likely he did. Of course, that would be expected of him. As I imagine him sitting in church, I feel sad and left out of things. Ezra is at church and I'm sitting here in my nightgown. Why didn't my aunt and uncle invite me to church? Probably because I'm not Amish. But my church at home's not like that. Everyone and anyone is welcome. In fact, our pastor is always encouraging us to invite outsiders. Why don't Amish people do that?

Realizing it's past eleven and I have no idea when my relatives will actually return from church, I decide I'd better get dressed. The idea of being discovered running about the house in my nightie is not pleasant. I go wash my bowl and breakfast things, then hurry back upstairs. I consider putting on my own clothes, but the thought of Aunt Katrina scowling at me makes me decide on the Amish clothes. Perhaps I'll try out the purple dress today.

I manage to get the undergarments on okay, but when it comes to pinning the back of the dress, I am all thumbs. Bloody thumbs. I glance at the crisp white *kapp* and, not wanting a bloody scalp, decide to skip it. I doubt anyone will be too concerned about that. Especially since Rachel said it wasn't necessary to wear it around the house. Besides, I doubt I could smooth my hair back as well as she did.

Satisfied that I look somewhat respectable, I go downstairs and write a note on the back of the one my aunt wrote to me. Mine is even simpler than hers. I want to add that I felt left out by not being invited to church, but I decide that would be rude.

Dear Aunt Katrina,
  I have gone to visit my mother.
  Thank you for breakfast.

Shannon

As I walk through the grass pasture between my uncle's house and the dawdi house, I can tell it's going to be a hot day today. I remember how my mom hated to waste money on air-conditioning. Perhaps that was good because it has prepared her for life in Amishland where AC is about as likely as TV.

"Hello?" I call into the house after I knock a couple of times. "Mammi?" For some reason I assume she will be here. I don't think she'd want to leave my mom alone. But not hearing any answer, I go in and knock on the door to my mom's room. When she doesn't answer, I get concerned. Surely Mammi and Dawdi couldn't have taken her to church. More likely she's sleeping.

I push on the door but am surprised to see that it only opens a few inches. Something on the floor seems to be blocking it. I push harder, sticking my hand in to discover that it's my mom's body that's blocking the door. "Mom!" I cry out. "Are you okay?" I shove my shoulder into the door, pushing with all my strength, but hearing her groan, I'm afraid I'm hurting her.

Remembering the open window, I run outside, take a chair from the porch, prop it up beneath the window, then climb inside. "Mom?" I cry as I run to her side. "What happened?"

"Dizzy," she tells me as I help her sit up.

"Are you okay? Anything broken?"

"I . . . am . . . okay . . ." She looks at me with relieved eyes. Throwing her arms around me, she starts to cry. "Oh, Shannon."

As we hug I realize that the floor is wet and her clothes are wet. When I point this out, she explains she had an "accident."

I clean her up and find her some dry clothes, then help her back to her bed. "Where's Mammi?" I ask as I position pillows behind her.

"They went to church."

"And left you here alone?" I say indignantly.

"I told them to go. I thought I would be fine."

"What happened?"

"I needed to use the bathroom. I thought I could do it. But I got dizzy, and then I fell."

"How long were you on the floor like that?"

"I don't know."

I hand her a glass of water. "Here, drink this."

"I need a pill," she says.

"Did Mammi give you one?"

She shakes her head. "Mammi says I don't need them."

"What?"

"She says they aren't good for me."

I consider this. On one hand I agree with Mammi. On the other hand, after finding Mom like this—on the floor—I'm not sure. "Well, I think you might need a pill now," I say. But when I look around the room, I don't see the bottle. "Where are the pills?"

She shrugs. "Mammi keeps them somewhere."

I go out to the kitchen, and after looking around a bit, I finally locate them in the pantry, next to a jar of cinnamon. I shake a pill out and take it to Mom. She is so grateful that tears fill her eyes again.

As she takes her pill, I clean up the wet floor. Then I take her soiled clothes out to the back porch, wondering where Mammi keeps the dirty laundry. Not seeing a hamper, I set the sodden pile by the door, then wash my hands and return to check on Mom. She seems more relaxed now but looks perplexed as she stares at me. "What are you wearing?"

I explain about Aunt Katrina wanting me to wear Amish clothes and about Rachel's help.

"Oh. Well, I suppose that's okay. As long as they're not recruiting you to become Amish." She chuckles like this is a good joke.

"Judging by the way I pinned this dress together, I don't think that's likely."

"Come here," she says. "Let me see."

I sit on the edge of her bed, waiting while she fixes the mess I've made of the pins. "I forgot you used to dress like this," I say as I turn around. "So pinning a dress is kinda like riding a bike?"

"I suppose." She still has a pin in her hand. "Let me show you how it's done, Shannon." She folds fabric from my skirt, then pins it, showing me how to slip the pin in and out of the fabric. "See how it holds?"

"Yeah." Now I try it a couple of times, finally getting it without drawing blood. "I'm not so sure I can figure out the *kapp*, though. It might help if I could use a mirror."

She smiles. "It's actually pretty simple." Using my skirt again, she explains how the hair would go and how the pin would go through the *kapp*, weave into the hair, and then come back out into the *kapp* again. "See, this part of the pin would hold the *kapp* in place because it's fastened to the hair."

"I guess that makes sense."

She frowns. "But I really don't like seeing you dressed up as an Amish girl, Shannon. It's giving me the creeps. I didn't raise you the way I did just to let you get stuck in a place like this."

I laugh. "Don't worry. That will never happen to me. And it's no big deal dressing like this. I have to admit, though, it was nice sleeping in a real bed last night." I tell her how I slept in and then got up and wandered about the house in my nightgown. "It was kinda fun."

"Well, that kind of fun will only happen once a week," she warns. "On the Sabbath." She makes a sleepy yawn, and I can tell the pill is starting to work.

"Well, I think I'd better spend Sunday mornings with you," I say. "I don't think you should be left home alone."

"No . . ." She sighs. "Maybe not."

"I can come over during the week too," I assure her. "Although I suppose I should make myself useful to Aunt Katrina and Uncle Ben, to show appreciation for taking me in."

"Yes, please do that, Shannon. Benjamin is a good guy."

"Yeah," I say. "And he's a minister too."

Her sleepy eyes look surprised. "My brother Benjamin is a minister?"

"Yeah. I guess that puts some pressure on the family."

Her head barely nods. "Oh, yeah. For sure."

"Just rest," I tell her. "I'll stay here until Mammi gets back."

After I'm sure that she's asleep, I go back to the kitchen for a drink of water. Standing by the sink, I drink it and stare blankly at Mammi's calendar and notice that she's flipped the page to July. Since July 1 is a Sunday, that means Wednesday is Independence Day. I've always enjoyed fireworks on the Fourth of July; however, since I haven't heard anyone mention it, I suspect that the Amish don't observe this holiday. Things like "independence" aren't exactly encouraged in this community.

I go outside and sit on the porch in the shade. I am wishing and wishing with all my might that Ezra might happen to come by. Maybe he has another tool to return to Dawdi, or perhaps his mother wants him to borrow an egg—some neighborly excuse to come over here and discover me sitting on the porch by myself. I run my fingers through my hair, which is curling around my shoulders and glowing in the sunshine. I suspect he would be pleased to see me like this.

That is, unless he's still in church. I wonder how long church lasts. It seems like it's been hours already. I hope it's not an all-day deal. Too bad I didn't think to ask anyone about this.

Thinking about them all at church together, I feel left out again. I know I'm not shunned like my mom is, but I do feel snubbed. As if I'm not good enough to be invited, just because I'm not Amish? But what if I wanted to become Amish? How can I find out about their religion if they exclude me? I remember when Ezra said he wouldn't mind being Amish if I was Amish. Despite assuring Mom that I would never become Amish, I am not so sure. If that is what it would take to win Ezra—I mean, win him for life—well, I might consider it. Okay, I know that sounds crazy. I can't even imagine what Merenda would think. Or my mom. But it's my life, isn't it? I have the right to live it as I want. I know that sounds selfish, but if I don't look out for myself, who will?

As I gaze out over the peaceful green countryside, mentally comparing it to the noisy, messy chaos of life in the city, I wonder why I shouldn't want this. What would be wrong with living in a place like this for the rest of my life? Seriously, what would I possibly have to lose?

14

To my relief, Mammi seems very concerned when I explain my mom's need for more supervision. "I could move back here," I offer, thinking it might be for the best since Rachel would probably prefer seeing less of me anyway.

"No, no," Mammi says firmly. "It is better for you to stay with your aunt and uncle. I will take care of your mamm. Even if it means I must miss church. It is all right."

"Maybe I can come over here when you go to church."

She frowns. "You do not think you will want to go to church, Shannon?"

I shrug. "I don't know. Is it okay if I go?"

"*Ja*," she says eagerly. "It is good for you to go."

"Well . . . maybe we can figure it out by next week."

"*Ja*. That is what we will do. And you can stay with your aunt and uncle."

It seems decided that I am to continue rooming with Rachel. As a result, I'm determined to be as congenial as possible to my pretty cousin. And if she ever shows interest in talking about whatever it is that's bugging her, I am more than willing. However, I don't think I'll try to force this conversation out of her. Usually she's so busy that there's little time for a cousin-to-cousin chat anyway. Perhaps that's for the best.

If I thought Mammi and Dawdi were hard workers, Aunt Katrina could actually put them to shame. Honestly, that woman almost never stops moving. Rachel is only a few steps behind her. I've been in their house for nearly a week now, and the Amish might not believe in automation, but I've decided my aunt is practically a machine. Whether it's food preparation, washing clothes, gardening, or whatever, she is in constant motion, and her house is always in perfect order. The only time she sits down is to eat or to work on her quilts.

"I would love to learn to sew," I tell her as I'm sweeping the dining room floor after the midday meal on Friday. She has colorful quilt pieces spread out over the table and is arranging them into an attractive geometric design.

"You do not know how to sew?" She peers up at me.

"No, but I'd like to learn."

"Do you want to help with my quilts?"

"Could I?"

"*Ja*, but you must do as I say, Shannon."

"I will," I promise.

So instead of working in the garden with Rachel, where it's getting pretty hot, I spend the afternoon inside the relatively cool house. My first task is learning how to cut out shapes, which feels sort of like kindergarten to me, but I keep my opinions to myself.

"You might think that cutting is not important," my aunt tells me as she pins some pieces together. "But you would be wrong. The pieces must be cut *exactly* right. Then the seams must be sewn exactly right. Otherwise the quilt will not fit together perfectly. Cutting the pieces perfectly is like building a good foundation for a house. It must be square and true and solid." She locks eyes with me. "It is the same with your life, Shannon. If God is not the foundation of your life, your life will not be square and true and solid."

"Oh?" I pause in the middle of cutting a purple triangle. "But God is the foundation of my life," I say. I've already told her that I believe in God and that I used to go to church with my mom. But she didn't seem to think that meant anything. At least not in her world.

"You can say the words, Shannon. But are they true?"

I consider this. "I *think* it's true," I say as I set the purple piece on a small stack of others. "I *want* it to be true."

"Your uncle is a minister," she tells me, as if I had somehow missed out on this. "If you want to build a good foundation for your faith, and if you want to learn more about what we believe, perhaps you should speak with him."

"All right," I say as I start cutting another triangle. "I'd like that."

As we quietly work together I question myself. Am I really as interested in learning about their ways as I'm acting? Am I motivated by God? Or by Ezra? I think I know the answer to that question, and I have a feeling my uncle will be able to see right through me.

Next Aunt Katrina shows me how to pin the pieces together in the right order for how they are sewn together after basting, which she explains means loosely pre-sewing pieces together in order to hold them in place—not what you do to a turkey. "I think of these pieces like people," she says as she bastes some pieces. "See how they are cut in different shapes and colors? In the same way, people are created differently by God."

I nod. "That makes sense."

"The way they are similar is that each one is cut exactly right. God prunes us so that we will fit in with one another."

"*Ja.*" I nod, taking this in.

"The sewing part," she says as she carries a section of basted pieces over to her treadle sewing machine, "is like God uniting his children together so that we can be strong—all together in one useful piece. Like a quilt."

She invites me to come over and watch as she runs the sewing machine. She explains how to use the foot pedal to make the needle go up and down. She shows me how to use one hand on the wheel that moves the needle up and down, as well as how to guide fabric through the machine as it sews a seam. "Would you like to try?"

"Can I?"

"*Ja*, but only on scrap fabric," she tells me. "Let's see if you can sew a straight line."

I take her place in the straight-backed chair, trying to remember what she showed me as I lower the presser foot onto a doubled piece of blue fabric.

"Go ahead," she tells me. "Move your feet. Just do not get your finger under the needle. That hurts."

Being careful of the sharp needle, I work to move my feet, and before long I am guiding the fabric along, making the seam into a fairly straight line. She has me try it again and again until I finally feel like I can do it.

"Now you can try it with this." She hands me a section of quilt, showing me how to line it up so that the seam will be exactly a half inch.

"Are you sure?" I ask uncertainly. "I don't want to mess it up."

"If you mess it up, you will have to rip it out. That too is part of sewing."

Although I'm nervous, I focus on what I'm doing and make it all the way to the end of the piece with what I think is a pretty straight line. But my aunt is frowning.

"Isn't it good enough?" I ask as I examine the seam.

"No, it is not." She shakes her head as she reaches for a tool. "This is a seam ripper." She shows me how to poke it into the threads and cut them. "Carefully pick out all the threads. It must be redone."

"I'm sorry," I tell her as I go back to the dining room table to take apart the seam I sewed.

"You do not need to be sorry," she tells me. "Just learn to do it right. And do not damage the fabric as you remove the seam."

As I pick out the stubborn threads, I hear Rachel washing something in the kitchen. Probably some produce from the garden. Although Rachel has been polite and kind to me, she has not been nearly as warm and friendly as she was when I first met her—before we went to that party together. Several times, when we've been alone, I've considered talking to her about Ezra, but for some reason I have been unable to make myself do it. I'm not sure if it's because I don't want her to know how much I care about him or because I hate to see her hurting. I can't seem to forget how she cried herself to sleep last Saturday night—and I can't help but think it has something to do with me and Ezra.

Thinking of this is a painful reminder that I haven't seen Ezra since last Saturday. I really thought he'd come by here to see me, and I've even taken evening strolls by myself in the hopes that I'd run into him, but I haven't seen him once. I tell myself this is simply because he is hard at work on his parents' farm. I see how hard my cousins Isaac and Jeremiah work with my uncle and grandfather. Everyone, including me, gets up before sunrise. But while Rachel and I help Aunt Katrina in the kitchen, the guys go directly outside to tend to the animals and start in the fields even before they come back inside for breakfast. Then they work until the midday meal, coming in hot and tired and dirty and hungry. After that, they slave until suppertime, when once again they are hot and tired and dirty and hungry. I cannot believe the amount of food we prepare—or how much of it they are able to eat. Yet no one has a bit of fat on them. The guys don't even stop working after supper. They'll polish off a big serving of dessert, and then without a word of complaint they'll return to their work. They don't usually come back into the house until after dark. By then it's bedtime.

At first I felt alarmed at how hard everyone works. After a couple days of this exhausting routine, I asked Aunt Katrina how it was humanly possible to keep this up. She explained that summer was always a busy time of year. "Our lives slow down in the wintertime," she told me.

"That must be a relief," I said as I switched hands on the

handle of the butter churning jar and continued to turn it. The first time I did this task, I thought it was fun. But by the second time, I realized it was just work.

"This is only July," Rachel warned me. "Wait until harvest time. You will work harder than ever then. In August and September we will be canning and drying and smoking food."

"*Ja*," Aunt Katrina agreed. "That is our busiest time. But the reward is having our pantry filled with good food for the winter."

I've noticed the colorful jars of preserved food in their pantry—impressive rows of green beans, tomatoes, peaches, pears, applesauce, jams, and jellies. As curious as I am to see how this is all done, I suspect it will be hard work. Everything here is hard work.

It's funny how my aunt often speaks of living simply, but none of the chores here seem particularly simple to me. For instance, to clean the floors, which has turned into my chore, instead of using a vacuum cleaner, like Mom and I used to do on the weekends at our apartment, first I must sweep the floors, without missing a corner or under the furniture. This includes the wooden stairway and the rooms upstairs. Then I must mop all the floors, which means heating the kettle and filling a bucket with hot, soapy water and then scrubbing every square inch with a rag mop. But it's not enough to stop there. After that I must fill the bucket with clean water and rinse the whole thing. It is exhausting. I did it for the first time on Tuesday afternoon and the second time earlier this morning. Sure, the floors are super clean after I finish, but in no time at all they will be dirty again. After all, this is a farm. Of course, I can't say this to my aunt.

So as I'm picking out the seam, I remind myself that this isn't nearly as taxing as cleaning the floors. "Will you have a quilting group here tomorrow?" I ask Aunt Katrina.

"No, that is only on the first and third Saturday of the month. Not again until next week." She holds out a portion of quilt that she's put together. "So we have time to get some quilt tops ready." She shows me how to use a wet dish towel and a heavy metal iron that's sitting on the cookstove to press the seams open. I want to point out how much easier this would be with an electric iron, but I know it's pointless. Being Amish means doing everything the hard way.

It's hot in the kitchen, but Aunt Katrina insists that I keep the ironing board set up next to the cookstove, so I am sweating. Plus I manage to burn myself several times as I press the seams of the quilt pieces open. Suddenly the idea of working out in the garden is becoming more appealing, and I suspect Rachel knows what she's doing to be out there instead of in here. Eventually it's time to start preparing dinner, and my aunt tells me to put the quilting work away.

As I peel potatoes, I notice how red and chafed my hands have become. Mostly it's due to washing dishes. It's up to Rachel and me to wash up after every meal, and lately Rachel has stuck me with the washing part while she dries. She says it's because she's older, explaining how for years she had to wash while her sister Grace dried. It's pointless to argue.

To say that my initial infatuation with being Amish is starting to fade some is an understatement. Especially since I haven't seen Ezra once. I've also started to wonder about going back to the dawdi house to live because the work over there doesn't seem as difficult or endless as it is here. However, every time I go to visit Mom, which has only been a few times this week, I get the impression that Mammi prefers I stay put.

"I am helping your mamm to get stronger each day," she quietly told me yesterday. Mom was asleep, but Mammi assured me that she was resting because she was tired, *not* because she'd taken a pill.

"Really?" I peeked in through a crack in the door, satisfied that Mom appeared to be sleeping peacefully.

"Every day I get Anna out of bed in the morning and we walk around. Today we even went outside."

"She walked outside?"

"*Ja.* And Jacob took a chair out there and she was able to sit in it."

"That's wonderful," I told her.

"She will be well soon," Mammi assured me. "I know it."

"That is so good to hear," I said happily. Part of me wanted to ask if she would be well enough to go home, but another part of me didn't want to know this yet. Because of Ezra, I'm not ready to leave this place.

On Saturday morning, I make a point to find Jeremiah on his way into the house for breakfast. After greeting him, I quickly inquire as to whether the young people will be getting together again tonight. "Since it's Saturday," I say quietly, worried that my aunt or uncle or Rachel might pass by and question my interest in these nighttime activities.

"You mean a party?" he asks with a twinkle in his blue eyes.

"*Ja.*" I shrug, trying to appear nonchalant. "Does that happen every Saturday?"

He chuckles. "In the summertime it does."

"Will you be going?"

He rubs his chin, then nods. "*Ja*. I think I will go."

"Do you mind if I go too?"

"Is Rachel going?"

"I—uh—I don't know." I glance back toward the house. "Does she have to go?"

"No. I think it's better if she does not go. Rachel does not like it so much."

"So it's all right if I go without her?" I ask hopefully.

He shrugs. "*Ja*. You can if you want. I will pick up my friend Jonah and his sister Lydia too."

Feeling as if I've been given permission, I hurry back into the house to help with breakfast. My goal is to keep my plans for this evening to myself. It's not that I want to leave Rachel out, but I know she doesn't enjoy the gatherings anyway. There seems to be no need for her to feel pressured to go for my sake. Besides—and I know this is the real reason—I think it will be better for Ezra and me if Rachel stays home. And really, she'll be happier too.

15

As Jeremiah drives the buggy to the party tonight, I start making a plan. As much as I enjoy kissing and being kissed by Ezra, tonight I'm going to try to focus more on talking to him. I want to hear how he really feels about being Amish. And I want to hear his reaction to the news that I plan to go to church with my relatives tomorrow. I've already talked to my uncle, and after asking me a few basic questions, he agreed that I was ready. He seemed pleased.

The truth is, I feel like I'm really putting myself out here. It's like I'm conforming to being Amish, and primarily because of Ezra. I mean, I could just be laying low at the dawdi house, waiting for my mom to get well. I could still be wearing my own clothes, doing my own thing, helping Mammi when she needs it, but taking it a whole lot easier than I have been at my aunt and uncle's house this past week. I feel like I'm playing by the Amish rules in order to prove to myself—and maybe to Ezra too—that I can do this. But what if I'm doing it for nothing?

Still, I can't believe that could be true. I believe that Ezra loves me. I believe we belong together. But after a hard week like this has been, I need to hear it from his mouth.

"This is the Schrock farm," Jeremiah calls out as he turns into a driveway. "Where Jonah and Lydia live."

As the buggy pulls up to a house that looks similar to my uncle and aunt's house, Jonah and Lydia come out. I remember Jonah from last week, but not Lydia. "How old is Lydia?" I ask Jeremiah as they jog over to us.

"She is Rachel's age."

I peer curiously at his face, noticing how he seems to be watching Lydia with great interest. "She's pretty, isn't she?" I say quietly.

He smiles. Jonah climbs in front, sitting next to him, and Lydia sits in back with me. I tell her who I am, but she just nods.

"*Ja*. I know who you are." She looks slightly disappointed. "Where is Rachel?"

"At home," I tell her.

"I thought she was coming," she says as the buggy starts moving. "Jonah told me she came last week."

"*Ja*," Jeremiah calls from the driver's seat. "She did not want to come tonight." He turns around to smile at Lydia. "But I am glad you came," he tells her.

"Oh . . ." She giggles and gives me a funny look. "Rachel and I are both studying for baptism," she confides to me.

"Are you and Rachel good friends?" I ask.

"*Ja*. We both want to be baptized in August."

"That's nice."

"I hear that you and Ezra are . . . well . . ." She makes a perplexed frown. "Are you a couple?"

My cheeks warm as I nod. "*Ja*," I say quietly.

She presses her lips tightly together, as if she's uncertain about this. But then she reaches up and pokes her brother in the back. "Jonah, you should be talking to Rachel these days . . . ya know?"

He doesn't respond.

"Jonah, can you hear me?"

"I hear ya, Lydia."

"You told Daed you want to be baptized," she says to him. "You should talk to Rachel about it, ya know?"

"*Ja, ja.*" Jonah elbows my cousin. "You too, Jeremiah," he says in a joking manner. "You should be getting yourself ready to be baptized too. If you want to be talking to Lydia." He laughs loudly like this is very funny.

I'm certainly no expert in such matters, but I'm beginning to see how courtship and baptism go hand in hand for Amish young people. I suppose it makes sense.

The gathering tonight is at a different barn. I don't catch the name, but if I didn't know it was a different barn, I doubt that I would've noticed much difference. The trampoline has been set up in this one too. According to Jeremiah, the trampoline travels around in the summertime. It seems like it would be work setting it up each time, but then these people seem to thrive on work.

To my relief Ezra is already here. I was secretly worried that he might not come tonight, but he comes directly to me and seems genuinely glad to see me. "I've missed you," I tell him.

He grasps my hands, pulling me close to him. "I missed you too."

I can smell beer on his breath, but his eyes still seem clear.

"I hoped that I'd see you sometime during the week," I say as he starts walking me away from the barn.

"We've been putting up hay," he says. "The heat made it come early this year. We hope to get another crop by August."

"Oh." I glance over my shoulder, back to where the others are gathered. "Where are we going?"

"Someplace we can be alone," he says mysteriously.

Okay, as much as this idea appeals to part of me, it worries me too. I remember how far things have gone with us already, and I don't want to get too carried away. He walks me alongside a creek until we come to a brushy clump of trees. There I can see something glowing in the dusky light. He pushes back the brush, and we enter a small clearing where there's a battery-operated lantern next to a blanket that's spread on the ground. There's also a bucket of water with a number of beer cans floating in it. I suspect the water is to keep them cool.

"What's going on here?" I ask. "Private party?"

"I made us a place to be alone," he says innocently, pulling me close to him again and leaning in for a kiss.

As badly as I want to kiss him, I put up my hand between us like a stop sign. "Can we talk a little first?" I say somewhat timidly.

He looks surprised but then nods, tossing his hat aside as he sits down on the blanket. *"Ja."*

I sit down across from him, studying his handsome face in the flickering lantern light. It would be so easy to forget my earlier plan and go straight to kissing. Except that I know where that could lead.

"What do you want to talk about?" he asks as he reaches for a beer, holding it out to me.

I consider saying no but don't want him to think I'm a party pooper, so I take it and carefully pop it open. I will pretend to sip it while we're talking. "This week has been really weird," I tell him.

"Weird?" He looks confused. "What happened?"

I explain how I'm living with my aunt and uncle, how I'm working so hard, how I'm pretending to be Amish. "I even talked to my uncle about going to church," I say. "I plan to go in the morning."

Ezra frowns.

"What's wrong with that?" I ask.

He shrugs, taking a big swig of beer.

"You see," I say slowly, "I'm wondering what it would be like to really be Amish. I want to find out more about it."

"Why?" he demands.

Feeling confused, I look down at my lap. "Why not?" I ask quietly.

"You don't want to be Amish," he says gruffly.

"Why?" I look back at him.

"Because it's too hard."

"Too hard?"

"*Ja*. For an English girl." He shakes his head. "It is too hard."

"I've been doing it all week," I point out.

"No, you are playing at being Amish. You are not really Amish."

"But I could be Amish," I argue.

With a beer in his hand, he points at me. "You want an Amish husband telling you what you can and cannot do?"

I make a half smile. "That depends on what he's telling me to do."

He starts to grin. "*Ja*, that is different, Shannon."

I shrug. "If it was the right husband, I might not mind being told what to do," I say honestly.

"I cannot believe that," he says sternly. "You have had freedom. You have lived in the English world. You do not know what you are asking for."

"You honestly think I couldn't fit in here?" I demand.

"I think you would be crazy to want to fit in here." He takes a long swig of beer, finishing it off, then crunches the can in his fist and tosses it aside. "I don't even want to fit in here."

"You don't?"

"I told you already." He reaches for another can. "I have my doubts about committing to the church."

"Why?" I ask.

"*Why?*" he echoes in a slightly hopeless tone.

"Do you doubt God?"

He shrugs, taking another long sip.

"I do believe in God," I tell him.

"*Ja* . . . that is good. But do you believe in the Ordnung?"

I pretend to take a sip.

"You do not even know what is in the Ordnung, do you?" he challenges me.

"You're right. I don't. But my uncle could teach me."

"But could he make you understand it?" Ezra sticks his thumb under one of his suspender straps. "Could he make you understand why it is sin for us to wear a different kind of suspender than these? Or why we must rely on a horse and buggy instead of a car? Or why we cut our hay by hand instead of using a machine? Can he make you understand and accept all those things, Shannon?"

I press my lips together.

"No, I didn't think so. I have lived here all my life and I do not understand."

"But there are things about this life that I really like," I say. "Things that I think I am beginning to understand."

"That's because you haven't been here long enough."

"You make it sound like you hate it here," I say quietly.

"Sometimes I do hate it here."

"Then why don't you leave?" I ask.

He finishes that can of beer now, crunches the can, and tosses it aside. "Sometimes I think about it."

I study him. "You'd leave your family and friends and your home?"

"I might." He reaches for another can.

"But you'd be shunned."

He nods.

"Where would you go? What would you do?"

He shrugs as he takes another long swig.

I'm feeling lost now, like everything I've been dreaming of and working for has been ripped out of my hands. "Ezra," I say quietly. "I thought you said that you loved me." He looks into my eyes, but already his eyes are starting to look blurry again, similar to last week.

"I do love you."

"I love you too," I whisper.

He leans forward, and grasping the back of my head in his hand, he pulls me toward him for a kiss . . . then another. After several, I pull myself away, struggling to catch my breath.

"Don't you think we could be happy together?" I ask him. "You and me . . . living here? Wouldn't it be a good life?"

He throws back his head and laughs. I feel as if I've been slapped.

In the same instant, I jump to my feet. "Fine." I toss my full beer can down to his refuse pile. "Go ahead and laugh! I can see I've been a complete fool." I turn and push my way out of the thicket and start to run. Tears are streaming down my cheeks, and I feel stupid and sentimental and just plain foolish. I half expect him to follow me, but I don't hear footsteps. So I stop running and just keep walking. But after a while, I realize that I don't know where I am. The sky is black since the moon hasn't risen, and all around me, everything looks dark. I can see lights in the distance, but they seem too far away to be the barn where the party is located.

I stop walking and listen, hoping I'll hear the sounds of voices and be able to follow my ears, but all I hear are crickets and frogs. Now I'm starting to get scared. Why did I run off like that? And why didn't Ezra follow me? I consider making an attempt to retrace my steps, but my pride won't let me. Instead I sit down in the grass, which smells faintly of cows, and then I lie down on my back and I cry . . . and cry . . . and cry.

I can't remember ever feeling this kind of hurt before. Even when my dad died, although it was horrible and sad and confusing, it didn't seem to hurt like this does. Maybe it's because I know my dad didn't intentionally abandon me. He never meant to hurt me. But this feels like Ezra has willfully driven a knife right through my soul. Like I've been cut to the core and am bleeding to death. And it feels like he doesn't even care.

After a while, though I have no idea how long, I figure I

should get up and get moving. I should find the barn and find my cousin, but I have no idea which way to go. So I just sit here feeling emotionally drained and mortally wounded and unbearably sad. A part of me says I should be scared out here alone in the dark. Maybe there are wild animals about—I have no idea if that's true or not, but even if there was a pack of hungry wolves prowling, I'm not sure that I really care. Let them tear me apart. It can't hurt as badly as it hurts to know that Ezra doesn't care.

As I'm sitting there I can see a light moving side to side, as if someone is walking with a lantern. I remember how my cousin found me last Saturday and assume it's him again—Jeremiah coming to rescue me. I hop to my feet and run through the grass toward him. But when I get close enough to see his face, I realize that it's Ezra.

"Shannon!" he cries out as he runs toward me, swooping me into his arms. "Where have you been?" He hugs me close to him. "I'm sorry, Shannon. I'm sorry."

I'm crying again. The more I cry, the tighter he holds on to me, telling me over and over that he's sorry.

"I'm sorry too," I say. "I expected too much from you. It wasn't fair."

"It's just that I don't know anymore." He lets me go now, stepping back to look at me in the lantern light. "I know I need to make some decisions. But I don't know what I want."

I look down at the ground, feeling my heart tumbling to the dirt.

"I mean what I want for my life," he says suddenly. "I want you, Shannon. I *know* that."

I look up, feeling hopeful again. "You do?"

He gathers me into his arms. "*Ja*. I do." He leans down and kisses me. The smell of beer is even stronger than before, but I decide I don't care. All I care about is that he wants me. He still loves me. I know he does. "Here." He hands me the lantern, then scoops me up into his arms as if I'm a child. With me giggling, he proceeds to carry me.

"Where are we going?" I ask between giggles.

"You'll see," he says. Before long, we're back in the thicket, and the blanket and bucket are still in place. "Here you go." He sets me down on the blanket, falling over on top of me, making us both laugh. Then he is kissing me again—with more passion than ever—and I start to feel nervous again. "Wait!" I say firmly, pushing him off of me.

"What's wrong?" he asks.

"Jeremiah is going to be worried," I say as I sit up. "I should get back."

"No." He reaches for me again. "You just got here. You can't leave."

I place both my hands on his cheeks and kiss him again. "I wish we could stay like this forever," I tell him. "And maybe someday we will. But not tonight, Ezra. My aunt and uncle will be worried if I don't come home with Jeremiah tonight."

"I can take you home."

"Not without telling Jeremiah first," I say as I stand up. "Do you want my uncle coming out to search for me?"

I can see the concern in his eyes as he stands. "You're probably right."

I hold the lantern for him as he gathers up his "camp," and then we walk back to the barn, which thanks to the bonfire is clearly visible. I can see Ezra weaving left and right as he walks, and sometimes he stumbles. I notice that his bucket is empty too. Did he really drink all those beers? And if he did, wasn't it partially my fault? After all, I was the one who ran away from him, leaving him alone like that.

It looks as if the party's starting to break up when we get to the barn. Already some buggies have left, and I discover my cousin and his friends have been searching for me. Although they seem relieved to see me, they are also aggravated at me for worrying them. Naturally, they tease me without mercy as we ride home. I pretend to ignore their nasty little jabs, but it bugs me that they assume I've been doing something "shameful" when I actually spent most of the evening feeling brokenhearted and lost, sobbing by myself in a cow pasture. Oh well, let them think what they like. I know what I was and was not doing.

It's weird—just when I think I'm getting a grasp on what it means to be Amish, I witness a whole different side to these people. Although they are definitely different from the English in many highly visible ways, beneath the surface they are very much the same. Perhaps that's simply because we are all human. And all flawed.

16

Amish church is nothing like the church Mom and I have attended over the years. I'm not just talking about the building either. I was surprised that the Amish, who seem sort of hyper-religious, do not believe it is right to own an actual church building. Instead, families take turns hosting the Sunday services in their barns.

It wasn't so bad since it's summertime, but I can imagine it might be cold in the winter. Benches and chairs are set in rows in the barn—the women and girls sit on one side with the men and boys on the other. I was a little disappointed that I couldn't sit next to Ezra. I had imagined myself silently flirting with him, maybe even holding hands under my apron. However, that was so not happening.

These people take their church service very seriously. Of course, it is almost entirely in Pennsylvania Dutch. Even the singing, which was more like chanting, was in this other language. The service was so long. I think I know why they don't wear watches. Everyone would be looking at theirs and wondering when it would all be over. Although, to be honest, no one seemed the least bit concerned. Even the children were okay with it. I actually think they all enjoy these services. I am mystified.

After the service ends, we all go outside to where tables are set up with food. The men eat first, followed by the women and children. Mostly it seems to be sandwiches and cookies and moon pies. I'm well aware that these people like their sweets, but their obsession with marshmallow cream is rather amusing. I worry a little about the children's teeth as they gorge themselves on marshmallow and peanut butter sandwiches. I hope they go home and brush, but I have my doubts since I've yet to see a toothbrush in my aunt and uncle's house.

As we ride home, this time in the larger two-horse buggy since Isaac took the smaller buggy to pick up his fiancée, I sit in the back with Aunt Katrina and Rachel. My uncle and Jeremiah are in front. Everyone is fairly quiet, and I use this time to think about things. I wonder if I would have liked the service better if I understood the language. Maybe I should try to learn it. But when I mention this to Rachel, she laughs. "Why would you need to speak our language?" she asks with a slightly creased brow, as if she is guessing my real motivation.

"I don't know," I say nonchalantly. "It might be interesting."

"If you want to learn, we have books. We can help teach you," Aunt Katrina assures me.

"Okay," I agree with some uncertainty. "I think I'd like to try it."

"Your uncle tells me that you have interest in learning

about our faith," Aunt Katrina says. "He is willing to give you instruction. But only if you are willing to work hard to learn." She nods to Rachel. "Our children have grown up learning all these things. You will have much catching up to do, Shannon."

"I want to learn," I assure her. "I really do."

"Why?" Rachel asks me again.

Aunt Katrina peers curiously at her daughter. "Why do you ask her why, Rachel?"

Rachel looks down at her lap. "I think she is doing it for the wrong reason," she says somberly.

I take in a quick breath, wondering how much Rachel knows and how I should respond.

"The wrong reason?" Aunt Katrina's eyes narrow slightly as she studies her daughter. "What reason is that?"

"Ask her," Rachel replies quietly.

"Shannon?" My aunt turns to peer at me. "What is Rachel talking about? Do you know?"

I look at Rachel, who is still looking down at her lap. "I don't know," I say to my aunt. "What makes one reason right? Or another reason wrong? I am interested in the Amish faith for a number of reasons."

"*Ja?*" My aunt nods. "What reasons?"

I go over my usual list, saying how I love the countryside and having family around and the simple way of life. "I already believe in God," I say. "I've gone to church most of my life. And I thought my faith was strong. But living here with you people, I'm not sure it was as strong as I thought."

"That is true," my aunt tells me. "The English do not understand how to serve God. They are too concerned with

171

vainglory. Even when the English profess to have faith, it is not the kind of faith that pleases God. Faith without works is useless."

I nod, trying to absorb this.

"Tell Mamm about you and Ezra," Rachel challenges me.

"What?" I try to play innocent.

"Jeremiah told me. You were with Ezra again last night. Jeremiah says that you want to marry Ezra . . . that perhaps you will *have* to marry him."

"What?" Aunt Katrina's eyes flash with alarm and maybe even anger. "What is this, Shannon?"

My cheeks are flushing and my heart is pounding, but I am determined to keep my voice calm. Although I doubt Jeremiah and Uncle Ben can hear us back here, I don't want this to turn into an ugly family feud. "I don't know what Jeremiah told you," I say to Rachel, "but it is gossip. And it is untrue. The Bible I know says that it's wrong to gossip and to lie." I turn to my aunt. "Does it say that in your Bible too? That gossip is wrong? That telling a lie is wrong?"

"*Ja.*" She barely nods. "But why would Jeremiah say something that is untrue?"

"I don't know," I tell her. "But it is hurtful."

Rachel looks up at me with a confused expression. "Were you with Ezra last night?" she asks in a challenging way.

"I was with him," I answer. "But not in the way that Jeremiah has suggested. You have no need to worry that I would *have* to marry him." I make an indignant scowl. "I am not like that."

"But you would like to marry him?" Rachel demands.

I just shrug, but Aunt Katrina looks even more concerned.

172

"I believe that is the true reason Shannon wants to learn about being Amish," Rachel tells her mom.

"Even if that was true," I begin, trying to think of the right way to put this. "Even if I did want to marry Ezra, would that be any different than it is for other Amish young people? I've heard other kids saying that they are getting baptized so that they can marry and be part of this community." I stare at my aunt. "Isn't that right?"

She barely nods again. "But when they meet with the ministers and the bishop, they must show that their faith is genuine."

"My faith is genuine," I declare, although even as I say the words, I feel doubtful and unsure. Is it really genuine? Oh, certainly, I believe in God. But is God as central to my life as he is to my relatives'? I don't think so.

"If your faith is genuine, there is no reason for concern," my aunt tells me. "Your uncle will help you to understand these things better." She squeezes my hand. "I am happy you want to learn, Shannon. Your mammi and dawdi will be happy too."

"What about your mamm?" Rachel asks me. "Will she be happy?"

"I don't know," I tell her. Then I decide to change the focus from me to her. "How about you? Will you be happy for me, cousin?"

She tilts her head to one side. "*Ja*. I will be very happy for you to become Amish, Shannon. There will be celebrating in heaven too."

"And what if I did marry Ezra?" I continue. "Would you be happy for me—for Ezra and me—then?"

"*Ja*," she says with sad eyes. "I would be very happy. I would pray for God to bless you both."

Aunt Katrina looks troubled but says nothing. I decide that this is a good place to end this uncomfortable conversation. So I ask them to tell me what today's sermon was about. I pretend to be patiently listening as they talk about the humility of serving one another the way that Jesus served by washing his disciples' feet, but the truth is, I'm daydreaming about Ezra again. Somehow this conversation—talking to my aunt and cousin about marrying Ezra—has made it all seem very, very real.

I'm aware that girls marry young in this community. After church today I met a cousin named Emma who is married and pregnant with her first child. And she only turned sixteen last month! Okay, it's a strange world . . . but if these people see nothing wrong with it, why should I?

After we get home, I tell my aunt that I need to go visit my mom, and she seems relieved to see me go. I have a feeling that whole conversation about Ezra and whatnot has slightly rocked her world. I'm not sure if it's because she is concerned for my welfare or because she had hoped that he and Rachel would marry, but I suspect it is the latter.

Finding my mom highly agitated because Mammi and Dawdi are not home yet and she has not had a pill, I feel guilty and neglectful. "When did you have your last pill?" I ask contritely.

"Days ago." She lets out a groan.

"Did you run out?"

"I don't know." She presses her hands to her temples. "Mamm says I don't need them."

"You don't need them?" I feel alarmed. "But how are you getting along?"

"Not well, Shannon. I think we may have to go home."

"But I—"

"I don't want to hear any arguments," she snaps.

"How about if I get you a pill?" I offer.

"Yes!" She exhales loudly. "Please, do. Now!"

I hurry to the kitchen and find the pills right where they were last time, and I'm surprised to see there are still about six left. They should've been used up by now. In fact, I had planned to find a way to go to town to get more. I rush back to Mom, give her the pill, and watch as she washes it down with water.

"Thank you," she mutters, leaning back and breathing heavily.

Wondering about my missing grandparents, I straighten her bed and her room and talk pleasantly to her until I can tell she's drifting off. She seems even more exhausted than usual, and the smudgy shadows beneath her eyes are darker than ever. I place my hand on her forehead, curious as to whether she has a temperature or not, but as usual, I can't really tell. Thankfully, she seems to be resting quietly now.

As I leave her room, I hear my grandparents coming into the house. I know it will not go well if I express anger at them for leaving her alone so long. Besides that, I feel partly to blame since I had offered to spend Sundays with her, and then I went off to church instead. Interesting that I feel guilty for going to church.

"Mammi," I say as I find her in the kitchen.

"Shannon. You are here," she says as she fills the kettle with water. "But you were at church too."

"Yeah. I came over right afterward to check on Mom."

"*Ja*? How is she?"

"Not very well, Mammi."

Mammi turns to me with concern. "Did she fall again?"

"Again?"

"*Ja.*" She sets the kettle on the stove. "She has fallen some."

"She said she hasn't been taking her pills?"

"*Ja.*" Mammi nods. "I think you are right. Those pills are not good for her."

"I didn't say they're not good for her," I clarify. "I only meant that I worry she relies on them too much. I know she needs them. I gave her one just now."

Dawdi comes into the kitchen now. He has changed from his dark church clothes to his regular clothes. "You gave your mamm a pill?" he asks.

"Yeah. I think she needed it." I glance from one to the other. "She told me she wants to go home."

Mammi looks shocked. "Home? Back to the city?"

"*Ja.*" I nod, waiting for them to respond.

"That is not good." Mammi turns to Dawdi. "Did you know this?"

He shakes his head, then looks at me. "What about you? Do you want to go home?"

"I—uh—I don't know."

"Do you like living here?" Mammi asks hopefully.

"*Ja,*" I tell her. "I do."

"Benjamin tells me you are interested in being Amish," Dawdi says.

"That's true," I admit. "But I am worried about my mom. I think she needs to see a doctor."

Mammi purses her lips. "I do not know if that will help. We believe God is wanting to help Anna, but we do not think she is ready for his help."

"What do you mean?"

"God cares more about our souls than our bodies," Dawdi tells me. "We believe God wants Anna to care more about her soul too."

I agree with this in some ways, but at the same time I feel confused. I believe my grandparents love my mom, but I'm not sure about their thinking on this. "Do you mean that God is making my mom suffer so that he can get her attention?" I ask.

"Our earthly life is short," Dawdi tells me. "The next life, eternal life, lasts forever. God is more concerned for Anna to enjoy the next life than this temporary one."

"So are you saying I *shouldn't* take Mom to the doctor?"

"We are saying it is more important to think about the next life than to worry about this one." Dawdi gives me a sad smile as he reaches for his straw hat. "God will do what God will do." He gives me a quick nod, then goes out the back door.

Mammi looks concerned for my sake. "Do you want me to keep giving your mamm her pills?" she asks.

"Yes," I tell her. "And I want to see about taking her to a doctor. Do you think Dawdi can help me get her to town?"

Mammi looks uncertain.

"Or maybe Uncle Ben or one of my cousins can help," I say.

"*Ja* . . . maybe." But her eyes look doubtful.

Feeling let down and slightly hurt, I tell Mammi good-bye and leave. But instead of going back to my aunt and uncle's house, I decide to walk over to the pond to think. When I reach the pond I realize I still have on the black bonnet that Rachel insisted I must wear over my *kapp* for church. With the sun beating down on it, as well as onto the black cape and apron that I also wore to church, I am sweltering. When I reach the pond, I remove all these extra pieces as well as my black shoes and stockings. Feeling somewhat rebellious, not to mention hot, I remove my *kapp* and let my hair down, and then I hoist up my skirt and wade out into the pond, curling my toes into the cool, slimy mud on the bottom. I'm considering peeling off this dress and totally submerging when I hear a rustle in the bushes.

Concerned that Dawdi spotted me heading this way and that he might not approve of me being out here in the pond like this, I scramble back up the bank, dropping my skirt down over my dripping legs and digging through the pile of clothes in search of my *kapp*. I'm not even sure why I'm so obsessed with this kind of propriety, considering that a couple weeks ago I would've thought nothing of putting on a stringy bikini and jumping right into this pond and floundering about. Suddenly I'm all anxious and nervous about being discovered with a bare head and bare legs? Is that really possible?

17

'm still fumbling to find my hair band and pins when the brushy shrubs are pushed open and a figure appears. "Caught you!"

To my relief, it is not my grandfather but Ezra. "What are you doing here?" I ask as I drop the white *kapp* on top of the pile of black garments.

"I saw something dark cutting across the field," he tells me as he removes his own straw hat, followed by his shoes and socks. "I realized it was you, still dressed in your church clothes. I was worried something was wrong, but it looks more like you're only taking a swim."

I sigh. "Just wading . . . but something is wrong."

"What is it?" He looks up from where he's rolling up his pants, exposing a sturdy looking pair of legs, which are strangely pale.

"Oh, nothing." I try to force a pleasant expression to my face.

He looks unconvinced as he rolls up his shirtsleeves and

steps into the pond, splashing some water onto his face. "Tell me what's troubling you," he urges me. "Maybe I can help."

As I watch him wading deeper into the pond, I quickly explain my concerns for my mom's health. "In fact, I'm wondering if it might be best to go home."

"You're going to leave?" His eyes darken with concern. "I thought you were staying all summer . . . or even longer."

"I never really knew how long we were staying. We didn't actually have a plan." I gaze longingly at the cool water.

"Come back into the pond," he tells me. "I promise not to splash."

I gingerly lift my skirt as I step into the water again, and I wade out until it reaches my knees. Standing there with the heat of the sun on my head, the chilly coolness of the water seeps into my skin.

"So what are you going to do?" Ezra is standing a few feet away from me, and the water is soaking into his rolled-up pants.

I frown. "I don't know. My grandparents aren't sounding very helpful about getting my mom to a doctor."

"Does she need a doctor?"

"I think so. But I don't know how to get her to one without going home."

"I can take her to a doctor," he offers. "I'm going to town on Tuesday to do some errands."

"Really?" I say hopefully. "You could take us with you?"

"*Ja*. I know a doctor too. I had to take my daed in last fall."

"So Amish do go to the doctor then?" This makes me curious because the impression I got from my grandparents was that medical attention was unnecessary.

"*Ja*. If something is real bad. During harvest time my daed cut his arm on the mower. He had to get thirty-four stitches."

"Wow, that sounds bad."

"*Ja*. It was bad. He bled a lot."

"So if someone's life is in danger, you can go to the doctor?"

"*Ja*. But most of the time we don't need to. We are pretty good at taking care of ourselves."

"What about when women have babies?"

"The women help each other." His blue eyes twinkle with mischief. "Are you thinking about having a baby, Shannon?"

"No, of course not." I scowl at him. "I was thinking about my cousin Emma. Her baby is due next month."

He reaches for my hand, pulling me over to him in the deeper water and causing most of my skirt to get soaked. "I like seeing your hair like that . . . all down." He touches my curls and smiles.

"Careful," I tell him. "I don't want to get all—"

But it's too late. He has pulled me completely into the pond with him. Although I'm irritated that he's gotten me soaking wet, I can't deny that the cool water feels delicious. We play in there together for a while, but then I get worried that this time my grandfather really will show up and surprise us. The idea of being found like this by Dawdi is more than a little unsettling.

"I need to get out," I finally say, pulling myself away from him.

"*Ja*. Me too."

We both climb out, dripping wet, and he suggests we lie down in the tall grass, allowing the sun to dry our clothes. "Okay," I agree, "but only if you promise to keep your hands to yourself."

He laughs and flops down.

"I mean it," I tell him. "The last thing I need right now is for my dawdi to show up and find us . . . well, you know."

"*Ja*." He folds his arms behind his head, looking up at the sky. "You are right about that."

I lie down next to him, spreading out my wet skirt so that it can dry. "In fact, I had to defend my honor on the way home from church today," I tell him.

"What?" He turns to peer at me.

"Rachel got it into her head that you and I were doing something . . . well, something disrespectful, if you get my meaning."

He chuckles. "She did, did she?"

"*Ja*." I sneak a peek at him and am surprised to see that he looks a little smug. "Do you want her to think that?"

"I don't care what she thinks."

Something about the hardness of his tone makes me question his sincerity. "You don't care what Rachel thinks? Not at all? What if she was thinking about you?" I say in a teasing way. "Would you care then?"

"What do you mean?" He sits up now, staring curiously at me. "What has Rachel been saying to you?"

I sit up too, realizing that I've probably really stuck my foot into this. "Oh . . . nothing." I start fluff drying my hair in the sun.

"Tell me, Shannon," he insists. "If Rachel has been talking about me, I need to know."

"Why?" I lock eyes with him. "Why is it so important for you to know what Rachel said?"

He looks away from me, squinting in the sunshine. "It's just that I don't want her talking about me . . . and you. I don't want her talking about us. You know?" He picks up a rock, tossing it into the center of the pond, watching as it makes a small circle and a larger one and then another.

"Well, that's what I told her too," I say. "I reminded both her and my aunt that the Bible says it's wrong to gossip and lie about people. I think she was sorry too."

"Oh." He stands, reaching for his socks. "I better get home."

"Yeah . . . me too."

Neither of us speaks as we put on our socks and shoes. Naturally, he is finished with his redressing before me. "I plan to leave for town right after breakfast on Tuesday. Will you and your mamm be ready then?"

"*Ja*," I say as I attempt to smooth my unruly hair.

"I will stop by your dawdi's house then." He adjusts his hat and tells me good-bye, then leaves.

I decide to forgo my *kapp* and other pieces of clothing. I doubt anyone will notice or care since I'm only walking from the dawdi house to my aunt and uncle's. But when I come into the yard, Rachel immediately sees me. "What have you been doing?" she asks curiously, plucking at my still damp and slightly soiled skirt. "To look like this? And in church clothes too?"

"I was very hot," I tell her. "So I jumped in the pond."

"With your clothes on?" She frowns skeptically.

"*Ja*," I say sharply. "With my clothes on." I go into the house and up to the room we share, and after putting away the black apron and cape and bonnet, I change into a clean, dry dress. I smooth out my hair and pin it into a bun, but since I don't plan to leave the house again, I don't put on the *kapp*. Since it is Sunday, the Sabbath, I know that work is kept to a minimum, so although I know my aunt will not approve, I remain in the room and read one of my paperbacks. I feel that after working so hard all week—harder than I've ever worked in my life—I must be entitled to a little downtime.

But after about an hour or so, Rachel appears and tells me it's time to help with supper.

On Monday I make it known to my relatives that I will be taking my mother to see the doctor in town tomorrow. Although I can tell they don't approve, no one makes any attempt to keep me from going. Nor does anyone offer to help me. It's both baffling and aggravating. Is it because Mom isn't Amish, or because they don't believe in intervening with medical help?

On Tuesday, instead of helping Aunt Katrina with breakfast like usual, I go directly to the dawdi house to make sure that Mom is ready to go. I already asked Mammi to be sure that Mom is dressed in clean clothes and takes a pill around seven. My hope is that it will keep her comfortable and sedated while we travel, but by the time we get there, she'll be awake enough to be examined thoroughly.

Thankfully, Mammi has followed my instructions. She even seems a little relieved that I'm doing this. "I hope the doctor can help her," Mammi quietly tells me. "I am afraid that she is not getting better. She is out of her pills. Yesterday she fell down two times. And she is very forgetful. Much more so than when she came here."

"Pray for her," I tell Mammi as I see a buggy pulling into

the driveway. "Pray that we get her to town without too much trouble."

"*Ja.*" Mammi holds out to me what appears to be a hand-made cloth shopping bag. "Food for the trip," she tells me. I drop my dead cell phone and Mom's wallet into it and thank her. Then I hurry to grab up the bundle of blankets and pillows I set by the door. My plan is to make Mom a bed on the floor of the buggy. That way she won't fall off the bench and hurt herself. As I arrange the bedding, I wonder if I've just created an Amish ambulance.

Ezra helps Mammi and me get Mom into the buggy, and once I'm satisfied that she is safe and her head is bolstered by pillows, I climb into the front seat to sit next to Ezra. "Thank you for doing this," I tell him.

"*Ja.*" He nods somberly as he releases the brake and then shakes the reins. "I did not know your mamm was so sick. It's good she is going to the doctor."

"*Ja,*" I repeat quietly.

"I called the doctor for you yesterday," Ezra informs me as the buggy turns onto the road. "I hope you don't mind. But I wanted to be sure Dr. Hoffman could see your mom today. Otherwise it would be a long trip for nothing."

"Oh!" I say suddenly. "Thank you for thinking of that, Ezra. Is he a good doctor—this Dr. Hoffman? Do you think he knows what he's doing?"

"It is not a *he* doctor. Dr. *Diane* Hoffman is a woman."

"Well, that's okay." I actually feel slightly relieved.

"*Ja.* I did not think you would mind so much. Although my daed was not pleased when he saw Dr. Hoffman was not a man. But I told him that women are better at sewing than men anyway." Ezra chuckles. "And that doctor, she stitched him up good."

"I think my mom will like that the doctor's a woman." I glance back to be sure that she's still okay, but she seems to be in exactly the same position as before. "I just hope Dr. Hoffman can help her."

We ride along for quite a while without speaking, but I don't mind at all. The sky is blue, the countryside is so pretty, and I am sitting here next to my man. Because that is how I see Ezra now. My man. And I am his woman. Okay, I know it sounds a little silly. But in his culture we are considered man and woman. We are old enough to marry, if we so choose.

I smooth my skirt down. I'm wearing the teal dress that Rachel said matched my eyes. I talked to Aunt Katrina about learning to sew clothes, and she seemed like she'd be happy to teach me—in exchange for me doing more chores. I wonder how that's even possible, but I agreed. I'm looking forward to making a dress that's truly my own. Not a hand-me-down.

I had actually considered wearing my old English clothes today because I knew it would make Mom feel better. I know she doesn't like seeing me dressed like this. But when I thought about being with Ezra—not to mention what others might think if they saw us—I decided not to. Besides, I'm starting to feel more comfortable in these clothes. They're sensible and modest. I think I like that. It's like I've turned a corner and I feel more Amish than English these days. Sometimes I hear myself saying *ja* and I realize that I'm even starting to talk like them.

I sigh and tilt my head back, allowing the morning sun to wash across my face. I can hear birds twittering and chirping over the rhythmic clip-clop of the horse's hooves. So peaceful and so picturesque. I wonder if I'll ever have time to do some paintings of these fields and barns and animals. Although my aunt has specifically told me that art is considered a "graven image." I'm not sure what that means, but I plan to ask my uncle. Anyway, I refuse to be distracted or discouraged by that now. It is a beautiful summer day, and sharing it with Ezra like this makes it absolutely perfect. Well, except for the fact that my mom isn't doing well. Being reminded of that seems to steal some of the sunshine. I glance back to check on her, but she still hasn't moved.

"I was thinking, Shannon . . ." Ezra adjusts the brim of his hat to shade his eyes from the morning sun.

I gaze at him, waiting for him to finish his sentence, but soon find myself caught up in his appearance, which seems even more striking in the golden morning light. I can't help but admire the firm jaw, the nice straight nose, those cheekbones, and those strong, broad shoulders. He is so handsome! Then I remember he was about to say something.

"What are you thinking about?" I ask pleasantly. I hope that he's been thinking about me. Better yet, thinking about *us*. I know that I have.

"I am thinking that you are right."

"I'm right? Well, that's nice to hear. What am I right about?"

He clears his throat. "That you and your mamm should go home."

"What?"

"If you go home, your mamm can get the medical help she needs. I think maybe it would be for the best. For everyone."

I bite my lip, trying to decide what this really means and

trying not to feel hurt. Although how can I help it? It's like I've been slapped. Or maybe I just misunderstood. "But what about us?" I ask in a mousy sounding voice.

He shrugs, keeping his eyes straight ahead.

"Wouldn't you miss me if I left?" I say in what I hope is an enticing tone.

"*Ja*. Sure. But I think it's for the best, Shannon."

"How can you even say that?" I demand.

"Because you and your mamm . . . you are English. And your mamm has chosen to not be Amish. She has been shunned."

"*Ja*, I know."

"Do you know what that means?"

"Sort of. People in the Amish community aren't supposed to be around her."

"Including me," he says. "And you too, if you were really Amish, which you are not."

"But I am trying to—"

"You can *play* at being Amish, Shannon. And maybe it is a fun game to you. But in the end you will see that you are not Amish. You will never be Amish. You are English, and I think everyone knows it. Everyone except for you."

"But English people can convert to Amish," I point out. "My uncle said so. He said he will help me."

"*Ja*. I am sure he is willing. You are his niece. He is a minister. He must be willing. But I think it is a waste of time. You will not become Amish."

"But I've been trying my best," I plead. "I even want to learn Pennsylvania Dutch. My uncle gave me a book."

"Learning a language will not make you Amish."

"I know. There is more to it. Like hard work." I remember what Aunt Katrina has told me. "I've been working very hard."

"Hard?" He laughs, but not with any warmth. "You think that living with your aunt and uncle—doing a few chores—you think that is hard? You do not know what hard is."

"Look!" I hold out my red, cracked hands. "I've never worked so hard in my entire life. I go to bed exhausted every single night. What do you mean by saying that I don't know?"

"I mean you do not know," he says firmly.

"Then tell me," I demand. "What am I missing here?"

"You think you want to be Amish," he says sharply, "but you do not understand what that means. You are living in a home that is established. Your uncle has had many years to make life better for his family. A young couple does not have that. A young couple must work hard for every single little thing. And everything—*everything*—is hard work. Right now you share the work with Rachel and your aunt—that is easy. But what if you had all the household work to yourself? And what if you had no indoor plumbing? No propane refrigerator? What if you had to wash the clothes in a tub outside in the yard? In wintertime too. And then the babies come. Sometimes one a year. You might have seven children before you are twenty-five."

I feel tears in my eyes as he goes on like this. Not because of the grim and gloomy picture he's painting but because of the tone of his voice. It is so cold, so unfeeling, it's as if he doesn't love me. I feel like he is telling me that he doesn't want to marry me—not ever. As he continues talking about hardships and deprivations, about how people sometimes die and no one ever speaks of them again, I feel trampled and buried by his words.

After he's finally done, we both sit there in awkward silence for a long while. I can hear the horse's hooves but not the birds. Now the sun is beating down on me, making my head throb. I am so crushed by what he's said that all I want to do is get away from him. If my mom wasn't lying helplessly in the back of the buggy, I would jump down and run away and leave him.

"I'm not saying this to hurt you." His tone is a little more gentle now. "But you need to know, Shannon. You need to understand."

"I know what you're doing." I glare at him.

"What?"

"You're acting like this is all about being Amish, but what you're really saying is that you don't love me . . . that you will never marry me. Even if I succeeded at being Amish, it would make no difference to you."

"You will not succeed at being Amish." He says something in Pennsylvania Dutch—it sounds like a curse. "I was born in this world and I cannot even succeed at it."

"But you *are* Amish."

"You know that's not how it works," he says sharply. "I have not committed to the faith. I have not asked to be baptized."

"But you could," I point out. "It would be easy for you."

"You do not know everything about me, Shannon. You don't know that I was ready to leave last winter. My best friend, Josiah, and I made plans to leave together in January."

"You were really going to leave—never come back?"

He nods. "Josiah's brother left three years ago. He lives

in Missouri now. He has a good job and a place to live and a car. He said we could join him there."

"But you didn't go."

He grimly shakes his head. "No. Josiah went without me."

"Why did you stay?"

"You do not want to know." His eyes narrow as he watches the road ahead. I can't tell if he is angry or something else.

I study him closely as he twists the reins between his fingers, and now I can see what I feel certain is pain in his eyes. As if he's been deeply wounded. Maybe as deeply as I've been wounded today, although that seems impossible. He is right; I do not want to know. I suspect his pain is related to my cousin. But I really, really hope he doesn't tell me.

"You will not become Amish, Shannon." His words sound gentler now, almost apologetic. "I will leave to join Josiah and his brother in Missouri. Right after harvest."

"You plan to leave? How long have you known this?"

"I'm not sure. I guess I've known it since . . . for a while."

"Since Rachel rejected you?" I can't stop myself from saying this, but the words come out sounding flat and dead.

Ezra doesn't answer. He doesn't need to. It is written all over his face. He still loves Rachel. Maybe he will always love her. There is nothing I can do about it. She has hurt him, and now he has hurt me. Maybe that's just how love works.

I turn away, watching a cornfield going by on the right. The tall green stalks blur together as tears slide down my cheeks. I have been such a little fool. A complete and utterly lovesick little fool. And now I am a brokenhearted fool.

Neither of us speaks for the duration of the trip. It feels like the longest hour of my life. I check on Mom frequently, almost hoping that she'll wake up and need my help, but she does not stir. In fact, she is lying so still and quiet that I begin to wonder, *What if she is dead?*

Oh, I know she's not, but the thought of this sets me to crying all over again. I try to hide my tears from Ezra, but then I decide I don't really care. What difference does it make now? After a while I can't even be sure what I'm actually crying about. Is it because Ezra does not love me or because I fear my mother is dying? Or both?

18

I am somewhat recovered, at least on the surface, when Ezra parks the buggy in front of a medical complex. He hops down and secures the reins to a post, then offers me a hand to get down. "They told me I can get a wheeled chair for your mamm," he says. "I will go and find it now."

"Thank you," I say solemnly as I start to rouse my mom. I don't even want to look at him. Not because I'm angry, but because I don't want to start crying again. "We're here," I tell Mom. She sits up fully with an anxious expression.

"Where?" She holds her head in her hands. "What is happening?"

I remind her about coming to Hochstetler to see the doctor. "It's a woman doctor," I say as cheerfully as I can. "I think she's going to really help you."

"Will she give me more pills?" Mom asks in a shaky voice.

"I think she will," I assure her. "Ezra has gone to get a wheelchair for you."

"Who is Ezra?"

I explain once again who he is and that he brought us here. I'm just finishing up when he returns with a wheelchair. He helps me to load Mom into it and then proceeds to push the chair. "I'll show you where the doctor's office is," he says as we go into a building.

Eventually we enter a waiting room, and Ezra politely introduces me to a gray-haired receptionist who looks like she's been sucking on a lemon. Without further ado and to my relief he excuses himself, promising to return in a couple of hours. The receptionist hands me a clipboard with paperwork. "Can your mother fill out these forms?" she asks. "Or should you do it for her?"

"I'll have to do it," I say.

"You have your insurance information?"

"We don't have insurance."

She frowns at my clothing as if that explains everything. "No, of course you don't have insurance," she says in what seems a slightly superior tone. "Well, just fill out the rest of the spaces. Do the best you can. And make sure you give us the correct billing address. And a phone number where you can be reached, if you have one."

I roll Mom's chair over to the seating area, then sit down and start filling out the forms. It's not that difficult, except that I feel rattled—like my brain's not fully functioning. I'm not sure if it's because my heart just got trampled, or because my mom is slumped in her chair like a marionette whose strings have been cut, or because that snooty old receptionist seems to be putting me down for being Amish— even though I'm not! I eventually get the form filled out correctly, and with fairly neat penmanship as well. I take it up to the grumpy receptionist, setting it on the counter and waiting.

"The doctor will be with you as soon as she's available," she says curtly.

"Thank you." I return her curtness with a forced smile. I am suddenly aware that I am my mom's advocate. I'm all she has, and I recognize it's vital that everyone in this office, including this receptionist, respect me. "I'm very grateful that the doctor could see my mom on such short notice," I say politely. "She's had a really rough time with this illness. Before we moved here, so her parents could help out, she was diagnosed with BPPV." I pause, seeing that the receptionist looks fairly surprised by my little speech. "I'm sure you know what BPPV is—benign paroxysmal positional vertigo. The diagnosis seemed plausible since she was so dizzy and unstable that she had to quit her job. But then her doctor changed the diagnosis to Ménière's disease, which also causes a form of vertigo. He prescribed diazepam for her, and although it does relieve some symptoms, she has never improved. Lately she's been much worse. So I hope Dr. Hoffman can give her a more thorough examination, and maybe even suggest a different form of treatment."

The receptionist looks surprised and slightly perplexed. "Yes, well, I hope so too."

"Thank you for your help," I tell her.

"You're welcome." She smiles at me as if she's suddenly realized that I'm human and have feelings.

"Oh, by the way, would you mind if I plugged my cell phone into an outlet? It's been dead for weeks, and I'd really like to charge it."

"No problem." She points one out to me.

I thank her again, then plug in my phone and go back to sit with my mom. She's still pretty out of it, but being here and talking to the receptionist like that renews a spark of optimism in me. Despite my agonizing morning with Ezra, I feel surprisingly hopeful. I'm not even sure why, but I suspect it has to do with these past few weeks of talking and acting Amish. I know it's impossible, but it almost feels as if my brain cells had been shrinking. As if I was forgetting how to think. I've always been considered fairly intelligent in school, but it's almost as if I've been playing dumb.

Okay, *dumb* is not the right word, but I was definitely not being myself. Maybe the word is *suppressed*. Because it's crystal clear to me now that I was pretending. There is no denying it. I was so smitten with Ezra and my unrealistic dreams of our future together that I was willing to suppress my personality, my intelligence, even my spirituality, just to please him. I totally compromised myself simply to fit into his world. And here is the irony: it is a world that Ezra doesn't even want to fit into. Or so he says.

"Anna McNamara?" a nurse calls out.

"Yes," I say eagerly. "We're over here." I push Mom's wheelchair toward her. "It's time to see the doctor, Mom," I quietly tell Mom, but she doesn't respond.

As I go by the front desk, the receptionist gives me a thumbs-up sign. "Good luck," she says quietly.

"Thanks." I give her a sincere smile, then follow the nurse into what appears to be an examining room.

"Are you going to stay with Anna?" The nurse peers curiously at my slumped-over mom and then back at me.

"Yes," I say. "She needs me."

She hands me a pale blue gown. "I guess she can remain in her chair for the exam. Just have her remove her upper clothing," she says. "The doctor will be in shortly."

As I help Mom take off her T-shirt, she seems to be growing more alert. I explain what's happening, but as I'm helping her into the cotton gown, I can't help but notice that besides being thinner than before, she also has a lot of bruises on her arms and torso. "Are these bruises from falling down so much?" I ask with concern.

"I don't know," she mumbles. "I fall a lot."

As I tie the gown behind her neck, I am assaulted with guilt. My poor mom! So sick and dizzy, and although Mammi was probably trying, she wasn't really caring for Mom in the best way. If I hadn't been so distracted with my pathetic love life, so obsessed with Ezra, so caught up in becoming Amish, I might've noticed. I might've done something sooner.

A tall, dark-haired woman in a white coat comes in and introduces herself as Dr. Hoffman. She has kind eyes and a gentle voice as she asks Mom some preliminary questions. When Mom struggles to answer, I try to explain. I basically tell her the same thing I told the receptionist, only with more detail this time. I can tell the doctor is carefully listening as she writes things down.

The doctor asks me some specific questions about Mom's behavior and symptoms and the timeline of her illness as she begins her examination. She does all the typical things, checking her blood pressure, heart rate, and breathing. She taps Mom's elbows and knees and asks about the bruising. I explain how the dizziness makes her fall.

"She's been staying with my grandparents, and I'm not sure my grandmother understood how sick she really is. You see, my grandparents are Amish, and, well, they don't have much respect for modern medicine."

The doctor gives me a puzzled expression. "Aren't you Amish too?"

I glance down at my clothes. "No, I dress like this to fit in better. But I am definitely *not* Amish."

"I see." She looks into Mom's ears, mouth, and eyes, but she seems most interested in her eyes, particularly the right one. "Did your other physician run many tests on you?" she asks Mom. "Any MRIs or CAT scans?"

"Cat skins?" Mom gives her a confused look.

"Did you go to a hospital to get your head looked at?" the doctor says simply, pointing to Mom's forehead. "To see if something was inside there."

"Besides my brain?" Mom asks. I don't think she's trying to be funny.

"Yes." Dr. Hoffman nods. "Did you lie down in a machine?"

Mom frowns. "No . . . no, I don't think so."

The doctor looks at me. "Do you know if she's had any scans done?"

"I honestly don't think so." I try to remember. "Our neighbor was a retired nurse, and she had said the doctor needed to do more." I sigh. "But we didn't have insurance. Maybe that's why he didn't. And he said she had Ménière's disease, so maybe he thought that was that. I put his name on the form in case you need to contact him, but I don't have his phone number."

"Well, that's ridiculous." Dr. Hoffman stands up straight.

"Something is going on in there. We need to find out exactly what it is." She reaches for a pad and starts writing something down. "And I intend to see that we do."

"Do what?"

"Get your mom an MRI. As soon as possible."

"Really?"

She nods as she continues writing. "I wish she could have it today, but I know that's not possible. Still, I'll call right away and tell them it's urgent." She hands me a slip of paper. "This is for the scan. Stop by the receptionist on your way out and Betty will give you some more forms to fill out. Hopefully we'll get it scheduled before the end of the week." She hands me another slip of paper. "This is a prescription for more diazepam. If I didn't think Anna was getting the scan this week, I'd change her to a different med, but as it is, I don't want to rock her boat too much." She smiles at Mom. "We're going to get you well, Anna."

"Thank you," Mom mumbles.

"Yes," I tell the doctor eagerly. "Thank you!"

"The paperwork Betty gives you will explain exactly what you need to do to get your mom ready for her MRI."

"What about not having insurance?" I ask hesitantly. "We don't have much money either."

She sighs. "Don't worry about that yet." She explains that the nurse will be back in to draw some blood as well as gather some other information. "While she's doing that, I'd like a word with you."

When the nurse returns to the examining room, I go find Dr. Hoffman.

"I don't want you to be alarmed," she tells me as I sit in

her office. "But I think this is very serious. I'm almost certain your mom doesn't have Ménière's."

I nod. "I thought so."

"The MRI will show us more, but based on everything I saw today, I'm concerned it might be a tumor."

"A brain tumor—as in *cancer*?" A wave of fear rushes through me.

"Yes, but don't assume the worst prognosis here. There are dozens of kinds of brain tumors, some benign. Or it could even be a cyst or a clot. But don't get me wrong—all of these left untreated are dangerous."

"Oh."

"It's clear your mother is suffering. The MRI will help us determine what the next step is, and it's possible it will be surgery. I'm telling you this now so you can prepare yourself, Shannon."

"Thanks," I say in a shaky voice. "I appreciate that."

"You seem like an intelligent and caring girl. Your mother is blessed to have you helping her like this."

I nod.

"As I was saying, after the MRI, depending on how it turns out, it's very likely that your mother will be scheduled for surgery."

"Will you do it?"

"No," she says quickly. "I'm only a general practitioner." Her eyes light up with a smile. "However, I can recommend an excellent neurosurgeon who goes by the same name as me."

"There's another Dr. Hoffman?"

"My husband—Dr. Mitch Hoffman." She grins. "And if I do say so, he is good."

"Oh. That's reassuring."

"So even though this is very serious, your mom is in good hands now. It's fortunate you brought her in here when you did. I'll have Betty request copies of all her medical records from her doctor in Indianapolis before she has the MRI. Although, based on what you've both told me, I doubt they'll be too helpful."

The nurse is finishing up when I return to the examination room. It's a good thing because I can see that my poor mom is completely worn out, and her pill has completely worn off as well.

I act perfectly normal as I help Mom get dressed. I assure her that things are looking up and that help is on its way. Of course, her biggest concern at the moment is getting her next pill. She is feeling dizzy and nauseated. I find a bag for her to hold on to as I wheel her chair back to the reception area. I settle her into a dimly lit corner, then go over to speak to Betty, the receptionist. First I give her Mom's debit card to settle today's bill, which saves us 15 percent, and then she hands me the paperwork for the MRI appointment.

I quickly fill out the MRI form and hand it back to Betty. "My mom needs her prescription filled ASAP," I explain. "She's feeling really miserable, and she still needs to make the buggy ride back home."

"How long is the buggy ride?" Betty asks with concern.

"Almost two hours," I say glumly.

She grimaces. "Probably less than fifteen miles, I'll bet."

I nod.

"What if I can get someone to give you a lift?" Betty offers. "In a car."

"Oh, wow!" I feel like hugging her. "Could you really do that?"

"I think so." She reaches for the phone. "Why don't you run down to the pharmacy. Walgreens is two blocks down on the right. You get that prescription filled while your mom stays here with me. In the meantime, I'll see if I can find you girls a ride home."

I quickly thank her, then grab up my cell phone and explain to Mom that I'm off to get her pills. "We might even have a car ride back to the dawdi house," I say hopefully as I reach for the bag Mammi gave me.

"Really?" She makes a little sigh.

I pull a wrapped sandwich from the bag, as well as a sugar cookie and a bottle of water, and set them in her lap. "I want you to do your best to eat some of this," I tell her. "Otherwise you won't be ready to take a pill when I get back."

"Okay," she agrees reluctantly. "But hurry, Shannon. I need that pill."

"I'm on my way." Looping the strap of the cloth shopping bag over my arm, I rush out of the medical center and down the street to the pharmacy. Unfortunately, there is already a line ahead of me. I'm not sure how much time passes until it's my turn, but when I reach the counter I tell the pharmacist that this is urgent.

He reads the prescription, then gives me a bewildered look. "Is this for you?"

"No, it's for my mom."

His expression turns to suspicion. "Your mom takes this?"

"Yes," I tell him. "And she needs some right now." He's still staring at me as if sizing me up, and I suddenly get it.

"Oh." I point to my clothes. "You think I'm Amish, don't you?"

He looks even more perplexed now. "Well, I, uh—"

"I'm not Amish. Neither is my mom. But my grandparents are Amish, and we're staying with them this summer." I point to the paper still in his hand. "You can call Dr. Hoffman's office if you want to verify it. My mom is waiting for me there right now. She may have a brain tumor, and she needs the diazepam to deal with her dizziness and—"

"Fine," he says quickly. "I believe you."

"Thank you. Please hurry."

"There's a line of orders ahead of you, but I'll see what we can do. Give me ten minutes."

I thank him again, and then, remembering my charged phone, I step outside and push the speed dial for Merenda's number. As I'm waiting for her to answer, I notice that I am being watched—not just watched but stared at—by a group of what I suppose are tourists. I've heard that they come by the busload to gape at the Amish, and some of them even try to take photos, which is forbidden by the Ordnung. I turn my back to these rude onlookers and face the pharmacy as Merenda answers the phone.

"Shannon!" she says urgently. "What is going on with you? I've texted you like a million times and even called your landline over and over. I was starting to think you and your mom had been kidnapped or something. Are you okay?"

"Yeah, we're okay. Well, kinda okay. It's a long story, and I only have a few minutes." Even so, I give her the quick lowdown about staying in Amish country with my Amish grandparents and relatives. She is stunned.

"You're kidding!" she cries. "That's unbelievable."

"I know!" I can't believe how good it is to hear her voice—her normal, enthusiastic voice. It makes me so happy that I feel like crying. "It's been a strange few weeks," I confess. "Seriously, it's like being in a different world. Or on a different planet."

"You could be on one of those reality shows."

I frown down at my clothes. "Yeah, I guess. You wouldn't believe what I'm wearing right now." I describe my outfit.

"No way!" she exclaims. "Can you send me a photo?"

"Sure." I laugh as I hold out my phone, taking a shot of myself. Of course, as I'm sending it I see the faces of the shocked tourists who are watching me. "Uh-oh," I tell Merenda. "I've been spotted photographing myself, and that is a real no-no for the Amish."

"Will they throw you in Amish jail?" she asks.

"No, it's just some tourists." I explain that I'm at a pharmacy, waiting for Mom's pills, and without going into all the details, I tell her Mom is worse.

"I'm sorry."

"She'll get an MRI this week," I say weakly. "So I feel a little bit hopeful."

"Wow, that's a lot to take in."

"So much has happened to me here," I confide. "I mean *so much*, Merenda. You wouldn't even believe me if I had time to tell you everything."

"I'm guessing you didn't get the butterfly tattoo then?"

I laugh. "No, but seriously, compared to what I've been through, getting a tattoo would be a walk in the park."

"I know what's happened to you," she says. "You've fallen in love, haven't you? I can tell by your voice."

"It's a long story, Merenda." I let out a weary sigh. "But yeah, you're right. I guess I kinda did."

"Who is he? Is he Amish? Is he—"

"I honestly don't have time to tell you about it now. Besides, it's all over with anyway. It all ended this morning."

"Oh. Are you okay?"

"I think so." I take in a deep breath. "I mean, I've never felt so hurt, ever. But at the moment, well, I need to focus on my mom getting well. I don't want to go into it now, but her condition is really serious. At least there's this really great doctor helping us."

"An *Amish* doctor?"

"No, silly, there's no such thing. Don't you know their education ends after eighth grade?"

"Seriously?"

"Yeah. But I gotta go. Hopefully Mom's pills are ready by now. And she really needs them. Keep praying for her, okay? There's the MRI this week . . . and, well, it's likely she'll need surgery too." I try not to consider all this implies.

"I'll keep praying. Call me when you can."

I promise to keep her posted, then go inside where Mom's prescription is just being put into a bag. Once again I use her debit card, thankful that the Social Security check must have been direct deposited in the bank by now. Then I thank the pharmacist and hurry back to the doctor's office to discover that Betty's daughter-in-law, Leah, has come to take us home. She's an ordinary looking woman, slightly overweight, dressed in baggy jeans and a faded pink T-shirt, but her eyes are kind.

"Betty signed out this wheelchair for you," she tells me

as I'm giving Mom a pill. "So you can keep it until after the MRI."

I thank her again, but as we're leaving I remember Ezra. I quickly explain the situation to Betty, but she assures me he's already been here. "I told him you didn't need him anymore," she says as her phone starts to ring.

"Yeah." I wave to her as I wheel Mom out. "I *don't* need him anymore."

As Leah drives us through the countryside in her air-conditioned minivan with her radio tuned to an upbeat Christian station, I know that what I told her mother-in-law was true. Despite feeling so hopeless and like I could not live without Ezra just this morning, I know that I do not need him anymore. Oh sure, my heart still aches from it. And as we pass a familiar-looking horse-drawn buggy, I avert my eyes, realizing it might take some time to get completely over him. But I do know I can live without him. After all, here I am, alive and well. As I help Mom lean back into the seat, using the weight of my own body to hold her steady, I'm not so sure about her, though. The grim expression on Dr. Hoffman's face when she told me it could be a brain tumor seems to be etched in my memory.

I suspect the next few days are going to pass very slowly for both Mom and me. It would be very easy to get consumed with worry, but that's a good reminder that the only thing I can really do is pray. I realize that since I've been asking others to pray for Mom, it's time I started doing this myself. So as the minivan continues zipping down the road, I pray.

19

After Leah helps me get my sedated mom into the borrowed wheelchair at the dawdi house, she hands me a slip of paper with her phone number on it. "You call me and let me know when your mom needs to go in for her MRI. I'll pick you up, or else I'll find someone who can."

"Thank you so much," I tell her. "You have no idea what that means for us."

"Well . . ." She glances over to the barn, then slowly shakes her head. "You might be surprised about that."

"What?" I peer curiously at her as I set the shopping bag in Mom's lap.

"I grew up in a settlement not so different than this one." She holds her hands to shade her eyes, looking all around with a hard-to-read expression.

"And you left?" I say quietly. "Like my mom did?"

She nods. "I didn't fit in. I never did . . . never would."

"Oh." I sigh.

"You better get your mom inside." She pats my shoulder. "But you call me when you know about the appointment."

I thank her again, then hurriedly wheel Mom up the graveled path to the house. I've never felt like I've seen an angel before, but today I feel like I've met three—Dr. Hoffman, Betty, and Leah—although I admit my dire and desperate situation might be influencing my deductive skills.

"You are home," Mammi says as I struggle to wheel Mom into the house. I'm huffing and puffing from getting her up the porch steps, and now I discover her chair won't fit through the bedroom door.

"Yes," I say as I try to get Mom to stand.

"Let me help you." Mammi comes over, and the two of us manage to get Mom out of the chair and into her bed. But because most of the bedding is still in Ezra's buggy, I'm forced to roll up a blanket for a pillow. Fortunately, Mom is so out of it that she barely notices.

As I put Mom's wallet back into her purse, I explain to Mammi that Ezra has the other bedding. "Hopefully he'll bring it by before bedtime," I say.

"*Ja*, or I will send Jacob to fetch it," she assures me.

"Mom needs to rest for now," I tell Mammi as we leave the room. "It's been a long day for her."

"*Ja*. I was afraid of that." She frowns as we stand in the living room. "What did the doctor say?"

I explain about the possible brain tumor and that she's to have an MRI, but Mammi doesn't seem to absorb this. If she does, she is pretending that it's not very serious. Or else she is in deep, dark denial. However, I'm too tired to figure it all out.

"I want to stay here again," I tell her. "If you don't mind. I think I can be more help to Mom here than at Uncle Ben's house."

"*Ja.* Maybe that is a good idea. The garden is coming on good now. I will start preserving cucumbers and tomatoes this week. You can help."

I want to point out I'm coming here to aid Mom, not to make pickles, but decide not to go there right now.

"You can move back here tomorrow," she tells me. "Dawdi will get you a bed by then."

I remove Mom's bottle of pills from the shopping bag. "She can have one of these every six hours or so, as she needs them."

Mammi studies the bottle. "This is the same as before?"

"Yes. The doctor says she needs to keep taking them. Until she has the MRI."

"MRI?"

"The test that tells us about the brain tumor." I remove my cell phone from the shopping bag and hand her bag back to her.

She frowns and shakes her head.

"Make Mom eat food before she takes her medicine," I remind her. "She'll probably be ready for a pill around suppertime."

"*Ja,* supper. Jacob will be here soon. I better get to work on that."

Feeling slightly dismissed, I go outside and look around. I'm curious as to whether Ezra is back yet but suspect he still must have a fair amount of road time before him. I wonder if he is feeling any regrets for this morning—if he misses me at all—and then I tell myself not to think about it. I am over him. Okay, more honestly, I am getting over him.

As I walk back to my uncle's house, I realize that Ezra was

right: it is for the best. I was living in an Amish fantasyland to think that it could truly work—that I could really transform myself into Mammi or Aunt Katrina. Oh, I might get used to the work, in time, but I don't think I could ever get used to all these restrictions. And I could never get used to shutting down my brain. I've always dreamed of going to college and having some independence and freedom. Why would I want to give up all that to become subservient to a bearded man wearing weird suspenders?

Still, as I notice what could be Ezra's buggy going down the road, although it could easily be someone else's since they all look very similar, I feel a sharp pang deep inside of me. I suspect that my broken heart has a ways to go before it catches up with my recovering brain. To distract myself, since my cell phone is still charged and can take a photo even if it can't connect, I snap a shot of the horse and buggy. Then I take several of the barn and silos and other scenic shots before I slip the phone inside my bodice. I still don't know why Amish clothes don't have pockets. So inconvenient.

"You are just in time," Aunt Katrina tells me when I go into the kitchen. "Rachel is not back from my sister's house. She went to get me some fabric. But the cows need milking."

I nod, realizing she's not asking me to do this detested chore, she is telling me. She doesn't know that Rachel already gave up on trying to transform me into a milkmaid. Instead, Rachel made sure I was stuck with even more mundane chores—the ones she was happy to pass down to me.

As I struggle to milk the first cow, I remind myself that this is my last night at Uncle Ben's house. I will no longer be under Aunt Katrina's rule. Besides, I decide as I finally move on to the next cow, I'll have some good stories to tell Merenda.

For that purpose, I decide to snap some photos of myself milking a cow. Chuckling at the results, I know these shots could be priceless someday. Who would believe this when I'm in college or even next fall back at high school? Just as I'm taking a shot of me holding the bucket in one hand and posing by the cow, Uncle Ben walks in.

"What are you doing?" he asks.

Still holding the cell phone in the air, I give him a sheepish look.

"Is that a camera?" he demands.

"It's my cell phone," I confess.

"You know that the Ordnung forbids taking photos," he tells me.

"I've heard that," I admit. "But I don't really know why."

His expression softens some as he hangs a coiled rope on a peg by the door. "Exodus 20:4 states, 'Thou shalt not make unto thee any graven image, or any likeness of anything that is in heaven above, or that is in the earth beneath, or that is in the water under the earth.'"

"But I'm an artist," I tell him. "Does that mean it's wrong for me to draw a picture of, say, a horse?"

"*Ja*. According to Scripture, that is true."

"Oh." I shake my head. "That's why Aunt Katrina doesn't like seeing me drawing on my sketch pad."

"*Ja*." He walks up to peer more closely at me. "I am pleased that you want to learn about becoming Amish, Shannon. It will not be easy for you. I hope you are ready to put English ways behind you."

I bite my lip, wondering how best to put this. "Actually," I begin slowly, "things have changed. I don't think I'm going to become Amish after all."

He frowns. "Why is that? What has changed?"

"I have realized that I don't really belong here."

"But you have been doing so good. We've seen you make progress. Why do you want to give up?"

"The truth is, I was interested in becoming Amish for the wrong reasons, Uncle Ben."

"What reasons?"

I sigh. "I thought I was in love with a boy, an Amish boy. I imagined I could be happy living here . . . married to him. But now I know I was wrong."

"Are you sure you were wrong?"

I nod.

"I will continue to pray for you, Shannon. I will pray that God will show you his right path and that you will learn to follow it."

"Thanks. And thanks for all your help and encouragement," I tell him. Then, not wanting to feel like I've ditched him with no notice, I explain my plan to move back to the dawdi house to help with my mom tomorrow. "She needs me, and Mammi has a lot to do with her summer chores."

"*Ja.* That is good you can help her." He seems a little disappointed but doesn't attempt to talk me out of leaving.

"But I really enjoyed my visit and getting to know all of you," I say.

He briskly nods. "I have more chores before supper."

As he leaves I turn back to the milking. I'd like to say I have him all figured out, but the truth is I don't. I like my uncle.

I respect him. But I do not fully understand him. I suppose I don't completely understand any of my Amish relatives. Not really.

During supper no mention is made of my intended departure tomorrow. I suppose I thought Uncle Ben might say something, but he doesn't. I consider making an announcement myself, but there never seems to be an opportune moment. I decide I'll break the news to the rest of them tomorrow. I doubt that any of them will care. In fact, I suspect they'll be relieved.

It's not until bedtime that I decide I should say something to Rachel. I'm not even sure why, but I feel a need to have a private conversation with her. "Ezra drove Mom and me to Hochstetler," I tell her as we're getting ready for bed.

"*Ja*, I know." Without looking at me, she continues braiding her hair.

"But you don't know everything," I say in a somewhat mysterious tone. I have no idea where I'm going with this, but I feel compelled to say something.

"What do you mean?" She puts a band around the end of her long, dark braid, then turns to peer at me. Once again, I'm struck by how pretty she is. Even in a plain white nightgown, she is really lovely. Creamy skin, clear blue eyes, perfectly shaped mouth. No wonder Ezra loves her. Thinking of this creates a lump in my throat again, and I question why I even opened my mouth.

"Oh . . . nothing." I focus my attention on hanging my dress on a peg.

"No, what do you mean I don't know everything?" she asks. "I want to know."

I realize I've opened this can of worms, and I need to either put a lid on it or get everything out in the open. Why not go for the latter? "Ezra has convinced me that it's a mistake for me to stay here," I blurt out.

She looks slightly confused. "What?"

"It's just that I know I can never be Amish," I say glumly. "You told me this some time ago."

She barely nods. "*Ja*. Why are you telling me this, Shannon?"

"Because Ezra is in love with you."

She turns away, picking up the lantern. "Do you need more light?"

"No." I climb into my bed now, wondering why I even broached this topic. Really, what do I hope to accomplish? Why should I even care?

She blows out the lantern, and in the light from the dusky square of the window, I watch her getting into her own bed. "Shannon?" she asks quietly.

"Yeah?"

"Do you love him?"

I take in a long, slow breath. I know I should give her an honest answer. "I believed that I did," I confess. "I suppose I actually did love him on many levels. But now I have some serious doubts. Do you know what a crush is?"

"Crush?"

"It's when you feel like you love a guy, but maybe it's more about the feeling than real love. Like you're kind of in love with being in love. Do you know what I mean?"

"I'm not sure."

Outside I can hear the sound of cows in the pasture and the faraway cry of a nighthawk. "Do you love Ezra?" I ask her.

Now it seems as if the room is draped in a heavy kind of quiet, and Rachel says nothing.

"I know you do," I say.

"How do you know that?"

"I think I've known it right from the start," I admit.

"You are right. *Ja*, I have always loved Ezra," she says quietly. "For as long as I can remember, anyway. But he never seemed to notice me. Not truly. I was just the little sister."

"Uh-huh?"

"But then a couple of years ago, the summer when I was fifteen and finished with school, Ezra noticed me." She lets out a sigh. "It was wonderful. We spent time together. We both said we love each other."

"Really?" I'm not sure why I feel surprised. Even though no one had said as much, I think somewhere inside of me, I knew this.

"*Ja*. Ezra said we would get married."

"And you wanted to marry him?"

"*Ja*. I wanted nothing more. We were promised to each other."

"What happened?"

"A year passed, then part of another. Ezra and his friends, they got more carried away with the parties and drinking and all that. I didn't mind it so much at first. I know young men need the chance to test everything. Daed explained that to me. But trouble is easier to get into than out of. And that is where Ezra was headed. This last spring I believed it was time for the nonsense to stop. Time for us to grow up. I wanted to get baptized. And I wanted Ezra to get baptized too." She gets quiet again. "Ezra said he was not ready. So I told him I would not marry him."

"I feel terrible," I tell her. "Like I came between you two. I had no idea your relationship had been that serious. Oh, I knew you'd been involved with him, but I didn't understand that you'd spoken of marriage."

"You should not feel bad."

"But if I hadn't been with Ezra, maybe you guys would've worked this out before it was too late."

"Too late?"

"Ezra said he's going to leave. He's going to join his friends in Missouri."

"Oh."

"But he's not leaving until after harvest time," I say hopefully.

"It sounds as if Ezra knows what he wants, Shannon. He has made up his mind. That is the end of it."

"But maybe you could—"

"I am tired, Shannon. Tomorrow is a busy day. Good night, cousin." She sighs. "I am sorry to hear that you are leaving. I think we could have become friends. I will miss you."

"I'll miss you too." As weird as it seems, especially since we've been at such odds these past few weeks, I realize that I really will miss her. I wish I'd gotten to know her better while I had the chance. Instead I was running around trying to steal her boyfriend. Okay, that might be overstating it, but it sure could seem like that. After a while, I hear a quiet sniffling and I know Rachel is crying again. I'd like to think that she's sad about my decision not to stay here, but I know better. She is crying over Ezra. And it is partially my fault.

Once again, it seems my only recourse is to pray. Since I'm determined to pray more, I decide that it's time to pray for both Rachel and Ezra. I pray that somehow they will figure this thing out before Ezra runs off to Missouri. If they are truly meant for each other, if the best thing for them is to be together and be married, I pray that God will do the miracles required to help them reach this place.

20

In the morning, Rachel acts as if nothing whatsoever is wrong. She greets me with a pretty smile and even offers to help me pack my things. We chat congenially as I organize my bags, and she asks me questions about my cell phone and iPad. "You English have so many funny things," she says as I zip a bag closed. "I would not know what to do with them."

"Would you even want to know what to do with them?" I wonder if she is thinking of leaving. "Would you ever consider becoming English?"

"No, no. I would not want that."

"Not even if it meant you could be with Ezra?"

She seems to consider this, then firmly shakes her head. "That is not who I am. I belong here. I would never want to leave."

"You're fortunate to know that, Rachel. So many people our age don't have a clue what they want."

"I want to live a life that pleases God," she says with what seems true conviction.

"I do too," I say with a little less certainty. "I'm just not always sure how to do that."

"God will show you." She reaches for the teal dress she loaned me, starting to fold it.

"Should I take these things to Mammi's house?" I ask as I hold up a *kapp*.

"*Ja*, why not?"

"You're right." I nod, remembering how Dawdi didn't approve of my English attire. "I guess I should keep wearing them until I leave. That will make Dawdi happy."

After I express my gratitude and say my good-byes to everyone at the breakfast table, I gather up my belongings as well as the paper sack containing my borrowed Amish clothes and tromp on over to the dawdi house. I don't know what I'll be sleeping on or even how long we'll be there, but my primary mission will be to take good care of my mom. I feel as if her very life is hanging by a thread right now. Until she gets that MRI and Dr. Hoffman can tell us exactly what's going on, I will be uneasy. But I will keep on praying.

I am relieved to discover Mom is sitting in the wheelchair. The chair is situated in the living room, near the front window, but she is slumped over to one side and doesn't look very comfortable.

"Good morning," I tell her, bending down to kiss her cheek. "How are you feeling?"

"I, uh, don't know." She reaches up to touch her head. "Pain . . . dizzy."

"Have you had a pill?" I ask. "Did you eat breakfast?"

"I don't remember."

"I'll go ask Mammi. Do you know where she is?"

Still rubbing her head, Mom gives me a blank, confused look. I'm sorry I even asked her. It's as if the smallest question is too much to handle. "No problem," I say lightly. "I'll find Mammi." As I go to the kitchen, which appears to be cleaned up after breakfast, I try not to feel overly concerned at Mom's disoriented state. Soon she will get that MRI. Soon we will know what's going on and how best to treat her.

But as I go outside, I pray with intensity, begging God to keep Mom safe until she can get the help she needs. "Or if you want to heal her," I mumble out loud, "that would be fine too."

"Shannon." Mammi stands up from where she's been bending down in the garden. "Who are you talking to?"

"To God," I tell her.

She smiles, rubbing her back. "*Ja*, that is good. I talk to God in the garden too." Her gray eyes twinkle as she holds up a small red tomato. "Look at this. They are coming on early this year. God has blessed us with good weather."

I inquire about Mom and find out that she was unable to eat breakfast. "Did you give her a pill?" I ask.

"No." Mammi puts the tomato in her basket. "You said she must have food with the pill."

Hiding my frustration, I simply nod. "Yeah. I'll go take care of her now." As I hurry back to the house, I feel guilty again. Maybe I should've spent the night here last night. Then I remind myself that at least Mom was sitting upright in a chair. That was something. At least Mammi is trying. And she was simply following orders regarding the food.

In the kitchen I pour a glass of milk and then get a pill. I take this to Mom. "Here, you can drink this with your pill, okay?"

She looks confused but then sees the pill and holds out her hand. "Thank you," she murmurs.

"Are you comfortable sitting in the chair?" I ask.

"I . . . uh . . . think so."

I go to her bedroom and see that the bedding from Ezra's buggy has been returned. I get a pillow and take it out to use to pad her chair, helping her to sit in a more reclined position. "Is that better?"

"Yes. Thank you."

"Can you finish your milk?" I ask. "Or perhaps eat something? A piece of toast maybe?"

She holds up a hand to signal no.

"How about a cookie?"

Her eyes barely light up.

"Yes," I tell her. "I'll get you a cookie, and you can have that with your milk."

As Mom slowly nibbles on a cookie, taking reluctant sips of milk, I talk pleasantly to her. I tell her about the tomatoes in the garden and how I've moved back to stay with her and how she'll soon have her MRI. "Dr. Hoffman is going to make sure you get well," I promise her. "And lots of people are praying for you."

Finally, as she's finishing her cookie and milk, I can tell she's getting drowsy. I try to make her even more comfortable, and she slowly slips off to sleep. I can tell that every day until the MRI is going to pass slowly. Very slowly. But I remind myself that it is much worse for Mom than it is for me.

Later in the day, as I'm helping Mammi with supper, Dawdi and Uncle Ben come from the barn. As they get closer I can see they're carrying something that looks like a wooden bed. "Is that for me?" I ask Mammi as I peer out the window.

"*Ja.* Your dawdi was making you a bed today. That must be it."

Because Mom is asleep in the bedroom, I run out to meet them, asking them to be quiet if they plan to put it in there. "She's had a rough day," I explain as I run my hand over the wood. "This looks like a nice bed," I say, hoping I don't sound ungrateful. "Thanks!"

I go ahead of them, opening the door and clearing a space by the wall across from Mom's bed. Standing back, I watch as they almost silently set the bed in place. It's very rustic looking with ropes crisscrossed back and forth, I assume to hold up the mattress.

"Come to the barn with me," Dawdi tells me after I quietly close the door to the bedroom. I follow him out and am soon put to work stuffing a big canvas sack with straw. This, I am told, will be my mattress.

"You make it how you like it," Dawdi tells me.

"I've never slept on a straw mattress before," I tell him as I reach for another handful of straw.

"When I was a boy it was all we had." He looks up from where he is sharpening a metal hand tool. "It was all we needed."

"Did you enjoy your childhood?" I ask.

"*Ja.* My parents were good, hardworking people. They had ten children, but we never went without food or love."

"That sounds nice."

"It was good." He smiles as he turns the tool over. "A happy memory never wears out."

"My childhood wasn't that great," I say as I shake the canvas sack to make the straw go down.

"*Ja*, I know your daed died when you were young. And no brothers or sisters. No family." He sets the tool aside. "But your mamm made her choices. She has had to live with them. Now you are of an age when you can make your own choices, Shannon."

Although I haven't told Dawdi that I've already decided not to become Amish, I can tell he knows. Uncle Ben must've said something. I pause from mattress stuffing and look up. "I've already made an important decision," I say as I stand up. "I've decided that I won't become Amish."

"It is your choice, Shannon. If you cannot learn from your mamm's experiences, perhaps you cannot learn at all."

I walk over to the workbench where he is rubbing his bearded chin and studying me. "There is a lot I like about being here," I tell him. "I love having family around. I think the farmland is beautiful. But there is a lot that I cannot live with. I know I will never really fit in."

He nods, but there is sadness in his eyes. "You are like your mamm."

"Maybe . . . but I didn't grow up here like she did. If I'd grown up here my whole life, maybe I would want to be Amish." I pick a piece of straw from my bodice and drop it to the ground. "Why did my mom leave, Dawdi? I would ask her, but she is so sick. Mammi doesn't seem to want to talk about it. Why did my mom leave here when she was only fifteen?"

His brow creases as he shakes his head. "She was a willful child."

"What do you mean? Was she naughty?"

"No, no, not willful like that. Anna was the baby of the family. Your mammi would tell you that it's her fault, that she spoiled Anna too much as a little girl. Scriptures say that a child left to itself brings shame to the mother. That is what Anna did."

"She brought shame to Mammi?" I feel sickened to hear this. "What did she do?"

He purses his lips as he picks up another tool. "Anna questioned everything. She questioned the way we lived and the way we worked and the way we worshiped. None of it was to her liking. It was little surprise when Anna left. That is how she brought shame to her mother."

"Oh."

"Elizabeth tried to rein in Anna as she got older, but I think it was too late. The twig was bent and the tree grew."

The way he's speaking makes it sound as if Mom is a horrible, worthless person, but I know she's not. "You don't really know my mom," I tell him. "You don't know her as an adult, Dawdi. First of all, she finished her schooling and then she met my dad going to church. They had a very good marriage. And she's been a great mom to me. She believes in God, and she's done everything she could to keep me involved in church. She is honest and upright and kind and generous. She's worked really hard to provide for us. Right up until she got sick." I feel tears in my eyes. "And she doesn't deserve to be sick."

"God is the judge," he says simply. "A knife cannot be

sharpened without friction, nor the man perfected without trials." Then he turns back to the workbench. "Finish that mattress, Shannon. Your mammi will need your help making supper."

I can hear voices in the yard and know others will be coming into the barn for various evening chores. Not wanting to be seen crying like this, I focus my attention on stuffing this mattress as quickly as I can. Finally, satisfied it's full enough, I sling it over my shoulder like a giant Santa's pack and hurry back to the house. I sort of understand Dawdi's perspective, but it still makes me sad—and slightly angry—that he thinks of his own daughter like this. As if she's good for nothing. I don't get that.

21

On Thursday morning I'm finishing up cleaning the breakfast things when Uncle Ben comes into the kitchen. "There was a phone call from Dr. Hoffman."

"Oh?" I drop the dishrag into the sink. "What did she say?"

"Anna has an appointment for . . ." He scratches his head as if trying to remember.

"For an MRI?" I prod.

"*Ja.*" He nods. "I think that is right."

"When? What time is it?" I say eagerly.

"Tomorrow morning, 10:00."

"Okay." I'm thinking of all that needs to be done before then—including the laundry.

"Something else too." He helps himself to one of the molasses cookies Mammi made last night. "Leah will pick Anna up at 9:00."

"Oh, good. Thank you."

"What is this appointment for? MRI?" He studies me as he takes a bite of the cookie.

"MRI stands for magnetic resonance imaging," I tell him.

I only know this because I've been reading the information Betty gave me, but I know if I give the technical description, my uncle will probably be lost. I mean, these guys don't even know what an iPad is. "It's a big machine that's able to see inside my mom's head. It'll tell the doctor what's wrong, why she's so sick, and how to make her well."

His brow is creased as he takes another bite, and I can tell he's thinking about something. "What if she can't get well?"

"What do you mean?" I pick up the rag again, scrubbing the already clean counter.

"What if she dies, Shannon?"

I turn to look at him. "She's not going to die."

"We are all going to die, when God says it is time."

"Well, it's not time for my mom to die," I say stubbornly.

"What would you do if she did? Have you thought about that?"

I toss the rag into the sink again. "No, I haven't thought about that. I refuse to think about that. I am doing everything I can to make sure that my mom does *not* die."

"Only God can do that, Shannon."

"Are you saying I should give up on her? That I should just let Mom suffer without medical attention? That I should let her die?"

"No. I am saying that it is up to God whether we live or die. It is God's decision to make. Not ours." He points at me. "The only decision you can make is whether or not you will follow God."

"I am following God," I say. "At least I'm trying."

He nods, but his expression seems doubtful. "It's possible that God has used your mamm's sickness to bring you here to us, Shannon. So that you can truly follow God. Have you thought of that?"

"But we want to go home," I tell him. "Mom and I both do."

"Unless it is too late, Shannon. For your mamm it might be. But it is not too late for you." He finishes off the cookie. "There is a saying: bend the tree when it is young; when it is old it is too late."

I turn to the sink, suddenly feeling as if I'm gagging on all these Amish proverbs and adages, but fortunately I don't need to respond because my uncle is already gone. I know he means well. So does Dawdi. But their comments come across as so coldhearted and unfeeling. It's like they don't care if Mom lives or dies. I have to wonder—where is their faith?

But right now I'm too busy to concern myself with these things. My focus needs to remain on today. That means caring for Mom, getting the laundry done, and ensuring my mom is ready for her MRI tomorrow.

On Friday morning, it feels like everything is working against me. Mom seems worse than ever and is not cooperating at all. First she refuses to eat breakfast, and then when I remind her of the conditions of getting her pill, she spills her bowl of oatmeal down her front and into her lap, ruining her second set of warm-ups. For a brief moment I remember my uncle's and grandfather's words and almost feel like giving up. But in the next instant, seeing my mom's troubled eyes, her helplessness, I know I can't.

"We can do this," I tell her as I peel off her jacket, then reach for another. I silently pray as I help her change again. I am begging God to help me this morning, begging him to make sure we make it to the appointment on time, begging him to show us some mercy.

It's nearly 8:30 by the time I've got Mom cleaned up and have coaxed her into eating a cookie and some applesauce and drinking some milk. I hold out her pill, and she reaches out with relief in her eyes.

"We can do this," I say again as I see Leah's minivan pulling into the driveway. Before long, we're loaded and on our way.

"You're not wearing Amish clothes today," Leah says as she drives toward town.

"Yeah. I thought I'd be more comfortable in my own threads." Yet as I look down at my jeans, fingering the hole in the right knee, I'm not so sure. It actually feels pretty weird not to have on a dress. I think Mom appreciated it, though.

As we ride, I check my bag to make sure the MRI paperwork and Mom's wallet are in there. Then I check to see that my cell phone, iPad, and charge cords are all inside as well. I even packed my sketch pad. I have no idea how long all this will take, but I plan to make the most of the available electricity and connectivity while I can.

Mom is starting to get drowsy as Leah and I load her into the wheelchair in front of the hospital. Leah gives me directions to the radiology department and tells me to call her when we're done. Then I am on my own.

I feel nervous as I wheel Mom toward the elevators, but then I remember what Mammi told me last night before I went to bed. Just when I thought I was sick to death of Amish proverbs too. "Courage is fear that has said its prayers," she said as she gave me a hug. "I know you are praying for your mamm, Shannon. I am too."

The receptionist in radiology seems kind and helpful and even asks if I want to go into the MRI room with my mom. "I wasn't planning on it. Do you think I should?" I'm bent over, trying to get Mom more securely into the wheelchair since it appears her meds have kicked in and she is slumping like a rag doll.

"No," the receptionist says. "Your mother looks as if she's pretty relaxed. She won't even know whether you're there or not." She calls over her shoulder to a nurse, asking her to help prepare my mom for the MRI. Then she smiles at me. "Why don't you go enjoy some downtime in the waiting room? It will take at least an hour. Maybe more."

Relieved to have this break, I carry my bag over to the chairs and immediately start plugging in my electronic devices. As soon as the iPad is running, I start to google information about brain tumors. Of course, the first thing I learn is exactly what Dr. Hoffman said. There are a lot of different kinds of brain tumors. I pick one of the more common ones and begin reading about the treatment. I realize right away that it's very involved. Sometimes even before surgery the patients have to be on medications. Then there is usually surgery, although some tumors are inoperable. In that case they might go straight to radiation therapy or chemotherapy. All in all, it looks like there's a long hard road ahead for both Mom and me.

I try not to dwell on what my uncle said yesterday—attempting to pin me down on what I would do if Mom died. I really don't want to go there. But I probably should prepare myself for the possibility that I'll be stuck here for quite some time. Based on what I'm reading, it seems unlikely

I'll be able to go back to my school in Indiana this fall. Even in the best case scenario—if the tumor was completely removed, followed by chemo or radiation—my mom would probably still need a lot of therapy. However, I tell myself, it's possible that it is not a tumor. So far I have no reason to assume that it is. And what about my prayers? And the prayers of others? God could still intervene and do a miracle.

Trying not to feel hopeless, I decide to call Merenda. If anyone can cheer me up, she can. Unfortunately, she seems to have her phone turned off. I leave her a pretty lengthy message and ask her to call back. Then I text her, just in case.

I pick up my iPad again, thinking I could catch up on the latest news, but then realize I don't really care. Plus I don't want to get caught up in reading more depressing stuff about brain cancer. I look at the clock behind the reception desk to see that nearly an hour has passed. Once again, I pray. I have to agree with my religious relatives on one thing—Mom and I do need God's help more than ever right now. Doctors and medicine are important, but God is more important. And more powerful.

It's nearly noon when I see my poor weary mother being wheeled out. Her eyes are open, but she looks pretty lost. I hurry to her, asking her and the nurse behind her how it went.

"We should know the results in a couple of days," the nurse tells me. "But your mother did fine." She pats Mom on the shoulder. "It looked like you were having a good nap in there, Anna."

"I need a pill," Mom says in a raspy voice.

"I have them," I tell her. "But we'll need to get something into your stomach first."

The nurse gives me directions to the cafeteria, and soon I am coaxing my mom to eat some chicken noodle soup. While she fumbles to eat a few bites, I call Leah and tell her we're ready to go home. As I hang up, it hits me that I've been calling my grandparents' house "home." I've been telling myself it's just a term of convenience, but after reading about brain tumors, I'm not so sure.

The next couple of days pass very slowly. At first I was making several trips to the barn every hour, hoping that Dr. Hoffman would call with the results from the MRI. Then I realized it was the weekend and decided that was unlikely.

Finally it's Monday, and as soon as I've finished cleaning up breakfast, I decide to call Dr. Hoffman myself. I explain to Betty about the phone situation and my concern that the doctor might call when no one is in the barn. She tells me to call back at 4:00. "I'm sure we will know by then."

Faced with another long day, I throw myself into chores and caring for Mom. Most of it is boring, mindless work, which leaves time for my brain to worry and fret. By afternoon, I feel like I'm having a full-blown pity party. As bad as I feel for Mom, I can't help but feel sorry for myself too. What sixteen-year-old wouldn't? Well, unless she was Amish. But I am not Amish.

As I wash jars that Mammi will use for canning relish, I imagine how my summer might've gone. How I'd probably have my driver's license by now and how I'd be driving Mom's car to a summer job, earning my own money while working at a fun thrift store. I imagine how I would have freedom and independence. With or without the tattoo!

Finally it's 4:00, and with my hands still red and wrinkled

from washing jars, I hurry out to the barn to make my call. Hopefully no one will be around to hear me. Betty answers and puts me right through to Dr. Hoffman.

"We've just been studying the scans," she tells me. "The other Dr. Hoffman and myself. My suspicions were correct, Shannon. Your mother does have a tumor." She starts going into some more technical medical terminology, but I am unable to fully absorb it. My knees feel weak and my heart is sinking. Of course, I knew this was how it could go, but I had been hoping for something else. A miracle, perhaps.

"Dr. Hoffman, my husband, has scheduled your mother for surgery on Thursday, Shannon."

"Thursday? This Thursday?"

"Yes. Is that a problem?"

"No . . . but it's only a few days away."

"We feel that sooner is better."

"Oh."

"I'm going to switch you over to Betty now. She can fill you in on all the details."

"Yes. Thank you." It feels like my head is spinning now. Like this is way too much to take in. But then Betty's voice comes over the phone and I immediately start to feel better.

"Don't you worry, dear," she tells me. "Your mother couldn't be in better hands. I'm working everything out for you. Leah will pick you and Anna up on Wednesday afternoon around 2:00. Your mother will be checked into the hospital to be observed overnight, and you will come stay with me."

"Stay with you?"

"I live just a few blocks from the hospital. I thought that would make it easier for you."

"Yes, it would. Thank you so much!"

"Your mother's surgery is set for 8:00 in the morning on Thursday. And it's always best to have an early surgery."

"Okay."

"It's hard to say how long they will keep Anna after the surgery. But you're welcome to stay in my guest room as long as you need it. It's only me and a couple of old cats."

I thank her again, but as I hang up I still feel like I'm on uneven ground. Trying to absorb everything, I slowly walk back to the house. I have no idea how I will tell Mom this news. How do you tell someone you love that she's got a tumor in her brain? And that in three days someone will be cutting her skull open? That is a lot to take in.

22

On Tuesday I'm feeling lost and confused and scared and totally apprehensive. I wish I had someone to talk to, a confidante to pour out my troubles to, a friend to reassure me. I'm even tempted to use the barn phone to call Merenda, but I am worried I'll get caught, and that would only make things worse. Especially since it honestly feels like no one here cares. It's as if they're so caught up in their own lives—or more accurately their chores—that they don't have time to be concerned for my mom. Or maybe they don't want to be concerned. Maybe they believe that because she left the Amish, she is not worthy of their concern.

Mammi tries to act sympathetic, and I can tell she cares, maybe even more than others, but she refuses to talk about it. If I try to express my anxiety, she simply changes the subject or quotes a Bible verse to me. I know she means well, but it makes me feel like screaming.

Finally, after I finish the supper dishes and know that Mom is resting, I go outside to get some fresh air. By this time tomorrow, Mom will be in the hospital, and then the next day, she will be undergoing a very serious operation. An operation that could take her life. The whole thing scares me to death.

But fear isn't the only emotion I feel as I walk through the pasture toward the pond. I'm mad too. I'm angry at my relatives for the way they've treated Mom. The way they refuse to care. As I push through the brush that surrounds the pond, I feel like throwing something. Or breaking something. Or maybe I'll jump into the pond with my clothes on, to cool off my hot head.

Instead I sit down and kick off my shoes and stick my bare feet into the cool water. I haven't been here since that day with Ezra. I really don't want to think about that right now. I cannot believe how obsessed I was with that stupid boy. Okay, maybe he's not stupid. But I sure was.

It's funny how having your mom at death's door diminishes other things. Thinking about what Mom faces tomorrow makes my silly crush on Ezra look ridiculous. In fact, I can hardly believe how totally smitten I was. It is embarrassing.

"Hello?"

I don't even need to look up. I recognize the voice. I say nothing.

"Do you care if I join you?"

I still don't answer.

"I know you hate me," he says as he comes over and sits on a stone that's a couple feet away from me. "I don't blame you."

"I don't hate you," I say quietly. "I just wanted to be alone."

"Oh." He takes off his hat, tossing it behind him. "I heard about your mom."

"What did you hear?"

"That she's having surgery this week. That maybe it's a brain tumor."

I turn to stare at him. "You heard that?"

"*Ja.* You know how people talk."

I pick up a stone and toss it into the water. "Well, I'm surprised anyone is talking about my mom's condition, since it seems like no one cares."

"People care." He picks up a stone, tossing it into the pond as well. This causes an interesting pattern of circles intersecting circles. "It's just that the Amish handle feelings differently than the English."

"Really?" I turn to study him. "How so?"

"Amish are taught to trust God for everything. The good and the bad. And when you are trusting God, you do not need to talk about it so much."

"We English like to talk about how we feel," I add.

"*Ja.*"

"Maybe some of you Amish would be wise to learn a lesson or two from the English."

"*Ja.* Probably so." His brow creases. "Do you have a lesson for me?"

I stand up and put my hands on my hips. "As a matter of fact, I do."

He looks surprised but interested.

I point at him. "You are such a good Amish boy that you have totally buried your feelings about something that's making you miserable. If you would only face the truth and admit how you feel, you might have a chance for happiness. As it is, you are running away."

"What are you saying?"

"How do you feel about Rachel?"

He shrugs and looks down at the water.

"See," I say with absolutely no patience. "You can't even acknowledge your real feelings. Ezra, you are pathetic!"

He looks up with startled eyes.

"You can't even admit how you feel about Rachel. Are you a man or a mouse?"

He almost smiles.

"Okay, let me make this easier for you. Maybe you'd like to hear how Rachel feels about you."

His eyes light up.

"But then you Amish don't like to talk about your feelings, do you?" I taunt him. "So maybe I shouldn't either. Let's just sweep it all under the rug."

"Come on," he urges. "What are you saying?"

"Why is that?" I continue in a slightly teasing tone. "Why do Amish hate to talk about their feelings?"

"That's not true. We talk about our feelings."

"Really?"

He seems to consider this. "You might be right. Maybe we don't talk about our feelings in the way the English do. But that's the way we are brought up. Think about it, Shannon. As a boy I might wake up on a cold dark winter morning and not feel like going out to milk the cows, but if I were to voice this feeling, what do you think would happen?"

I slowly nod. "Okay, I kind of get it."

"What were you saying before? I mean, about Rachel?"

"Only that Rachel still loves you."

"No," he objects. "She does not. She made that clear in May."

"Then that shows how much you were not listening," I declare. "Why does that not surprise me?"

"Why are you being so mean to me?" he asks. "Is it because I hurt you?"

"If I'm being mean, which may or may not be the case, it's probably because I'm worried about my mom. And because I'm fed up with all these Amish people who refuse to talk about their feelings." I turn to go.

"Wait," he calls out. "What if I tried to talk about my feelings?"

I think of Rachel now, remembering her quiet tears in the night and her hopelessness for her future. For her sake, I stay put. "Okay, let's do a little test," I say as I turn to face him. "Tell me, Ezra . . . how do you feel about Rachel?"

His expression grows serious. "I feel the same about her now as I ever did."

"And that is what?"

"I love Rachel. I think I always have." He grabs a fistful of grass, shredding it angrily. "But it doesn't matter. Rachel doesn't care about how I feel."

"I'm sure that's what you assume, Ezra, since you won't even talk to her. But I happen to know differently. And maybe if you got off your high horse and had a real conversation with her, you'd know differently too."

"She won't talk to me."

I shrug. "Yeah, maybe not. And who can blame her?"

"What do you mean?"

"I mean, look at how you've been acting. You go out party-ing and drinking and you take up with an English girl, acting like you love her, when you clearly did not. Why should Rachel trust you or want to talk to you?"

"But you said she loves me?"

"Love is a two-edged sword," I say tritely.

"What?"

"Never mind." I glare at him, wondering how he could have become such a dim-witted blockhead when he used to seem so charming and intelligent.

"Tell me what to do," he pleads as he leaps to his feet.

"Seriously? You want me to tell you what to do?" I am tempted to tell him to go jump in the pond, but seeing the pain in his eyes stops me. "Okay, you asked for it, Ezra. Why don't you get baptized?"

He frowns. "I always planned to get baptized."

"You *planned* to? When?"

"I probably would've started working on it this summer. But then Rachel did what she did. I figured, why bother?"

"Would you be getting baptized for Rachel? Or for God?"

He looks down at his feet.

"Maybe it doesn't matter." I feel a little too intrusive. "It's not like I understand all that anyway. I should go."

"Wait," he says. "What you said is true. I was going to get baptized for Rachel. But I do believe in God. And the truth is, I want to serve God."

"But you also want to leave," I remind him.

He's twisting his hat around and around in his hands. "That was to get away from her. I can't stay here, working for my parents, watching as she marries someone else—and she will. I know she will. Lots of guys want to marry Rachel."

"I'm sure they do. She's a wonderful girl. Why wouldn't they want to marry her? Why wouldn't you?" I fold my arms in front of myself, staring at him, waiting for him to respond.

"Why are you saying all this to me?" he asks.

I hold my hands in the air. "Probably because I feel sorry for my cousin, and because I've had enough of this whole Amish scene. I'm so fed up with so much . . . I just needed to vent a little." I sigh. "I guess I don't care what I say or how I sound. At least with you, anyway." I almost apologize for this harsh statement but then stop myself. Why should I be sorry for saying what's true? "I need to go," I say more gently. "I need to go help my mom get to bed. Tomorrow will be a long day for her."

"*Ja.*" He steps ahead of me, opening the brush so I can pass through. "I will be praying for your mamm, Shannon."

"Thanks," I tell him.

"Thank you," he says as we stand out in the open, "for talking to me like that. I needed to hear those things. I think that only an English girl like you could say them, Shannon."

"Oh." I shrug.

"I'm sorry I hurt you. I really am. I hope you will forgive me." He looks down at his feet.

"Yeah, I'm working on it. I think I'll forgive you in time." He looks up, and I give him a small smile as I start walking. "Truth is, I was probably asking to be hurt."

He looks slightly confused by this but just nods as he shoves his hat back onto his head, then turns toward his own farm.

"Don't wait too long," I call out as he's going. "Rachel might not wait forever, you know!"

As if I lit a fire beneath him, he starts to jog. Of course, he's headed for his own house, but maybe he'll start putting together a plan. I can only hope. As I walk back to the dawdi house, I feel better. I'm not even sure why exactly. Maybe it's because I let off some steam—and who better to let it off on than Ezra? In some ways I think he almost understood. At least he's promised to pray for Mom. Every prayer will help. I really believe that.

On Wednesday afternoon, Leah delivers Mom and me to the hospital. I fill out more forms, and eventually my mom gets settled into a room. With the bed adjusted to a forty-five degree angle, she leans back and for the first time in weeks seems almost comfortable. "It's kind of like your La-Z-Boy," I point out.

She sighs and closes her eyes. "I'm so tired, Shannon."

"I know, Mom. You've been through a lot."

"I'm ready for it to end."

Before I can respond, Dr. Hoffman and another doctor come into the room. "This is Dr. Mitch Hoffman," she tells us. "My better half."

"Don't be so sure about that," he says. Everyone visits for a while. Well, everyone except for Mom. She is just lying there with her eyes closed.

"She's really tired," I quietly tell them.

"All you need to do now is rest," Dr. Diane Hoffman tells her.

"That's right," her husband agrees. He shares a little more information, my mom signs a couple of release papers, and then they leave.

Mom tells me that I should go too, but I'm unwilling. "I'll stay for a while," I tell her. "Until you fall asleep."

She closes her eyes again, letting out a slow sigh.

I sit there, knowing there's nothing I can do. The nurses

will give her medicine and tend to her. She doesn't need me now. But I need her. I reach for her hand, holding it between my two hands. "I love you, Mom," I whisper. "If you don't mind, I'm going to pray for you."

"Yes," she says quietly.

I take in a deep breath, wishing for the perfect words for the perfect prayer, but they don't come. I think of how the Amish pray in silence and how I've gotten comfortable with that too. Still, this time I believe Mom needs to hear a prayer with audible words attached.

"Dear Father God," I begin. "I'm placing my mom into your hands right now. She's going to have a very serious operation in the morning. But you know all about that already since I've been praying for her for days now. I just want to ask you to give her a good night's rest tonight. And please give her peace about what is going to happen tomorrow. I ask that you would guide Dr. Hoffman's hands during the surgery, as well as all the other hands involved in this operation. Guide all of them to do their very best and make the surgery go perfectly well. I pray that whatever they find won't be too serious. I pray that Mom will get well as soon as she can. I place her in your hands now, Father God. I know that you are our Father. I know that you love us. And I know you want to take care of her. Amen." I squeeze Mom's hand.

"Amen," she murmurs, squeezing back.

"I'll sit here until you go to sleep," I say quietly. "Just because I want to."

"Thanks, honey."

As I sit there, I look around the room, realizing how different this world is from the one I've been living in. It's like being jerked out of a previous century and slammed into today's noisy, busy world. Very surreal and weird. I can almost understand how such an experience, particularly a hospital that's full of machines and electronics, would be overwhelming to my Amish relatives. Yet I don't understand how they could turn their backs on us now. Because that's what it feels like to me. Like when we left, that was it, and they wrote us off. Like they have already forgotten us. Like if Mom dies, they won't even cry. It just feels wrong.

23

I t's not much," Betty tells me as she shows me the guest room in her condo.

"Are you kidding?" I set my bags on the bench at the foot of the queen-sized bed. "It feels like a luxury hotel room compared to where I've been staying these last few weeks." As she shows me the closet and a dresser to put my things in, I describe my various sleeping experiences, including the mattress that I stuffed myself. "It's prickly and pokey and makes me sneeze," I tell her. "Guess that's what the old saying means—you make your bed and you have to lie in it."

Betty chuckles as she hands me a key. "Well, make yourself at home. I'm a little tired from a long day of work. I thought I might order a pizza to be delivered for us."

"Pizza?"

"Is that okay with you?"

I nod eagerly. "Oh, yeah! I'm already salivating."

She laughs. "What kind do you like?"

I list my favorite toppings, and she tells me to get settled while she places the order. As I unpack my bags, I cannot help but feel I have died and gone to heaven. Well, except for my mom. Thinking of her puts a slight damper on things. Still, I feel like doing a Snoopy dance when I see the hall bathroom. Betty already told me that it's all mine since she has another bathroom in her master suite. I cannot wait to have a nice long shower!

As we eat our delicious pizza, I confide to Betty how freaked I am for my mom. "I keep telling myself it'll be okay, and I try to pray for her instead of worrying. But it's hard." Then I tell her about how nonchalant my Amish relatives were. "It seems like they really don't care. Just because she left and has been shunned, it's like she doesn't exist."

"The shunning thing is hard," she says as she reaches for another slice. "Leah has really struggled with that. She and Bruce—that's my son—have three adorable kids, but they never see their other set of grandparents. I try to make up for that, and I enjoy all the time I get with them. But to be honest, I wouldn't mind sharing them. I do think it's a shame that they're cut off like that."

"I don't understand how the Amish can be so hardhearted."

"I don't think it's hardheartedness as much as it is their religious beliefs. Their rules are strict. Well, you must know that after living there. But it's those unbending rules that have preserved their way of life. Without that kind of order, their Ordnung, the Amish wouldn't even exist today."

"I suppose that's true."

"Almost everything they do—the way they dress and talk and work and live—is meant to set them apart. It's like their boundaries, keeping them separate from the rest of us. If they let down those walls, what would they have?"

I nod as I reach for another piece of pizza. "I guess you're right. It's funny, I was right there living among them, but I never quite saw it like that."

"Well, because of Leah and Bruce, I've given it some thought and a fair amount of study. As a result I've developed a deep compassion for the Amish. I know their lives are not easy. Some people overly romanticize them. In this town, tourists come to gape at them. But most people don't realize that there's a fair amount of heartbreak in a lot of Amish homes. Even so, those people keep on keeping on. Their lives are filled with hard work and rigid rules, and for the most part you would never hear them complain. I actually have a lot of admiration for them."

"Do you remember when Mom and I came into Dr. Hoffman's office?" I ask.

"Sure. It wasn't that long ago."

"Well, for some reason I thought you didn't like Amish people." I won't admit to her what a grump I took her for. "And I was absolutely certain you didn't like me—just because I was Amish, even though I wasn't. I was actually offended at first. But then I decided to try to win you over."

Betty chuckles. "I'd been to the dentist first thing in the morning that day. Had a filling that had fallen out and the dentist really worked me over. I was still in a little pain by the time you came in. I'm sorry if I seemed overly harsh and abrupt."

"Well, I'm sorry I misjudged you."

She shrugs. "I suppose we all misjudge sometimes. That's

why I've learned to give people second chances. And to be honest, I do remember thinking, 'Oh no, here come some more Amish patients.'" She shakes her head. "The problem is, we don't usually see them in the office until they've let an ailment go too long, and that's hard on everyone. Truth be told, because of their beliefs, they can be a little difficult sometimes too. But I'm not usually that crabby."

"Well, what you said about the Amish letting it go too long, that's how it was with my mom too."

"The important thing is that you got her in when you did, and now she's going to get help."

"Do you think she'll be okay?" I ask.

"She's in good hands." Betty gets up to get a glass of water. "Do you plan to go over in the morning before her surgery?"

"Yeah. I know she's scheduled for 8:00, but I figured I'd go earlier."

"They'll probably take her from her room an hour or so before her surgery," she tells me. "So you'll have to get up pretty early to see her."

"That's okay. I'm used to getting up early."

She chuckles. "Yeah, I'll bet you are."

I offer to clean up after dinner, but as Betty points out, besides putting our dishes in the dishwasher, there's not much to do.

"I cannot wait to take a real shower in your lovely bathroom," I tell her as I wipe down the countertops.

"What are you waiting for?"

Thrilled at the prospect of a long shower and a good shampoo, which my hair has been begging for, I decide to go for it. For a while I'm so immersed in scrubbing, shampooing, and conditioning that I completely forget about my mom. Later, as I'm drying my hair, I consider straightening it, but then I remember how much my mom loves my curls. For her sake—and maybe because I'm starting to appreciate them a little more too—I leave my hair as is. I must admit it's a time-saver.

"I'm so used to going to bed early," I tell Betty, who is sitting in front of the TV. "I think I'll turn in. I hope you don't mind."

"Not at all. I'm sure you need the rest. And if you're going to see your mom in the morning, you'll need to get up early too."

I tell her good night and then thank her for having me here. "Being in your home like this, well, it really is like a slice of heaven. You have no idea."

"No, but I can imagine." Betty smiles. "I'm glad you're here, Shannon. Be sure to call the office tomorrow and let me know how the surgery goes."

"I will."

Betty tells me good night and that she'll be praying for Mom tomorrow. Before I go to bed, I call Merenda because I really, really want to hear her voice, but she doesn't answer. So I text her, filling her in on the latest details and promising to call her tomorrow.

To my dismay, Mom's bed is already empty when I get to the hospital. How can I be late when it's only 6:30? Then, looking at the unmade bed, I start to freak—*did she die in the night?* I'm standing there with tears filling my eyes when a nurse's aide comes in.

"They're prepping her for surgery," she informs me in a nonchalant way.

"But it's only—"

"The surgical staff likes to get an early start in the morning because it always backs up later in the day." She pulls back the linens from Mom's bed, wadding them into a ball.

"Can you tell my mom I'm here?" I ask.

"No, I can't go in there. But she's probably sedated by now anyway."

Trying not to feel too dejected, I head for the lobby by the nurse's station. I pause to let them know I'm here, waiting to hear the news. Then I go and sit down. If it wasn't so early I'd call Merenda, but knowing my best friend, she is still soundly sleeping. I consider pulling out my iPad but don't want to get caught up in reading about brain surgery and get discouraged. Instead, I get out my sketch pad and decide to make a drawing for my mom. However, I can't find anything in the sterile waiting area to inspire me. Strangely enough, I feel like drawing barns and cows and horses and buggies. Somehow I don't think Mom would really appreciate that.

I put my sketch pad away and just sit there feeling frightened and sad and lonely. Very, very lonely. I know it's time to pray. I bow my head and try to form a prayer, but it feels like I'm saying the same things I've said before. I wish I could think of something more clever, something to really grab God's attention. Okay, I know that's silly, but it's how I feel. What can I say to ensure he will help Mom through this—maybe even do a miracle?

"Shannon?"

I open my eyes to see several people standing before me—all dressed in Amish clothes, but not regular work clothes. They are dressed in their dark Sunday clothes, which look totally out of place in this modern hospital. I stare in astonishment at Mammi, Dawdi, Uncle Ben, and Rachel. All of them look curiously down at me.

"What?" I stammer as I begin to stand. "What happened? Why are you—"

"We came to be with you." Mammi sits down next to me, wrapping her arm around my shoulders.

"To pray for your mamm," Dawdi adds as he sits across from me.

"And to pray for you too," Uncle Ben says.

"We are your family," Rachel tells me as she sits on the other side of me.

I'm too stunned to even speak. I cannot believe they came. What about the housework and the farm work? What about the shunning of my mom? Of course, I don't want to vocalize these questions. Instead I nod, muttering a quiet, "Thank you for coming."

"Let us pray," Dawdi says in a firm voice. Everyone bows their heads and, grateful for their company, I do too. Even though I still can't think of any special words to say—some fancy way to get God's attention—I'm thinking that this should get his attention. Four Amish people and one English, all praying together. You don't see that every day.

We pray silently like this for quite some time, maybe even an hour, but eventually I look up. Almost as if he was watching for this, Uncle Ben says, "Amen." We all echo him.

Mammi opens her cloth shopping bag, removing sugar and molasses cookies. "I thought you might be hungry."

I nod eagerly. "I didn't have breakfast. Thank you." I smile at my relatives, hoping that they will stick around a while longer. "Would anyone like coffee to go with the cookies?"

"*Ja*," Dawdi says, and the others agree.

"If you'll wait here, I'll go get some." I stand.

"I will help you," Rachel says.

Rachel and I head for the elevator. Making small talk as we go down, we get some curious looks from the others. I'm sure no one would ever guess we are cousins. Once we're out of the elevator, Rachel puts her hand on my arm.

"Shannon, I must tell you something," she says urgently.

"What is it?" I pause near a potted palm, waiting.

"Ezra," she says quietly. "You spoke to him about me."

"Oh, yeah." I nod nervously. "I hope you don't mind. I kind of dumped a lot on him the other day. I was so stressed out about my mom. I just let him have it. Are you mad?"

"No. It is all right." She smiles shyly. "Ezra came to speak to me last night."

"He did?"

"*Ja*. He told me he was sorry. He told me he still loves me."

"Of course he loves you," I assure her.

Her blue eyes shine happily. "He still wants to marry me!"

"That's wonderful."

"He said he is done with partying and drinking and all that."

"What about baptism?"

252

"He must get baptized before we marry."

"And he's willing?"

"*Ja*. And it is because of you, Shannon. You talked to him." She throws her arms around me, hugging me tightly. "I am so grateful to you."

I hug her back. "But God had a lot to do with it too," I say as we step apart.

"*Ja*, I know." She nods with a knowing expression. "But God uses people too."

It's nearly 11:00 and we've finished up the coffee and cookies when I see both the Hoffmans coming our way. I stand to greet the couple, quickly introducing them to my relatives, who stand back a ways while the doctors speak to me.

"We have good news," Dr. Diane Hoffman tells me. "Your mother's surgery went as well as possible." She grins proudly at her husband. "Our surgeon performed the craniotomy with perfection, and the tumor is completely removed."

"The growth turned out to be exactly what I hoped it would be," he explains to me. "An acoustic neuroma." He explains how that's a nonmalignant sheath of cells that sometimes surrounds the cranial nerve. "We don't know what causes the growth exactly, but it does cause vertigo and hinders a person's balance. This growth was larger than average. I could see the size of it on the MRI, and I was concerned that it had moved into the seventh cranial nerve. That would've changed the prognosis considerably."

"But it didn't go that far," his wife tells me. "Your mother should have a full and complete recovery."

"You said *non*malignant?" I repeat. "So that means she doesn't need radiation or chemotherapy?"

"That's right. She just needs some time to rest and recover from her surgery." Dr. Hoffman puts her hand on my shoulder. "So do you."

"Thank you!" I exclaim as I hug her. "Thank you for everything!"

She smiles at her husband. "It was his hands that did it."

"Thank you so much!" I tell him. But I'm thinking it was God's hands too.

"I'm pleased we had such a positive outcome. I was prepared for something with complications," he admits. "Now if you'll excuse me."

"How long until I can see Mom?" I ask Dr. Hoffman.

"She'll stay in ICU for several hours to be sure there's no swelling and to monitor her vitals." She checks her watch. "If there are no problems, she should be back in her room around 3:00, I'd guess."

"How long will she be in the hospital?" I ask.

"It depends on a number of things, but you should count on four to five days at the minimum."

"Okay." I nod. "Thanks again."

"Glad we could help. And not to diminish my husband's role in this, because in my book he is the tops, but I feel like there was a miracle at work here today."

"Why's that?"

"Like Mitch said, the size of the tumor on the MRI looked much larger than the one he removed. Yet we know he got all of it. It was as if the tumor had shrunk since her scan."

"Is that possible?"

She smiles. "With God all things are possible, right?"

"Right." I nod eagerly.

"Now I need to get back to the office."

After she leaves I turn back to my family, who are looking somewhat bewildered. "It is good news?" Dawdi asks me with concern in his eyes.

"Very good news." I explain Mom's prognosis to them as best I can using simple terms. "Dr. Hoffman told me that she thinks it was a real miracle." I describe the unexplainable shrinking of the growth. "If it had been bigger like they expected, there would have been serious problems. As it is, it sounds like she will be fine."

"It is an answer to prayer," Mammi declares.

"*Ja*," Dawdi says. "Thanks be to God."

We all hug, and everyone seems happy and relieved. But I can tell they're uncomfortable—so far out of their comfort zone. Being here like this has probably stretched them more than I know. "I understand if you need to go now," I say.

"*Ja*, that is true," Dawdi tells me. "There is work to be done for sure."

"We must get back to our chores," Uncle Ben chimes in.

"But your mamm will still be in our prayers," Rachel assures me.

"Will you come back and stay with us?" Mammi asks.

I tell her how I plan to stay with Betty, explaining how close her home is to the hospital so that I can easily visit my mom. I'm not sure, but I think she is relieved.

"You know you are always welcome," Dawdi tells me.

I nod. "Yes, I do know that."

"We will leave your bed in the spare room," he says.

Once again, I thank them all for coming, saying how much it meant to me to have them here. Then I watch in wonder as the four of them walk toward the elevator. They look so out of place, like characters torn out of a history book. Yet they are my family. And I feel blessed to have them.

24

After a few days of staying at Betty's place, I feel like a normal English girl again. Okay, I recognize that thinking of myself as "English" means I'm still under the influence of the Amish—but maybe that's a good thing.

Most of my time's been spent at the hospital with my mom. At first she looked so frail and pale, with her head bandaged up and dark shadows beneath her eyes, that I was concerned that she wasn't really doing well. By the second day, though, she was able to sit up in bed and eat and drink with no dizziness. And by the third day, she was up and walking around the hospital.

I'm so happy for her progress. It's almost like she's her old self again, except that she's weak and still has headaches. The doctor says that's normal after the kind of surgery she had. Plus she still needs to sleep a lot, but it's much less than before. While she's resting, I reintroduce myself to the internet and have conversations with Merenda. I've also been in touch with Mrs. Wimple. Our dear old neighbor has been back from her cruise for some time now. She was worried we'd never come home.

Dr. Hoffman has been working with Mom's pain meds, helping her to get off of the diazepam, which she'd clearly become addicted to. Fortunately, without the dizziness and nausea, Mom realizes that she doesn't need the diazepam anymore. And the new pain pills aren't addictive.

By the following week Mom's headaches are gone and she is restless to get out of here. I think it's mostly because of her concern about finances. I can't say I blame her. I've heard how expensive hospitals are. I can't even imagine the whopper of a bill we'll get at checkout time.

"I think we can sign you out today," Dr. Hoffman tells my mom on Wednesday morning.

"Really?" Mom looks uncertain but hopeful. "To go home?"

"Well, I'm not sure about making the trip all the way to Indianapolis yet. Plus we need to do some follow-up visits." Dr. Hoffman glances at me. "Did you tell her about Betty's suggestion?"

"Betty offered to let us both stay with her for a few days," I explain to Mom. "Until you get strong enough to go home. Otherwise we can go back to Mammi and Dawdi. It's your choice."

Mom slowly nods. "Betty's place might be best. Do you think so, Shannon?"

"Yeah," I assure her. "I think it'll be more comfortable for you."

"And you'll be in town for your follow-up appointments," Dr. Hoffman points out.

"Okay. Betty's it is." Mom gives Dr. Hoffman a nervous

smile. "I know I'll need to settle my bill with you and your husband and the hospital before we leave. I wish I still had insurance, or that I could afford to pay everything all at once. Especially considering how you folks have handed my life back to me." She sighs. "But that's simply not possible. I hope we can arrange payments."

"Your bill with my husband and me is already settled," Dr. Hoffman informs her.

"Wh-what?" Mom stares at her. "How?"

"It's just something we do once in a while." Dr. Hoffman smiles at me. "In very special cases."

Tears fill Mom's eyes. "I—I don't even know what to—"

"Not only that, but I've spoken to the hospital administrator, and she's agreed to reduce your bill here significantly."

"I'm so grateful. And amazed. How can I ever thank you?"

"Just take good care of yourself, and"—Dr. Hoffman points to me—"take good care of this girl too. I'm not sure what her plans for college are, but I happen to think she'd make a fine doctor."

I smile. "I guess I'll have to sign up for some AP science classes in the fall."

She pats my back. "Just keep your options open, Shannon."

After a week at Betty's, my mom seems almost as strong as before she got sick. She insists on helping with cooking and cleaning, and we take three walks a day. Considering how she was two weeks ago, it really feels like a miracle. Both the Drs. Hoffman have given her the green light to go home. On Thursday we buy our tickets for a bus that's scheduled to leave on Saturday.

"Do you want to go see your parents again?" I ask her Thursday evening. "We might be able to get a ride from Leah."

Mom's brow creases as if she's unsure. "Well, maybe that's a good idea, Shannon. Anyway, I'm sure they'd like to see you again."

I've already told Mom about how our relatives came to the hospital during her surgery, but she's certain that was for my sake, not hers. It's possible she's right. After all, I'm fully aware of the whole shunning business and how seriously they take it. All the same, it seems like a healthy thing for her to see her parents before we go home. It might be good for them to see her whole and well again. So I call Leah.

I can tell my mom is nervous, but I try to act calm as Leah drives us to the dawdi house on Friday afternoon. The plan is to visit with our relatives for an hour. Leah has brought a book and says she doesn't mind waiting. Naturally, Mammi is surprised to see us, but I can tell by her eyes she is happy. Even though she doesn't say a lot to Mom, I can tell she's relieved that she's well. She sends me out to get Dawdi so he can see her too, and I find him in the barn with Uncle Ben. While both of them go inside to visit with my mom, I dash over to say one last good-bye to Rachel.

Aunt Katrina doesn't seem terribly glad to see me, but I guess it might have more to do with how I'm dressed than anything personal. Since I've been wearing my own clothes this past week, I nearly forgot about all that. But seeing her grim expression is a vivid reminder of Amish propriety.

Once again, I thank my aunt for the time I spent in her home, and I tell her that Mom is better. "It was a real miracle,"

I explain. "Even the doctors said so. I know it's because so many people were praying for her." I start to thank her for praying but then am unsure whether or not she did. "Thankfully, God was listening."

"*Ja*. God is always listening," she says in a polite but chilly tone.

"Anyway, I wanted to tell you good-bye—and thanks."

"Rachel is in the garden if you would like to tell her good-bye."

I go outside to find a barefooted Rachel down on her knees, staking up bushy tomato plants, but as soon as she sees me she leaps to her feet and comes over to hug me.

"I'm so glad to see you again. How's your mamm?"

I tell her of Mom's progress, and Rachel seems genuinely happy.

"That is good to hear. I have been praying for her every day."

"Thanks! She's well enough that we can go home tomorrow," I explain. "I just wanted to tell you good-bye first."

"Thank you," she says with real gratitude. "I am going to miss you so much, Shannon."

I nod. "I know. It's like you're my real cousin."

She laughs. "I am your real cousin. And so are my brothers and my sister. And all your other cousins too."

"Yeah, but I feel like I have a bigger connection with you. And for someone like me—I mean, having no family—that means a lot."

"Will you write me letters?" she asks hopefully. "To let me know how you're doing?"

"Is that allowed?"

"*Ja*. I do not think there's a rule against writing letters."

"Okay," I agree. "I'll get your address from Mammi and I'll write."

"I will write you back. I can tell you about when Ezra and I get baptized. And when we get married."

"I would love to hear about it. I wish I could come to your wedding."

"You do?" She seems honestly surprised. "I guess you can if you want to, Shannon. I think it'll be in the autumn time, after harvest."

I imagine myself in my English clothes, sticking out like a sore thumb at Rachel's wedding. "Well, it's a long ways to come, and I'll probably be in school then. Maybe I can send you a wedding gift."

She brightens. "That would be wonderful."

I hug her again. "I'm so glad that it's all worked out between you and Ezra. I hope you're really happy together."

She looks uncertain. "There are no hard feelings?"

I consider this. "No," I answer honestly. "I think Ezra was more of an escape for me. Like I told you, I'm sure I was in love with love. The truth is, I didn't really get to know Ezra that well, or I made myself believe he was something he wasn't. Mostly I think I wanted to run away from my own life. I know now that I can't do that. It's like trying to run away from God. Everywhere you turn, there he is."

"For an English girl, you have spirituality."

I laugh. "Yeah, and for an Amish girl, you are—well, you are very cool."

Now she laughs. I tell her I'd better get back to the dawdi house. As I hurry back to my grandparents' tiny house, I know what I told Rachel is absolutely true. I was trying to run away from everything—all I wanted was an escape, and I believed that Ezra could give it to me. I know better now.

It's surprisingly hard telling Mammi, Dawdi, and Uncle Ben good-bye. I guess I didn't realize how much I really do love them. I mean, for a short while I felt like I hated them, or more likely that they hated me. Now I can tell that although it's an awkward relationship and they have difficulty showing it, they do love and care about us.

"Come and visit us again if you like," Uncle Ben tells me as he's leaving.

"I just might do that," I say.

"*Ja*," Mammi chimes in. "You can come and visit, Shannon." She gives Mom an uncertain look. "You can too."

"We'll keep that in mind," my mom assures her. We all hug, and it's time to be on our way.

"That wasn't so bad." Mom lets out a loud sigh once we're in Leah's minivan. "They're not so bad either. Not really."

"No, they're not bad at all, Mom. Just different."

"That is for sure," Leah adds in a philosophical tone. "But that is exactly how they want to be—different."

We've been home for a week and school starts up on Monday. Mrs. Wimple couldn't believe the difference in Mom's health, but when I told her it was a miracle, she nodded. "My sister and I were praying for you," she told Mom. "I should've known you'd be all right."

On the Sunday before school starts, I am sitting with Merenda in the park near the apartments. She got home from her dad's last night, and we're soaking up some sun next to the fountains and catching up. At her insistence, I've told her all about my brief "love affair" with Ezra. Although she got swept away in the "romance" of it all initially, she eventually comes to the same conclusion I did.

"You must've been temporarily insane," she declares.

I laugh. "Yeah, I think there was definitely a little craziness involved."

"To think you could marry an Amish guy and become Amish and never go back to school and just stay there cleaning house and having children?" She shakes her head. "That is unbelievably insane."

"Maybe . . . but you know what? I don't even regret it."

"Of course you don't regret it—you said Ezra was a hottie and a good kisser," she teases. "But even so."

I playfully punch her. "It's not because of that."

"What then?"

"Well, like I already told you, I was ready for an escape this summer. Remember how I wanted freedom and independence? For a while it seemed like Ezra was the key to all that."

"Becoming Amish is freedom and independence?" She frowns. "I seriously don't think so, Shannon."

"But at the time it felt like Ezra got me away from everything, including myself. He also distracted me from Mom's troubles. Then because of my interest in Ezra, I was compelled to become Amish for a while. I mean, I wasn't truly Amish because I never got baptized or anything. It's like I was obsessed with it, though. I tried it on for size. And I think that was a good thing."

"Why?" She looks confused as she squints into the sun.

"Because playing Amish forced me to take a good hard look at God. It made me see that as much as I was trying to escape my own life, I was trying to escape him too. I had been doing that for about a year."

A look of realization crosses her face. "Yeah, I'd noticed."

"But I don't feel like that anymore," I declare. "Instead of escaping God, I feel like I want to run directly toward him now."

"That's cool."

"Yeah." I nod happily. "It is cool." Just then a big yellow butterfly flutters down and gracefully lands on my ankle. I stare in silent amazement, barely moving as I point it out to Merenda.

"Shannon," she whispers with wide eyes. "Remember the tattoo you wanted?"

I grin. "Yeah. I guess I don't really need it now." As I sit here watching that beautiful creature, I realize that this is like God's tattoo. Except that his mark on my life is going to be a whole lot more than just skin deep.

Melody Carlson is the award-winning author of over two hundred books, including *The Jerk Magnet*, *The Best Friend*, *The Prom Queen*, *Double Take*, *A Simple Song*, and the Diary of a Teenage Girl series. Melody recently received a *Romantic Times* Career Achievement Award in the inspirational market for her books. She and her husband live in central Oregon. For more information about Melody, visit her website at www.melodycarlson.com.

Meet Melody at
MelodyCarlson.com

- Enter a contest for a signed book
- Read her monthly newsletter
- Find a special page for book clubs
- Discover more books by Melody

Become a fan on Facebook

 Melody Carlson Books

"Carlson hits all the right notes
in this wonderful story that grips you from
the beginning and does not let go."

—RT Book Reviews, ★★★★★ TOP PICK!

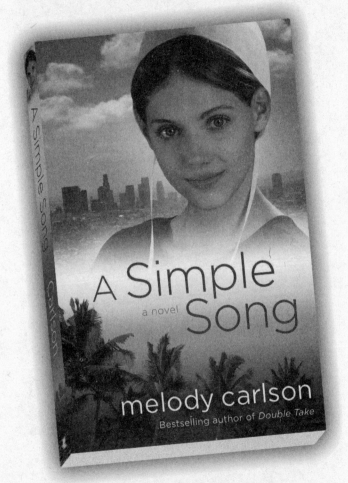

Katrina Yoder has the voice of an angel, but her Amish
parents believe singing is prideful vanity. When she wins a
ticket to sing in Hollywood, her life is turned upside down.

What do you do when your life's not all it's cracked up to be?
Get a new one.

Worlds collide when a Manhattan socialite and a simple
Amish girl meet and decide to switch places.

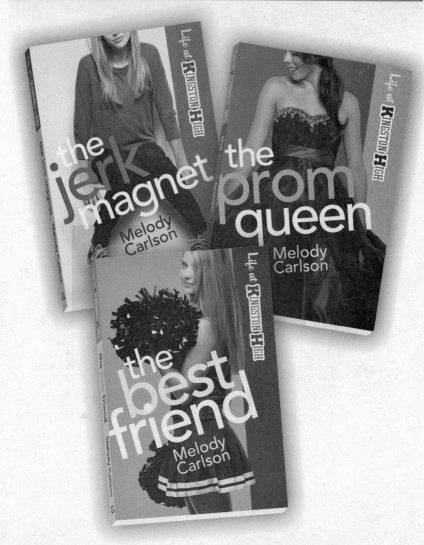

Patterns for
College Writing

A RHETORICAL READER AND GUIDE